Reed seized the handhold to stabilize himself after a particle beam impact on the dorsal hull rocked the bridge severely. "Captain, we need to engage deflectors!"

"Agreed," T'Pol said. "Lieutenant, activate forward deflector shields." She activated the comm channel to the engine room. "Bridge to engineering. Adjust warp field to compensate for deflectors."

"They've taken damage to propulsion," Kimura announced. "They're slowing."

"But so are we," Mayweather reported. "I can't maintain more than warp three-point-two."

"What is going on?" General Valk demanded. "Why are you slowing down?"

T'Pol noted Archer's grimace. He was reluctant to admit one of Starfleet's tactical weaknesses. But T'Pol judged that holding on to the Tandarans' tenuous trust in the here and now was more important. "This is an Earth ship, but the deflector shield technology is of Andorian origin," she explained. "There has been some difficulty in reconciling the two technologies."

Valk laughed. "Your shields interfere with your warp field!"

"Only for the moment," Archer said through clenched teeth. "We just need to work out a few bugs."

—STAR TREK—
ENTERPRISE®

RISE OF THE FEDERATION

A CHOICE OF FUTURES

CHRISTOPHER L. BENNETT

Based upon *Star Trek*®
created by Gene Roddenberry
and *Star Trek: Enterprise*
created by Rick Berman & Brannon Braga

POCKET BOOKS
New York London Toronto Sydney New Delhi

Pocket Books
A Division of Simon & Schuster, Inc.
1230 Avenue of the Americas
New York, NY 10020

This book is a work of fiction. Any references to historical events, real people, or real places are used fictitiously. Other names, characters, places, and events are products of the author's imagination, and any resemblance to actual events or places or persons, living or dead, is entirely coincidental.

First Pocket Books paperback edition July 2013

POCKET and colophon are registered trademarks of Simon & Schuster, Inc.

For information about special discounts for bulk purchases, please contact Simon & Schuster Special Sales at 1-866-506-1949 or business@simonandschuster.com.

The Simon & Schuster Speakers Bureau can bring authors to your live event. For more information or to book an event, contact the Simon & Schuster Speakers Bureau at 1-866-248-3049 or visit our website at www.simonspeakers.com.

Manufactured in the United States of America

10 9 8 7 6 5 4 3 2 1

ISBN 978-1-4767-0674-0
ISBN 978-1-4767-0675-7 (ebook)

*To the art department of Star Trek: Enterprise,
for creating a near-future environment
that's so much fun to inhabit.*

This isn't about finding someone else to watch our backs!

     —Jonathan Archer, January 2155

2162

1

HE COULD ONLY WATCH as the colony burned around him.

A minute ago, it was the children he'd been watching as they'd run through the bright blue grass of the colony's central square, using child-sized throwing sticks to try to hurl a ball through a ring that hovered above their heads on repulsors. They could have been human children back on Earth, if not for the color of the grass and trees, and if not for the subtle V-shaped notches between their brows. Some of the parents had been urging their children to victory, while other, less competitive-minded ones were content to let their kids just run and play, some recording the event with cameras while others simply basked in the light of the bright yellow-white star overhead.

And then something had come out of that light, faint specks against the sun's disk. Before they could even be resolved into ships, they had begun firing, bolts of fierce yellow-green plasma tearing into the ground, the buildings, the people. The parents in the square, quicker to understand what was happening, began to panic before the children did. A few managed to stay calm, tried to rally the others to gather up the children and flee to safety. But then a plasma bolt tore through the metal sculpture at the center of the square, sending out shrapnel that felled many of the parents and children nearby. The shock wave left him looking up at the sky from ground level as bodies fell around him. The ships flew overhead, and he recognized them: angular bronze polyhedrons, most only big enough for two people, but undeniably powerful. He watched helplessly as one of the larger, more elongated ships set down in the square and opened to disgorge the raiders, who began methodically shooting down the surviving parents, seizing the screaming, crying children and dragging them back to the ship.

He knew those faces too: bald, cantaloupe-green, textured like stucco. The faces of Suliban.

One of the raiders reached him, loomed above him, a rifle barrel pointed at his head. He studied that mottled face closely, unafraid of the weapon, knowing he could do nothing to affect what he saw. He could only watch as the raider crouched, a hand reaching forward to fill his field of view . . . leaving only blackness.

"There! Do you see?"

With a heavy sigh, Admiral Jonathan Archer reached up and took the virtual display visor off his head, the blackness lifting away to reveal the gray-walled conference room of the *Grentra*, a warship in the Tandaran fleet. His hands shook slightly as he lowered it, and he made an effort to still them, feeling a twinge of frustration. Doctor Phlox had assured him the latest round of treatments would hold off the tremors for months.

But after a moment, he realized that his shakiness

was probably an emotional response to the sensory playback he'd just experienced, recovered from a proud parent's holorecorder by the Tandaran soldiers who'd come to Kemsar Colony to aid the survivors and investigate the brutal raid. Anyone would have been shaken after watching the attack from the vantage point of one of its victims.

Archer gathered himself and turned his gaze to the portly, dark-featured Tandaran who had spoken. Valk wore the quilted gray tunic of the Tandaran military, his twin black sashes declaring him an officer and the golden rank pins on the sides of his brown leather collar marking him as a general. "No one's disputing what happened here, General Valk. It's a terrible crime, and the Federation extends its sympathies for your loss."

"Sympathies don't heal mortal wounds, Admiral," Valk fired back. "Nor do lies. Let me remind you, the only reason we agreed to tolerate your upstart government's grant of asylum to Suliban refugees was in exchange for your assurances that there would be no Suliban retaliation for our . . . disputes with them over the years."

Archer resisted an undiplomatic reply to the general's choice of words. They both knew the history perfectly well. In response to the Suliban Cabal's decade-long war against the worlds of the Tandar Sector, the Tandaran government had imprisoned innocent Suliban civilians, lifelong citizens of Tandaran society, in brutal internment camps—allegedly to protect them from the persecution of the masses or forced impression into the genetically enhanced ranks of the Cabal. It had been over eight years since the factions in the Temporal Cold War had ended their intrusions into the twenty-second century, leaving the Cabal with no instructions from the future to guide them or genetic enhancements to motivate them. The directionless Cabal had fragmented, some former members using their augmentations for petty piracy and crime, others simply fleeing from the Tandarans, Klingons, and others whom they'd wronged in service to their twenty-eighth-century sponsor's unknowable agendas. But it had been years more before the Tandaran government, having killed or imprisoned most of the Cabal's surviving leaders and suffering no further attacks, had consented to close the camps once and for all, under pressure from Tandaran activists who had learned of the conditions there from former prisoners like the ones Archer had helped free a decade ago.

But the Suliban had still faced fear and bigotry from many in the Tandar Sector, and while some had chosen to reclaim their homes there and try to rebuild their lives and relationships, many had chosen to resume their nomadic ways or relocate to other worlds, including some within the territory of the United Federation of Planets—the fledgling union of United Earth, the Confederacy of Vulcan, the Andorian Empire, the United Planets of Tellar, and the Alpha Centauri Concordium. Jonathan Archer, who had played a significant role in bringing that union about, had used his clout to persuade the Federation Council to grant the refugees asylum as one of its first acts. More importantly, he'd persuaded the Tandaran government to accept that grant, although in return they'd insisted that the Federation erase all records indicating that the Tandarans were aware of the Temporal Cold War, as part of some sort of disinformation campaign directed at the future. It sounded fishy to Archer, but he'd gone along with it for the sake of the refugees. "The Federation has kept its side of the bargain," he assured the general.

"Then why," Valk asked, "have all three of these attacks been along the border closest to your territory?" He nodded to his aide, a lean, ash-blond woman named Major Glith, to slide a data tablet across the table toward Archer. "And why," the general went on, "do the raiders' weapons signatures read as consistent with Vulcan and Andorian firearms?"

"The Vulcans and Andorians were fighting for a long time before they finally made peace," Archer said. "Some of their weapons must've fallen into other hands over the years."

"But which hands? Most of the Cabal's members and resources have been accounted for by our intelligence agencies. Yet the biosignatures of these raiders," and he worked a control on his own tablet to send new data to the one before Archer, "are not baseline Suliban."

"Nor do they correspond to any known enhancements," Glith added in a much cooler tone.

"Then they can't be Cabal, can they?"

Valk stood and leaned forward, trying to intimidate Archer with his bulk. "Or maybe the Cabal has simply found a new set of sponsors willing to protect them from discovery and dole out a different form of genetic edge. Maybe defeating the Romulans has given you humans and your allies a taste for conquest, and you've decided to go after the Tandar Sector using Suliban as your shock troops!"

"The Federation is not about expansionism."

"Isn't it? For generations, the Vulcan High Command imposed its 'benevolent' interference on its neighbors, often at the point of a plasma cannon. Now they claim to have retreated into pacifism, but only after their human protégés rise to power with unprecedented speed, build a massive war fleet that drives the Romulans into retreat, and assimilate the once fiercely independent Andorian and Tellarite nations! Giving your so-called Federation of Planets the strongest battle fleet outside of the Klingon Empire as a result, even with the Vulcan fleet in mothballs. And no sooner have you dealt with the Romulans than you begin pressuring the Denobulans, Arkenites, and others to submit themselves to your rule as well."

"We're offering them equal partnership for mutual support and defense. And we don't force it on anyone who doesn't want it."

Valk scoffed. "Says the man who spent years forcibly interfering in the affairs of the Tandarans, the Klingons, the Mazarites—"

"This is getting us nowhere, General!" Archer interrupted. The truth was, he couldn't offer a solid defense on this point. The Federation was too new, its identity and objectives still in flux. He knew that the minds behind the Federation saw its purpose as benevolent, but there was still much disagreement over how to fulfill that purpose, or how aggressively to pursue it.

"We can argue about the Federation's intentions all day long," he continued, "but it won't bring those raiders to justice or liberate the children they captured. I came here to offer you the means to do just that."

"How? If you're not in collusion with these Suliban, how can you track them down when we cannot?"

"Because we know you're looking for the wrong thing."

"How do you know this?" Glith asked. "What do you propose we look for instead?"

Archer hesitated. "I can't tell you that. I could tell you what I know, but you'd never believe me without proof, and my sources are . . . highly classified." The general scoffed. "But what I can do is help you find the raiders and *show* you who's really behind them— and help you get your children back. But you're gonna have to extend us a little trust."

"So that you can win your way into our good graces?" Valk blustered. "Maybe persuade us to submit to absorption into your Federation?"

Archer faced him squarely. "So that those children won't have to live in slavery. Isn't that enough?"

Valk held his gaze firmly a while longer, reluctant to give any ground, but the reminder of what was truly at stake penetrated his armor, to his credit. "Explain to us how you propose to track down the Suliban so long after their warp trails have dissipated."

"We'd be happy to. Travis?"

"Yes, sir." Lieutenant Travis Mayweather stepped forward from where he had stood behind Archer, waiting patiently to play his part. The handsome, dark-skinned, bright-eyed officer gave Archer an easy smile and nod as he stepped up to the table, a reminder that the tensions that had arisen between the two men at the onset of the Romulan conflict were now decisively a thing of the past. Admiral Archer was still getting used to the sight of him in the new Federation Starfleet uniform. Although the various space agencies of the UFP's five founding members still existed and oversaw their own ships and specialties within the combined fleet they jointly administered, they'd agreed they should adopt a common uniform with elements reflecting all its member states. Mayweather's black undershirt sported a Vulcan-style Mandarin collar; over it was a V-necked tunic worn above a separate pair of black trousers and boots. Archer's own command-division tunic was an avocado green not unlike the command color of the Andorian Guard, while Mayweather's operations-division tunic was reddish-brown per Tellarite military convention. The lieutenant's rank insignia—a single gold stripe, as opposed to five alternating wide and narrow stripes for Archer—adorned each of his cuffs and shoulder straps. The shoulders were set off by a shallow chevron of gold-fringed navy-blue piping extending from shoulder joints to mid-sternum, reflecting Vulcan designs from the twenty-first century. Below the piping, next to the vertical zipper of the left-hand tunic pocket, was the gold arrowhead insignia of the United Earth Space Probe Agency, the government department that administered Earth's Starfleet. To balance it, the mission patch had moved to the right sleeve, with Mayweather and Archer both bearing the generic Starfleet Command patch, a circular blue field of stars behind a horizontal gold chevron, rather than a specific ship's design. Mayweather's wide-ranging experience during the Romulan War had broadened his interests beyond piloting starships, and he'd been a valuable advisor to Archer in this current assignment.

"I don't mean to contradict you, General," Mayweather began in his usual laid-back, conversational tone, "but those warp trails haven't *completely* dissipated. There's still some ion residue out there."

"Disconnected traces," Major Glith said, "already blended into the interstellar medium."

"Almost, but not quite. See, the thing about reconstructing ion trails is that you need to know what you're looking for. You searched for a lot of small trails, right? One for each cell ship?"

"That's correct," the stern-faced major replied.

"Well, we have reason to believe these cell ships aren't capable of warp drive. They would've had to dock with the two motherships you detected in orbit. So you'd be looking for two larger trails instead of a few dozen smaller ones."

Glith pondered Mayweather's words for a moment, then turned to Valk. "It's a plausible notion, General. If the sponsors who provided the Cabal's advanced technology truly have been gone as long as we believe, then the Suliban would be unable to repair those micro-warp drives when they failed. They may have been forced to retrofit their larger vessels with standard drives and rely on the modular nature of the craft to cluster them together." She looked back at the Starfleet officers. "But we did scan for the motherships' traces as well and found nothing conclusive."

Mayweather smiled. "That's where we can help you, Major. There's a little trick we picked up a few years back in the Delphic Expanse. Helped us track down some Osaarian pirates who'd destroyed an alien ship and then ransacked *Enterprise*. See, what you have to do is model the effect of the warp field's own gravimetric distortions on the ISM's density profile, then correlate that with the ion concentrations to compute the most probable trajectory. We've already found their most likely course out of this system, which should put us on the right track."

Valk was taken aback. "If you already found that information, why haven't you shared it with us?"

"Well, we would've told you sooner, sir, but, well, you were talking and it would've been rude to interrupt." Archer suppressed a chuckle. From anyone else, the comment would've come across as snide. But Mayweather's natural good humor and openness softened the barb, getting the criticism across without provoking the general's ire. If Valk did take offense, it would be clear that his bluster, not Federation duplicity, would be the source of any further delays in tracking down the raiders.

Still, General Valk was slow to let go of his suspicions.

"So you would have us follow you in pursuit of a trail *you* claim only you can find. How do we know you won't lead us into ambush?"

"You're welcome to join us aboard my flagship, General," Archer proposed. "You can observe the entire operation yourself. And we'll share our sensor telemetry with your ships."

"Which have no means of verifying its accuracy without further analysis."

"But you'll have plenty of time to analyze it later," Mayweather told him. "If we did trick you to lead you into a trap, your people would have the proof, and that would look really bad for the Federation. So either we're not your enemy—or we are, but we're a really stupid enemy. Either way, what have you got to lose?"

Valk made a show of discussing it with his officers, but Archer could tell Mayweather had sealed the deal. He gave the lieutenant a tiny nod and smile, earning a bigger smile in response.

U.S.S. *Endeavour* NCC-06

Whatever flimsy filament of trust General Valk was willing to extend to Starfleet did not include trusting his bodily integrity to the transporter, a technology the Tandarans lacked. So Archer and Mayweather ferried him across by shuttlepod—which Archer was glad of, always appreciating a chance to see the new pride of Starfleet from the outside. *Endeavour* had been the sixth *NX*-class starship built by Earth, originally a twin to Archer's beloved *Enterprise*. But that class had suffered badly in the Earth-Romulan War—production of the state-of-the-art ships had been suspended in favor of mass-producing older, simpler designs, leaving only a handful of *NX*-class ships in service, and most of those had been lost to Romulan weapons. *Enterprise* herself had survived, but with her spaceframe too compromised in the decisive Battle of Cheron ever to fly again; so she was now in honorable retirement at the Smithsonian's orbital annex. Thus, *Endeavour* was now the last active survivor of the *NX* class.

Yet she was also the first of a new breed of Federation starships. After the war, she had undergone a massive refit, the results of which were visible to the shuttlepod's occupants as it drew nearer. From above, *Endeavour* looked much the same as it always had: a silver-skinned saucer with two large pontoons stretching back to connect to a pair of red-domed warp nacelles on upswept, winglike pylons. Yet as the shuttlepod descended alongside the ship, her newest feature came into view: a cylindrical secondary hull with a deep rear undercut, positioned and sized to occupy the secondary node of the vessel's warp field while in flight. The hull had been added to house the larger, more powerful warp reactor that allowed the ship to surpass warp factor six for finite periods of time, and also bore a large, circular navigational deflector dish on its prow to supplement the flattened oval of the saucer deflector. The new design—which would be the template for more ships to follow—had been redesignated the *Columbia* class at Archer's insistence, in honor of the first *NX* ship to be lost, the vessel commanded by his dear friend Erika Hernandez until her disappearance in the first year of the Romulan War.

At first, Archer had disliked the modifications, feeling *Enterprise* had been perfect the way she was. But the more he got used to the secondary hull, the more he felt it gave the design a balance it had been missing before. It still clashed a bit with the pontoons, but he imagined that future ship designs would integrate it more smoothly.

The thick, squat dorsal connector that joined the two hulls had taken the place of the main shuttlebay, so the two drop bays for the shuttlepods had been relocated to either side of it. Yet Mayweather still piloted the pod into contact with the umbilical as deftly as he ever had, and soon they were safely aboard. As Archer debarked, *Endeavour*'s captain greeted him at the top of the ladder. "Admiral," she said in her usual cool tones. "Welcome back."

"Permission to come aboard, Captain T'Pol."

"Permission granted." She gave a tiny tilt to her head. "It is, after all, your ship."

He grinned, appreciating his former executive officer's dry wit more than ever now that he saw her less frequently. Having *Endeavour* as his personal flagship meant they worked together fairly often, but still his duties forced him to spend much of his time Earth-bound. T'Pol looked good in her green command tunic. She had taken to wearing her brown hair a few centimeters longer than in the past, which also flattered her. She wore the UESPA arrowhead on her

breast rather than the circle-and-triangle IDIC patch
of the Vulcan Space Council; after all, it was an Earth-
administered ship she commanded, and she had been
a member of Earth Starfleet for seven years before the
services were combined.

T'Pol was flanked by two guards, their slate-gray
tunics a tribute to the former Military Assault Command Operations forces that had now been folded
into Starfleet's security division. The guards flanked
General Valk unobtrusively as Archer, T'Pol, and Mayweather led him to the bridge.

It had been less than an hour since Archer had
stood on this bridge, but it still struck him how
much it felt like old home week. Its layout was much
the same as *Enterprise*'s bridge, with only minor upgrades to some of the controls and readouts; aside
from the added hull, most of the improvements in
the redesigned ship were under the proverbial hood.
Archer knew there had been a project under way at
Alpha Centauri to devise downgraded equipment
that would be less vulnerable to Romulan telecapture weaponry; but with the Romulans no longer an
issue, the project had been abandoned—although
a few folks at Starfleet Engineering had been taken
with the minimalist aesthetics of the design and were
talking about incorporating a similar look into future ships, despite their greater advancement underneath.

But it wasn't the room that fired Archer's nostalgia
so much as the people. "General Valk," he said to their
guest, "this is Commander Malcolm Reed, *Endeavour*'s

first officer." The compactly built, brown-haired and trim-goateed Englishman looked crisp in his green tunic with twin commander's stripes and the *Endeavour* mission patch on the sleeve. He gave a stiff, proper nod to the Tandaran general, but nevertheless watched him as closely as if he'd still been Archer's armory officer on *Enterprise*. "And Lieutenant Commander Hoshi Sato, protocol officer and chief of communications."

"*Gaval nek bor, Valk-Darak,*" the lovely, deceptively delicate-featured Japanese woman greeted the general in Tandaran before extending an arm swathed in the cobalt blue of the science division. "I'll be seeing to your needs while you're aboard, sir."

"*Mer nalak,*" Valk thanked her, surprised at her courtesy. "But my only need," he went on to Archer, "is to find those Suliban raiders. You claim you can do so—now is the time to prove it."

"Certainly," Captain T'Pol said, settling smoothly into the command chair. "Lieutenant Mayweather, if you would care to take the helm?"

Travis beamed. "It's been a while, ma'am."

"Perhaps you should think of it like riding a bicycle. That seems to be effective among humans."

The lieutenant chuckled. "Yes, Captain."

Archer smiled to himself. *Old home week,* he reflected. Even Doctor Phlox was down in sickbay, waiting to confirm the raiders' identity. But then he grew somber, remembering those who were missing—one in particular, whose absence from the engineering console was still keenly felt. *I guess you can't go home again after all.*

September 26, 2162

By the second day of the pursuit, it became evident that the raiders' vessels were en route to the Qhem-bembem Outpost, a disreputable trading post orbiting one component of a dim, unremarkable binary red dwarf system in unclaimed space. Many criminals, both private and organized, took advantage of the system's obscurity and isolation to engage in illicit transactions, including slave trading. This made it imperative to intercept the ships before they reached the outpost; otherwise the abducted Tandaran children could be transferred to any of numerous vessels and become exponentially harder to track down.

Fortunately, *Endeavour's* chief engineer, Michel Romaine, was one of the designers of the vessel's upgraded engine, and thus was able to apply his expertise to get the engines up to warp factor 6.3 and keep them there for over eight hours, enabling the vessel to close on the two Suliban carrier ships while still on the outskirts of the binary system. The *Grentra* was the Tandarans' fastest available ship, but though it could reach warp 6.5 for brief periods, it could not sustain such velocities for long without slowing to let its engines cool. The *Grentra* was thus lagging behind *Endeavour* but closing in at best speed as the carrier ships came into the Federation vessel's visual range.

Captain T'Pol studied the ships carefully as Sato brought them into focus on the viewscreen. It was an illogical impulse, since surely the sensors could gather far more data than her eyes could; but it had been a long time since she had been able to suppress such impulses reliably. The Vulcan had learned instead, through careful training, to allow them, acknowledge them, and move on. She simply noted the distinctive modular design of the Suliban vessels. Each carrier had a lattice-like central spine on which the various cell ships were docked, extending perpendicularly outward from docking points at regular intervals, giving the ships a crosslike appearance from the rear. T'Pol recalled her only prior encounter with such a carrier vessel, during an incident a decade before involving the Tholians. There, all the ships attached to the spine had been of the larger, more elongated variety of cell ship, but these were more asymmetrically arranged, with some of the docking points empty, some occupied by the larger slab-shaped vessels, and the rest occupied by trains of three to four of the smaller, more symmetrical cell ships. The engine modules at the rear also appeared larger than those of that earlier carrier, reinforcing the idea that these raiders were using a cruder form of warp drive than the Cabal had employed.

"Closing to weapons range," Lieutenant Commander Takashi Kimura reported from the tactical station on T'Pol's right.

The captain turned to the other side of the bridge, where Lieutenant Elizabeth Cutler sat at the science station. "Scan for Tandaran biosigns," T'Pol instructed her.

"Scanning," Cutler replied, brushing back her straight, honey-brown hair. "They're jamming, it's hard to get a clear read . . . but I'm only getting indications consistent with Tandarans from the lead ship. Nothing in the trailing vessel."

"Then detaining that lead ship is our priority," T'Pol said.

"Leave that to us," General Valk demanded. "Those children are our responsibility. They must not be harmed."

"I have no intention of allowing any harm to come to them," T'Pol assured him. "This will be a precision operation."

"If they were your children, would you trust anyone else?"

"I might have to," she told him evenly, "if theirs were the only ship able to reach them in time."

Before Valk could respond, Kimura called, "Incoming fire!"

"Hull plating," T'Pol ordered. Kimura barely had time to polarize the hull material, strengthening its molecular bonds, before the raiders' torpedo struck. The impact rocked the ship. "Evasive," T'Pol instructed Mayweather at the helm.

"I thought we weren't in range," Admiral Archer said.

"Clever," T'Pol replied. "They remembered that the lead ship in a warp pursuit has an advantage."

"I see," said General Valk. "They let the torpedo drop to impulse behind them, using it as a mine."

"They won't have the advantage long," Reed announced.

Indeed, it was only moments more before *Endeavour*

was close enough to synchronize warp fields with the nearer ship and fire its phase cannons. "Target their engines," T'Pol ordered as the deck jolted beneath her feet from the return fire. If they could force this ship to impulse, it would no longer pose a threat and they could concentrate on rescuing the captives aboard the lead ship.

Unfortunately the trailing carrier proved too well armed and shielded for it to be that simple. Reed seized the handhold mounted atop the helm console to stabilize himself after a particle beam impact on the dorsal hull rocked the bridge severely. "Captain, we need to engage deflectors!"

"Agreed," T'Pol said. "Lieutenant, activate forward deflector shields." She activated the comm channel to the engine room. "Bridge to engineering. Adjust warp field to compensate for deflectors."

"They've taken damage to propulsion," Kimura announced. "They're slowing."

"But so are we," Mayweather reported. "I can't maintain more than warp three-point-two."

"Continue targeting propulsion and weapons," T'Pol instructed the tactical officer.

"What is going on?" Valk demanded. "Why are you slowing down?"

T'Pol noted Archer's grimace. He was reluctant to admit one of Starfleet's tactical weaknesses. But T'Pol judged that holding on to the Tandarans' tenuous trust in the here and now was more important. "This is an Earth ship, but the deflector shield technology is of Andorian origin," she explained. "There has been some difficulty in reconciling the two technologies."

Valk laughed. "Your shields interfere with your warp field!"

"Only for the moment," Archer said through clenched teeth. "We just need to work out a few bugs."

The general's humor quickly passed. "And while you contend with your 'bugs,' the other ship is getting away!"

"A temporary setback," Reed said confidently, even as Kimura's determined fire finally blew out the trailing carrier's warp drive and forced it back into normal space, where it quickly receded behind them.

"Deactivate deflectors," T'Pol said. "Mister Mayweather, resume maximum speed. Commander Sato, notify the *Grentra* of the carrier's location. General, if you will instruct your personnel to take the crew prisoner, they will be able to verify—"

"Captain!" Kimura cried. "The trailing ship just exploded!"

"Scanning," Cutler said, then shook her head. "No survivors."

"Mister Kimura?" T'Pol asked.

"I fired to disable, Captain. But I suppose I could've miscalculated . . ." There was no shock or remorse in his voice, only professional focus. Kimura was an experienced soldier, a former major in the MACOs, and had always been able to set his emotions aside when duty required.

"No," Sato said after a moment. "The lead ship sent a burst transmission to the other one just before it exploded. I think it was a remote detonation signal." She shook her head with a curt sigh. "They didn't even warn them first."

Archer's expression hardened. "They murdered their own people to conceal their identity."

"We know they're Suliban," Valk said, renewed suspicion in his voice. "Perhaps it's their new backers' identity they wish to conceal, eh, Admiral?"

"Has it occurred to you that the raiders might've had a reason for leaving that recording for you to find?"

"In any case," T'Pol stressed, "we now know the lengths they will go to in order to avoid capture. Extreme care must be taken with the remaining ship."

Unfortunately, by the time *Endeavour* caught up with the second carrier twenty-three minutes later, it was already beginning its descent toward the surface of the otherwise lifeless planet hosting the Qhembem-bem Outpost. "Our options for preventing it from reaching the outpost's defense perimeter in time are severely limited," Malcolm Reed observed. "Once it's inside, we won't be able to get to it, or scan through their jamming fields."

"Then we must prevent it from reaching the surface," T'Pol said. "Mister Kimura, deploy the tractor beam."

Kimura worked the controls that extended the graviton beam's emitter array from the underside of the secondary hull. "Ready," he said. "Locked on."

"Engage."

The false-color display on the viewscreen showed

the beam appearing between *Endeavour* and the carrier ship. Yet instead of locking onto the ship's center of mass, the beam went awry and only snagged a row of cell ships extending outward from the rear docking node. Moments later, the carrier jettisoned the cell ships and pulled free, its descent trajectory barely interrupted.

"Let me guess," Valk growled. "The tractor beam is Tellarite."

"Vulcan," T'Pol corrected. Still, the general's basic premise was correct; as with the deflectors, it was proving difficult to integrate the technology effectively with the human ship's systems—in this case, the targeting sensors, which were susceptible to the gravimetric distortion induced by the beam.

But Reed actually seemed pleased by the result. "Captain, I have an idea."

"Go ahead."

"Elizabeth, can you isolate which pods the Tandaran biosigns are in?"

"Yes, Commander," Cutler replied. "They're in the two large cell ships at twelve o'clock and nine o'clock in the second cluster from the front."

Reed circled the tactical console and came up to Kimura's side. "Takashi, do you think you can snag one with the tractor beam while I get the grappler lines on the other?"

"I think I can compensate for the beam drift manually, sir. But we need to take their shields down first."

"Shouldn't be a problem," Reed told him, and they exchanged a quick look and a knowing nod.

Working together, Kimura and Reed let loose three of the ship's phase cannon beams against strategic points around the second docking node, and T'Pol observed the characteristic shimmer of failing shields. Moments later, the tractor beam brushed the front of one of the cells, then locked on more firmly as the ship's forward momentum brought it more fully into contact. Seconds after that, the fullerene grappling lines snagged the other cell ship. The carrier strained against the pull for a few moments, then released both pods.

"Get them out of there!" Archer ordered, and not a moment too soon. As *Endeavour* drew in both cells, the carrier began firing at them as it continued on toward the defense perimeter. "Can you beam them out?"

"Something in the hulls is still jamming our scans," Cutler said. "We need to get them closer to force a beam through."

"Then do it!" Valk bellowed.

Fortunately, *Endeavour*'s refit had included the enlargement of the main transporter pad and the installation of a second unit, for both transporters were needed to beam off the occupants of both cell ships simultaneously, just before the carrier's fire hit home and destroyed them.

"The carrier's almost to the perimeter," Reed reported from tactical. "We're too far to reach them in time."

But a proximity alert sounded on the console. "It's the *Grentra*, incoming, sir!" Kimura reported.

Moments later, plasma bolts began raining down on the compromised carrier.

"Tell your people to take them alive, General!" Archer said. "We need to prove who's really behind this."

"Don't worry, Admiral," Valk said. "You'll be given that chance."

In moments, the carrier was neutralized and held in the *Grentra*'s own grapplers. But the forward cell ship broke free and shot for the planet surface, and moments later the carrier exploded. "*Grentra*, damage report!" Valk demanded. Major Glith's voice reported that the Tandaran warship had sustained only minimal damage.

"But what about our proof?" Travis Mayweather asked.

"That won't be a problem," Reed said, grinning. "Security reports we beamed over a couple of the children's abductors along with them. One was injured in the battle, the other's been stunned after trying to start something with our people. They're on their way to sickbay now along with the children."

Archer was already heading for the lift. "General, will you join me?"

General Valk's first concern on reaching sickbay was the well-being of the children, but Phlox assured him that they were all intact aside from some cuts and bruises, and of course the emotional trauma of their ordeal. Valk showed unexpected gentleness in speaking to the children and reassuring them they were safe— and Archer had a greater understanding for the steel underneath his words when Valk demanded that they be taken to his ship immediately so they could be reunited with their own people. Phlox agreed there was no reason they couldn't be discharged, and Archer had them escorted to the transporters.

That left the two captive raiders, both still sedated. One was currently on the main operating table in front of the imaging chamber, while the other was on one of the biobeds along the outer wall of the circular complex. "Suliban," Valk said, observing their cantaloupe-skinned appearance. He gestured to their formfitting red jumpsuits. "And those are Cabal uniforms."

"But appearances, as the humans say, can be deceiving, General," Phlox said with his usual good cheer, a wide smile splitting his chubby Denobulan features. He gestured to the large display screen above the imaging chamber, showing a tomographic view of the raider's anatomy. "Although these individuals have managed to obscure their biosigns sufficiently to fool external scans, a more detailed analysis confirms that their internal organs are very far from the Suliban norm."

"One doesn't expect 'the Suliban norm' from the Cabal, Doctor," the general replied, beginning to grow impatient.

"Ahh," Phlox said, his grin widening as he raised a scalpel. "But does one expect *this*?"

Valk stiffened in surprise as Phlox drew the scalpel deftly and efficiently across the side of the raider's mottled face. Archer was a bit startled as well; his source, well-trained in the ways of secrecy, had not fully briefed him on what to expect. But as soon as it became evident that there was no blood emerging from the cut, he began to realize what he was about to see.

Indeed, a moment later, Phlox pulled back the Suliban face to reveal a different alien face underneath—humanoid in structure with a compact nose and thin lips, but covered in gray reptilian scales, with low, gently curving ridges of raised scales adorning the cheeks and forehead and forming crests above the eyes. "What is that?" Valk cried.

"A Malurian, General," the doctor replied, the showman in him relishing the reveal. "The other is as well, and so, I daresay, were the rest."

"Malurians?"

"They run one of the major criminal operations in known space," Archer told him. "My crew and I first encountered them eleven years ago on a pre-warp planet, mining veridium for black-market munitions. Their operation was poisoning thousands of the native people, the Akaali, until we put a stop to it." Archer remembered the Malurians' leader, a man calling himself Garos. He had been a real piece of work, with the personality of a used-car salesman and the ruthlessness of a Romulan, contending with shocking casualness that a few thousand Akaali wouldn't be missed. Archer had always regretted being unable to do more than send him into retreat, free to wreak havoc somewhere else. "Other Starfleet ships have encountered them a few times in the years since. They're masters of disguise and deception."

"Their dermal camouflage is quite ingenious," Phlox said. "It stretches, respirates, perspires, even heals and grows hair, if necessary, just like the real thing. It can be worn for weeks without needing repair or replacement, barring accident. And it can even mask the Malurian biosigns within."

"When you analyze the captured cell ships," Archer added, "you'll probably find they're fakes too, which is why they didn't have warp drive on their own."

"But why did they attack our colony?" Valk pressed. "And why in Suliban disguise?"

Archer faced him. "To provoke exactly the reaction you had, General. To try to trigger a war between Tandar and the Federation. See, when the major spacegoing powers band together to promote peace, law and order, that's not a good thing for the criminal element. They want to nip the Federation in the bud before it gets too strong—or at least keep us so busy fighting our neighbors that we won't be able to focus on them."

"Hm." Valk contemplated for a moment. "From what I've seen, they needn't have bothered."

"General?"

The massive Tandaran chuckled. "You and your allies can't even get your equipment to work together effectively. I saw how it worried you that I discovered that. But you needn't be concerned. You pose no threat to anyone, least of all Tandar. So we will have no quarrel with you—as long as you continue to stay out of our business." He smirked. "Hmp. I daresay you've got enough problems of your own to deal with."

Qhembembem Outpost

Dular Garos knew better than to try to fight the well-muscled giants who had waylaid him shortly after he'd landed his ersatz cell ship, before he'd even managed to get back to the Malurian compound. He simply let them escort him to meet with their master, knowing his best chance of survival was to play along. He generally preferred more subtle means of dealing with a crisis than open confrontation. He didn't even resist when they unceremoniously ripped off his Suliban disguise, even though it stung as the adhesive pulled on his scales, and even though it had been a very expensive and meticulously designed piece of work.

He was a bit surprised, though, when the massive retainers plopped him down in front of a subspace transceiver. He'd expected to be brought before the local master of this particular syndicate, but evidently he'd drawn attention from someplace higher up—and someone too prominent to be caught anywhere near this cesspool.

"Mister Garos," purred the woman who appeared on the screen—evidently quite a striking humanoid female, judging from the seductive way she presented herself, though she was far from his type. *"You promised us some juicy young slaves."*

"I expected to have a consignment for auction to the highest bidder," Garos replied, matching her faux-amiable tone and the steel hidden underneath. "You were welcome to participate, but I made your people no promises."

"It's not the first time you've failed to deliver the goods, though. You do have the worst luck when Starfleet gets involved."

Garos wished he were still masked; it would have made it easier to conceal the impact her words inflicted on him. He had been rising in influence in his alignment until that upstart human captain, Archer, had exposed and scuttled his veridium-mining operation, earning him exile for his failure. Until he redeemed himself, he would never see his ancestral mating ground again.

"And was it really necessary to kill so many of your own people?" the woman asked, sounding more amused than shocked. *"I doubt your alignment will think very highly of that."*

"It was necessary if we were to convince the Tandarans that the Federation was backing their enemies." He hadn't enjoyed killing so many useful underlings, many of whom had been highly competent. Some had been quite pleasant company as well. But the good of Maluria would always come first.

"Except that didn't actually, well, work, did it? Instead you've just proven to two of the region's powers that they have a common enemy, and probably driven them closer together in the process. Now, why does that sound so familiar?" she asked, idly twirling her long hair with a finger. *"Oh, yes. That's just what happened when the Romulans tried to do the same thing. Rather than provoking a war between the Vulcans, Andorians, and the rest, they provoked an unprecedented alliance—and the result was that troublesome Federation."*

"Is that the only reason you brought me here?" Garos asked. "To critique my lack of originality?"

"Far more than that, my dear Garos. You have the right idea;

this Federation experiment could become a real threat to our free enterprise if it succeeds, so it's in our best interests to smother it in the crib. But dividing to conquer has been tried, and has failed."

"Then what do you propose as an alternative?"

"That we follow the Federation's own example—embrace the strength that comes from partnership," the woman replied, a cunning grin on her delicate face. *"If they want to ally with their neighbors against a common enemy, why, let's give them one—but one that suits our purposes.*

"For the same drive to unite that created the Federation . . . also contains the seeds of its destruction."

2

"So how convincing was this virtual technology?" Malcolm Reed asked between bites of his pineapple chutney–grilled chicken.

"Not as real as Xyrillian or Kantare holograms," Admiral Archer replied after taking a sip of his iced tea. They and T'Pol sat together in *Endeavour*'s captain's mess, and now that Malcolm was a senior officer himself, he had grown far more comfortable dining with his captain—as well as his former captain on occasions like this.

"Probably just as well," Reed replied, and Archer nodded in agreement. Both the Xyrillians and their Kantare trading partners had banned the sale of their holographic simulation technology to other worlds upon learning that the Klingons, who had obtained Xyrillian simulator tech in a trade that Archer himself had brokered, had been using it to torture prisoners. Luckily the Klingons were hard on their toys and lacked the expertise to repair the simulators, so the problem was well on the way to resolving itself.

The admiral shook his head. "But it was real enough. I can't forget that saving those children . . . it's not really a happy ending. A lot of them lost their parents, and they'll all be traumatized by this for a long time to come." He poked at his salad with his fork, then let it drop into the bowl. "I knew the Malurians could be ruthless, but this. . . ."

"Their goal was to enrage the Tandarans," T'Pol pointed out. "Jeopardizing children is an effective way of provoking an intense emotional reaction from most humanoids." She paused, then went on with veiled intensity, "Including Vulcans."

Archer gave her a little smile as thanks for her expression of understanding. Reed reflected on how much T'Pol had mellowed in her years among humans—and how much Archer had mellowed toward Vulcans in the eleven years he'd known T'Pol. The two of them made a fine, if unlikely, team, Reed had long thought, and he felt a renewed twinge of regret that they no longer served together on a regular basis. He had grown unwontedly close to his crewmates aboard *Enterprise*, and though he was lucky to have T'Pol, Hoshi, Phlox, and Cutler still serving alongside him, it just wasn't quite the same.

"It's not just the Malurians," the admiral went on. "What bothers me is how vulnerable the Federation is to stuff like this. We're . . . the new kid on the block. Nobody knows what to make of us yet. And that makes it easy for people like the Malurians to smear our reputation. I mean, I can see where General Valk was coming from. We've just come out of a six-year war—and we won. We don't exactly look peaceful and non-threatening to our neighbors."

"Some would say that's a good thing, sir," Reed

said. "Better to be in a position of strength, don't you think?"

"Not if it makes other people afraid of us. We need to show the galaxy that the Federation is about cooperation. Planets and species coming together for the common good. We need to show them our strength is for protection, not aggression."

"We are demonstrating that," T'Pol said, "by example. Our actions this week have demonstrated it to the Tandarans."

"But it's still one hell of a fragile reputation. And there are a lot of skeptical people out there—and more than a few rooting for us to fail." Reed could think of no reply, nor could he disagree with the admiral's assessment of the challenges ahead.

"Well," Archer said after a long, solemn moment, putting on a more cheerful mien. "That's enough depressing talk for one meal. Especially when I have some much better news to talk about."

Malcolm realized the admiral's eyes were on him, and bore a distinct twinkle. "Sir?"

"I've been sitting on this until we resolved the crisis, so it wouldn't distract you from the mission. And your good work yesterday rescuing the children just confirmed to me that Starfleet has made the right choice."

Reed was still confused. "About what, sir?"

"You've heard of the *U.S.S. Pioneer?*"

"It's . . . one of the newer *Intrepid*-class ships, isn't it?" The *Intrepid*s were an offshoot of the *NX*-class warp 5 technology, a smaller variant built from the same basic components. Like their parent class, they'd seen their construction put on hold during the Romulan War in favor of simpler vessels.

"That's right."

"I'm glad they've put them back into production, sir. They're good, solid ships. As advanced as an *NX*—er, *Columbia* class—but stripped down to the essentials. Lean and mean."

"I'm glad you approve." Archer's grin widened. "Because she's yours."

Reed blinked. "Sir?"

"The *Pioneer*. Starfleet wants you to be her captain."

After a moment of dumbstruck silence from Reed, Captain T'Pol turned to him and said, "That is quite an honor, Malcolm. Congratulations."

"Thank . . . thank you . . ."

"Something wrong?" Archer asked with a lopsided grin.

"It's just . . . sir, I'm very honored by the offer, but I'm not sure I'm ready yet. I haven't been a commander very long . . ."

"Nonsense. You and the rest of *Enterprise*'s old crew have more field experience than anyone else in Starfleet. And even with the added strength of the Andorians, Vulcans, and Tellarites, we're still recovering from all the losses we sustained in the war. Starfleet needs good people commanding its ships."

"I understand, sir. But . . . I feel we've always been strongest as a team. I . . . you know I don't make new friends easily, sir, and this crew, and before it *Enterprise*'s . . ."

The admiral gave him a gentle smile. "I appreciate your loyalty, Malcolm. And believe me, I know how you feel. I didn't like being kicked upstairs at first, but now I see it was necessary." He leaned forward. "We're part of something new now, something bigger. We're building a whole new nation, unlike anything we've known before. And that means we have to be ready to embrace change." Archer reached across the table and clasped Reed's wrist. "And the more trusted friends and comrades I see out there on the front lines, representing the Federation to the galaxy, the better I'll feel about its future."

Reed straightened with pride. "Then it will be my honor to accept command, Admiral. I promise I won't let you down."

October I, 2162
Smithsonian Orbital Annex, *Enterprise* NX-0I exhibit

Coming back to the bridge of *Enterprise* was always a bittersweet experience for Jonathan Archer. Nostalgia for his time aboard this ship clashed with regret at what he had been forced to give up—not only *Enterprise* herself, thanks to the crippling blows the Romulans had inflicted on her spaceframe and internal systems, but the freedom to command a starship at all, thanks to the neurological damage inflicted by the radiations and traumas of his years in deep space. He looked around the carefully restored bridge at the thick plastic shells that encased its consoles and his old command chair to protect them from the skin oils and exhalations of the thousands of tourists who tramped through here during the day, and saw them as a symbol of the inaccessibility of that extraordinary phase of his life.

Archer looked down at Porthos, who was hesitantly lifting his head and forelegs, considering whether to jump up onto the command chair, before deciding that the hard, clear surface encasing it was too uninviting. "I know how you feel, boy," Archer said to the small beagle.

To be sure, those nine years on this ship had been as full of bad memories as good, the majority of them spent fighting wars for the very survival of humanity. He looked back on those first two years of exploration and marveled at how naïve and optimistic he and his crew had been, how recklessly they had stumbled about in a frontier far more dangerous than they could ever have imagined. And yet he envied the younger Jonathan Archer for that very spirit of adventure, that sense of wonder and optimism about the universe beyond the known. Perhaps Archer himself could never recapture that spirit, but he hoped he could help build a future that would allow it to flourish, one where Starfleet could again become a tool of discovery and diplomacy. That was the bright side of being forced into a desk job by his own failing coordination: it put him into a position of greater influence, with the ability to help shape what the new Federation Starfleet would become, and even to make his voice heard in the civilian government. He felt an affinity for *Enterprise* herself: also forced into retirement by incurable system damage, but able to serve as an aspirational symbol for the Federation, an exemplar of its highest ideals and accomplishments in peace and war alike. Though she had endured her share of battles, Archer had seen to it that her primary role during the long Romulan War was a diplomatic one, a charm offensive to win allies and support through good works and neighborliness—not only to help Earth survive the war and ultimately prevail with the help of its sometimes grudging friends, but to lay the groundwork for the role Archer hoped the Federation would come to play in peacetime. Through his peripheral involvement in the Temporal Cold War, he had been given glimpses of a future in which the Federation had united much of the galaxy in peace and protected that peace from those who would destroy it; but those same glimpses had shown him how tenuous and mutable the future could be. He knew for a fact that such a future was attainable, yet he knew he couldn't sit back and trust in fate. It would have to be earned.

Some in Starfleet were clamoring for a new ship bearing the *Enterprise* name; but with a new government still feeling itself out, there was a lot of political jockeying for naming rights of new ships, so another *Enterprise* might have to wait its turn. Indeed, there was some political pressure to avoid using the name for a while, for it was still a controversial ship in some quarters, particularly the Klingon Empire. Promoting Archer to admiral had provoked enough grumbling from the High Council as it was; another *Enterprise* might be too great an affront for the

Klingons to ignore, at least until memories faded and tempers cooled (the latter of which could take an especially long time with Klingons).

And truth be told, Archer didn't really want another *Enterprise* to be commissioned during his lifetime. He appreciated the desire to honor the ship that was his father's legacy and his own greatest pride. But he didn't want another namesake vessel competing with the memory of this one. He was sure there would be other ships of the name someday; humans had been using it for over four hundred and fifty years, and other Federation members had traditional ship names with the same literal meaning of bold venture or ambition—*Vol'Rala* for the Andorians, *Hrumog* for the Tellarites. But for now, when people heard the name *Enterprise*, Archer wanted their thoughts to be directed to this vessel alone.

Not that he was the type to wallow in nostalgia when there was so much work to be done building tomorrow. It was convenient for people to think that was the reason for his occasional after-hours visits to the ship: to walk its corridors with only his beloved dog for company and reflect on the life he'd left behind. But no; this was where he came for his infrequent meetings with a certain individual, meetings that had to be kept off the books but which provided Archer with valuable insights.

Indeed, when Porthos grew edgy and retreated around the helm console, Archer knew his source had arrived. The man had a way of getting into a room without anyone detecting his approach. Archer turned to face the person who stood in the shadows of the situation-room alcove at the rear of the bridge, his dark suit helping him blend into them. "Admiral," the man said before Archer even finished turning.

"Your information was good," Archer told him. "Did you know it was the Malurians behind it?"

"We weren't sure enough to confirm it."

"Or you couldn't tell me what you knew without giving away something I'm not supposed to know."

"Maybe," his source admitted. "But you managed pretty well even without that little detail."

"I guess we did. Hopefully the truth about what happened will keep the real Suliban refugees from being persecuted. We owe you a lot—" He broke off. "I still don't know what to call you these days."

The other man smiled. "When it comes to old friends, I still answer to 'Trip.'"

Archer smiled back and nodded, a bit uneasily. In some ways, the man he'd known for so many years as Charles "Trip" Tucker III was still the same good-natured, unassuming, inventive man he'd always been. But his years as an intelligence agent, working for a section of Starfleet Command so secretive that it officially didn't exist, had changed him. He was very controlled when it came to what he showed on his face, and when Archer did glimpse an unguarded emotion in his eyes, they often seemed haunted.

"Trip," he went on. "I'm grateful for the help. But I have to say, I'm still uneasy not knowing how you got your information. Why can't you tell me that?"

"Don't you trust me, Jonathan?" Trip answered glibly.

"I trust *you*," he replied, though he would have said it with more conviction if Trip had trusted him just now. "But I trust you to follow orders. And I don't particularly trust the people who are giving you your orders."

"I know our methods aren't exactly kosher. Hell, that's the whole point of Section 31 of the Starfleet Charter. Extraordinary measures when nothing else will get the job done."

"In times of extreme threat," Archer countered. "For something like the Xindi Crisis or the Romulan War, I could see it. But I don't see why thugs like the Malurians couldn't have been exposed through more conventional channels."

"They coulda been, but they weren't. Isn't it enough that you stopped them?"

Archer sighed, unable to refute the sentiment. "I just . . . I worry about you, Trip. I don't like what this agency is doing to you." He went on after a thoughtful pause. "Why not come back to Starfleet? You only faked your death so you could infiltrate the Romulans. There's no more reason not to let your family know, let Hoshi and Travis know, that you're still alive. They still miss you, Trip."

Trip was quiet for a time, and Archer feared he'd retreat into enigma once again. But finally the younger man spoke. "I've thought about it a hundred times. But I always come to the same answer. They've had seven years to get used to me bein' dead and move on.

It'd hurt them too much to open those old wounds."

"They'd be glad to see you. To know you're okay."

"But I'm not!" He looked away, taking a deep breath to regain his control. "That is . . . I'm not the Trip they knew. Not anymore. The things I've seen these past seven years, the things I've lived through . . . the things I've had to do to survive. . . ." He shook his head. "I couldn't face them. Couldn't pretend to be the man they remember."

Archer waited, but Trip said nothing more. "Like at the Battle of Cheron?" he prompted gently. Only silence met him. "Trip, are you ever going to tell me how you survived that escape pod blowing up?"

For a time, after learning of Trip's escape from a Romulan ship and the subsequent destruction of his pod, Archer had feared that the death report he had fraudulently filed years earlier had finally become true. Eventually Trip had renewed contact, but since then, Archer sometimes feared that he'd lost his friend at that battle after all. He was so different now, more subdued and closed off. Something troubled him, and he refused to confide in his old friend about it. Archer suspected that it was linked with whatever had befallen Trip at Cheron.

But Trip was no more ready to reveal the truth now. "You wouldn't understand, Jonathan. You can't know what I've been through, how I think now, and neither can they. And I don't want 'em to know. They don't deserve that. Let them remember me as I was.

"Trip Tucker really did die seven years ago. And he ain't ever comin' back."

October 4, 2162
San Francisco Navy Yards Orbital Facility

Travis Mayweather was glad the newly minted Captain
Malcolm Reed had invited him to pilot the inspection
pod for his tour of the *U.S.S. Pioneer,* which hovered
inside an orbital spacedock frame while a Starfleet engineering team completed its refits. He'd always found
the *Intrepid* class an endearingly clunky breed, its makeshift nature reminding him of the Earth Cargo Service
freighters he'd spent the first two decades of his life on
and around. An *Intrepid* was basically the front half of
an *NX/Columbia*-class saucer plus a bit more, tapering
back from the centerline in a Y shape whose "tail" section contained the warp drive. The nacelles, mounted
to the engine tail with delta-shaped struts like those
of an *NX* but smaller, were in so close that their forward Bussard-collector assemblies actually rested atop
the half-saucer—necessitating an extra pair of cool-
ing fins extending from the nacelle sides farther aft so
that the occupied sections underneath the nacelle caps
didn't grow uncomfortably hot. Mayweather imagined
they must still get pretty noisy when the warp coils
were running near their peak, but those sections were
mainly cargo and hangar bays.

The tightly packed design allowed for a compact,
relatively low-power warp bubble, enabling the ships
to go faster with less power expenditure. The *Intrepid*
class had started out as a backup plan to repurpose
NX-class components for ships that could get up to
warp 3 or 3.5 in case the warp-5 engine program had

been a failure. But even though that program had succeeded, Earth Starfleet had seen no reason to let that hard work go to waste, and *Intrepid* herself was put in service within two years of *Enterprise*'s launch. She and her classmates had been a valuable contribution to the Earth fleet in the year of the Xindi Crisis and afterward.

"With the new engine core," Captain Reed was telling him enthusiastically as the inspection pod drifted under the ship's tail section, "we should be able to get *Pioneer* up to warp five-point-six in a pinch."

"Amazing," Travis breathed. "And with that tight warp silhouette, maneuvering should be a breeze. You made the right call, picking Ensign Tallarico. She's a great pilot. Trained her myself on the *Discovery*."

"Why do you think I chose her? You'd like Doctor Liao, too. She's a space boomer herself. Born and raised on the *Ibn Battuta*."

"Captain Hussein's ship?" Mayweather whistled. "That's one of the oldest cargo freighters out there. I could tell you stories."

"I've already gotten more than a few from Therese herself."

Mayweather shook his head. "What gets me is that you picked a Tellarite as your comm officer."

Reed chuckled. "I was skeptical at first myself. But Ensign Grev's quite the sociologist as well as a linguist. He's well-studied in other species' forms of courtesy and tact, and unfailingly polite on duty." He grinned. "Mind you, he's still properly rude and insulting to his family and friends back home."

They shared a laugh. "And I hear you're thinking of Alan Sheehan for chief engineer?"

"Well, I couldn't pry Michel away from *Endeavour*. But Sheehan's got experience with this class going all the way back to *Intrepid* herself . . . although he's still getting up to speed on the new engine."

The pod was flying over one of the nacelle caps now, and Mayweather shook his head. "Warp five-point-six. Amazing. I still remember the first time we broke warp five. We thought we were on a milk run to ferry a Vulcan ambassador, and we ended up getting chased halfway across the sector by a bunch of Mazarite gangsters who didn't want her to testify against them!" Reed nodded. He'd been there at the time, of course, but he'd long since gotten used to Travis's fondness for spinning a good yarn. Growing up on the *Horizon*, spending months or years crawling between ports at warp one-point-I-think-I-can, there'd often been little to do but tell each other stories everyone already knew. The trick was to make it interesting anyway. "Talk about a game of interstellar chicken. We were overheating our engines, they were overheating their engines, and it wasn't so much a race to see who was fastest as to see who blew up last. I tell ya, whatever those crooks wanted to hide must've been *really* terrible, since they pushed themselves right to the edge, warp four-point-nine-five. But Captain Archer said, 'It *is* called a warp five engine,' and Commander Tucker said, 'Yeah, on paper!'" They shared a laugh. "I was never so scared to push that throttle forward. I was sure I was gonna get the whole crew killed."

"But you didn't," Reed told him. "You were the first human being ever to pilot a starship above warp five. How does it feel to know your place in the history books is assured for all time?"

"I don't know, Mal—uh, Captain. I prefer not to look at it that way. I'd like to think I've still got some major accomplishments waiting for me in the future."

Reed studied him. "I'm glad you feel that way, Travis. Because *Pioneer* still needs a first officer."

Mayweather looked at him for a moment—and when he realized what the captain meant, he was so startled he almost swung the pod into the side of the drydock lattice. "Sir? You mean me?"

"It's only a two-person pod."

"But I'm just a lieutenant!"

"And I was just a commander a week ago. I'm happy to spread the wealth. And it's a small ship, only forty-six crew—it's not unusual for the first officer to be of lieutenant commander's rank."

"Even so, do you really think I'm ready for it? There must be other, more experienced officers. . . ."

"Travis, you've got all the qualifications you need. You gained a wealth of experience on different ships during the war, served with a number of different crews."

"And kept getting my ships shot out from under me."

"And survived every time, and came away wiser for it." Reed fidgeted. "But there's more to it than that. You fit into all those crews because you're good with people. And . . . as you know, that's not a big part of my particular skill set. It isn't easy for me to . . . overcome my natural reserve with new people."

"I don't know, you did fine with me."

"Which was largely because you made the effort to reach out to me. That's your gift. And that's what I need, Travis. I need a first officer who can relate to the crew, bond with them. Who can be my bridge to them. And I need it to be someone I trust . . . someone I already consider a close friend."

Mayweather was quiet for a long moment. He and Malcolm had been friends for a long time, and the latter had shown it many times through his actions, but had rarely chosen to put it into words. Travis respected his natural reticence, understood that he just communicated differently. But that just made it all the more moving that he'd finally come out and said it.

Mayweather extended his hand and spoke solemnly. "I would be honored, sir. I accept."

Reed gave his hand a firm, curt shake. "Welcome aboard, Lieutenant Commander Mayweather."

3

"YOU'RE FIDGETING AGAIN, COMMISSIONER," said Captain Bryce Shumar.

The Federation Commissioner for Foreign Affairs stiffened slightly and threw the mustachioed captain a look. "Vulcans do not fidget, Captain. I am . . . uneasy with this assignment."

"You've made that clear enough by now, Soval. But we're here," Shumar went on, gesturing at the water-rich Minshara-class planet on the *Essex* bridge's forward viewscreen, the fourth planet of its yellow primary star. He spoke in a dialect characteristic of the Earth island of Great Britain, while his complexion and facial structure indicated that he was one of the many inhabitants of that island whose ancestors had come from the Indian subcontinent. "Close enough that the Saurians have probably detected our approach by now. It's a little late to turn back."

Saurians, Soval thought, finding the term an awkward placeholder. He supposed the origins of the term were logical enough; the lacertilian bipeds native to this world were divided into dozens of nations and cultures, lacking a consensus name for their species. Thus the crew of the *E.C.S. Silk Road*—the Earth

freighter that had first contacted them five years earlier—had referred to them simply as saurians, a description which had undergone memetic mutation
into a demonym, leading in turn to the back-forma-
tion "Sauria" as an informal name for the planet itself.
Still, Soval would prefer to be able to address them
by one of their own names for themselves. Normally
first contacts waited until a species was unified enough
to have a single consensus language. But while Jonathan Archer may have learned the wisdom of limiting
contact with pre-warp cultures through his long asso-
ciation with Soval's former aide T'Pol, other humans
were still quite reckless when it came to contact protocols. Shumar seemed to be no exception.

"Nonetheless, Captain," Soval told him, "I urge
you again to approach this interaction with extreme
caution. Our priority should be to ameliorate whatever cultural contamination the *Silk Road*'s contact may
have caused."

Shumar's mustachioed lip twisted as though he had
tasted something sour. "Why do you Vulcans always
assume that any contact from outside is 'contamination'? No culture develops entirely in isolation, and an
influx of new ideas can be enriching."

"Or disruptive to their fundamental cultural un-
derpinnings. Especially if those ideas are imposed by
activist outsiders with superior technology and resources. Given your own heritage, you should be familiar with that principle from both sides."

"Perhaps in some cases, but here? A civilization
thousands of years older than Earth's, with advanced

theoretical sciences?" Shumar had a point. The only reason the Saurians lacked the technological advancement of Vulcan or Earth was that they were so naturally robust and adaptable that they had less need for technology in order to master their environment. But that had not limited their intellectual development. "Discovering extra-Saurian life only confirmed the theories they'd already formed about the universe. They even had relativity and something resembling the basic warp equation, though they hadn't bothered to develop it."

"And what if that hadn't been the case?" Soval had had this discussion with Shumar before, but humans had a proclivity for reiterating arguments in the belief that simple repetition would overcome resistance. Soval indulged the tendency in this case, as it was the first time they had conducted the debate in the hearing of the full command crew. "Or what if there are unknown cultural taboos we simply haven't discovered yet? There are solid, logical reasons for the Vulcans' contact policies, and it would be in the Federation's best interests to adopt them."

"The Federation doesn't have that luxury, Commissioner." The speaker was Commander Caroline Paris, who moved forward into his field of view. Shumar's first officer was a tall, robust woman of pale complexion and hair similar in hue to the sands of Vulcan, worn in a tightly knotted style that Soval believed was called a French braid. She had also made this point to him on two prior occasions. "Particularly not deep-space traders like the boomers," she went on, using the Earth nickname for the generations of humans who had been born and raised aboard low-warp cargo freighters. "Crews like that depend on first contacts with the species they encounter for food, fuel, repair supplies, medicines— things they don't have the luxury of waiting to find a warp-capable civilization to trade for."

"I'm well aware of the argument, Commander," Soval replied. Indeed, the interstellar traders of Earth, Tellar, and Alpha Centauri formed a significant economic bloc whose political pressure had stymied the Vulcan government's efforts to persuade the Federation to institute Vulcan contact directives. "But surely those with access to faster drives—Starfleet in particular, whose crews are trained to sacrifice themselves for the protection of others—should employ a less self-centered calculation."

"Starfleet's duty is to protect the Federation," Paris countered. "And the Federation's in the same boat as those traders right now. We're still rebuilding from the war, and we need a lot of resources." She nodded at the planet on the viewer. "And Sauria is drowning in resources. Dilithium, tritanium, rare earths, transuranics, whole rain forests of untapped pharmaceutical potential."

"Not to mention their art, their literature, their music," Shumar went on avidly. "Our souls could use nourishment too."

"And one hell of a brandy, according to the *Silk Road*'s captain," put in Steven Mullen, *Essex*'s science officer.

"Since the spirit was surely not distilled from Earth grapes," Soval said to the lieutenant commander, "I believe the correct term would be *eau de vie*, would it not?"

Mullen's broad, dark face split into a grin. "I thought Vulcans didn't drink."

"I have spent many years on Earth, studying your customs."

"We could also use new friends," Paris went on. "New allies, maybe even new members. There are a lot of people out there who still don't like us, so we could use some more who do."

"All the more reason, Commander, to approach this contact with care. However friendly they may have appeared initially, we have no idea what might offend or alienate them—or what might disrupt their social order, their cherished beliefs."

"I get it, Commissioner," Shumar said. "You're the diplomat, so you take the lead. That's what you're here for, after all."

Soval was not reassured. In his experience, Starfleet captains had a way of taking matters into their own hands. Otherwise he wouldn't have bothered to issue his cautions.

Something on Mullen's science console caught his attention. "Uh, sir?" he said. "I'm picking up what seems to be . . . yes, there's a large metallic object in low orbit of Sauria."

Shumar looked at him sharply. "An alien ship?"

"I'm not reading any engine signatures. It's . . . the materials are crude, power output minimal. . . . Sir, it's a space station!"

"Can you get a visual?"

Within moments, working with the communications officer, Mullen managed to magnify and focus the image enough to reveal the space station's structure: a small, primitive cluster of spherical and cylindrical modules, bearing a faint aesthetic similarity to the *Daedalus* class to which *Essex* belonged. "Sir, based on the *Silk Road*'s geological assays, I'd say the materials are strictly local," Mullen said. "Not just from this system, but from Sauria itself."

Paris stared. "The Saurians built it? Five years ago they had no spaceflight capability at all!" She laughed. "I think I'm gonna like these guys."

"Captain!" It was Miguel Avila, the communications officer. "The station is hailing us."

"Can you translate?"

"A moment . . . yes, it's in the language of the largest nation."

"Open a channel."

A soft, sibilant voice came over the speaker—or maybe it was the heavy static giving that impression. *"This is orbital outpost Tai'sheku to approaching Earth vessel. Welcome to Lyaksti'kton! This facility stands ready to provide anchorage and resupply to weary travelers."*

Shumar exchanged a wide-eyed look with Paris, then cleared his throat. "This is Captain Bryce Shumar of the *U.S.S. Essex*, representing Earth as a member of the United Federation of Planets. Your invitation to dock is a . . . welcome surprise. We would be interested to learn how you constructed your, er, outpost so swiftly."

"*You flatter us,* Yu'es'es'es'ex. *In truth, you returned sooner than we anticipated. Even with the cooperation of all members of the Global League,* Tai'sheku *is only half-complete. We only pray it will be adequate to your needs.*"

Ordering Avila to mute the return channel, Shumar turned to Mullen. "Global League?"

The science officer shrugged. "Nothing in the E.C.S. files about it. Must be new."

"Already exposure to outsiders has altered their society," Soval pointed out.

"And for the better, it seems." Shumar nodded at Avila, who reopened the channel. "*Tai'sheku,* our needs at this time are few, but we would be happy to acc—"

"Sir!" Avila interrupted.

"Stand by." Shumar turned expectantly to the ensign.

"We're receiving *another* hail from Saurian orbit."

"Another station?" Paris asked.

"It just came into line of sight around the curve of the planet. The frequency, the language, it's all different."

"A smaller station, too," Mullen added. "Cruder, little more than a tin can in orbit. But . . . it's in orbit!"

"Are you sure there aren't any *other* stations we haven't seen yet?" Paris asked in a flustered tone.

"Pretty sure, ma'am. I'll keep looking."

"In the meantime," Shumar said, "let's hear their hail."

". . . *station* M'Tezir One *extends welcome and invitation to Earth vessel. In the name of the mighty Basileus of M'Tezir, sole inheritor of N'Ragolar's most ancient lineage of rulership, we offer the unmatched bounty and hospitality of our nation."*

"N'Ragolar?" Paris asked.

Avila answered. "The name of their planet in the M'Tezir language."

"Outpost Tai'sheku to Yu'es'es'es'ex. You may be experiencing signal interference from an outside source. Let us reiterate: this outpost represents the Global League of Lyaksti'kton, a co-operative endeavor on behalf of all major nations of our world. We urge you not to be led astray by distracting signals. Tai'sheku is uniquely capable to provide safe haven to your vessel."

"It seems their Global League is not so global," Soval observed.

"So which invitation do we accept?" Mullen wanted to know.

"Well," Paris said, "we've got a multicultural alliance on the one hand and what sounds like a hereditary monarchy standing alone on the other. The League sounds more appealing to me."

"On the other hand," Shumar said, "we don't know how much power this M'Tezir nation wields, or how angry they'd be if we turn down their offer." He turned to Soval. "This is your game, Commissioner. Recommendations?"

"It would be best to avoid giving any impression of partisanship," Soval replied. "Take up an orbit equidistant from both stations and send a shuttlepod to each, docking simultaneously."

"Can't we just beam over?" Paris asked.

"We can't get into transporter range of both stations at once," Mullen pointed out.

"And I would prefer not to reveal the existence of transporters at this time," Soval added. "As we have seen, these 'Saurians' are an adaptive and ambitious people, possibly to the point of haste. Transporter technology is not something to be embraced recklessly."

"Very well," Shumar said. "Helm, plot an equidistant orbit from the two stations. Commissioner, you take one, I the other?"

"Logical," Soval granted. He would have preferred to send delegations of equal rank and position to both, but the Commission had not anticipated this situation. Soval did have an aide aboard, but she was a junior functionary. As Starfleet captains—particularly those in the Earth division of the service—often functioned as *de facto* ambassadors in first-contact situations, Shumar was the closest thing available to Soval's equal. "I recommend you visit the Global League station. I will represent us to the M'Tezir."

"Any particular reason?"

"With all due respect to your own diplomatic skills, Captain, I have a suspicion that dealing with the M'Tezir will require extra delicacy."

Shumar took it philosophically. "I won't argue, Soval. Frankly the League station looks a lot more comfortable." He and Paris shared a laugh.

Soval hoped their levity was warranted. Given how complex the situation had grown before *Essex* had even entered orbit, he suspected the difficulties of this contact were only beginning.

October 19, 2162
U.S.S. Endeavour

Doctor Phlox looked unusually somber as he came back over to the examining table where Malcolm Reed had just finished dressing—and admiring the new, narrow third braid on his uniform sleeves. Reed instantly grew just as serious. "What's wrong, Doctor?"

Phlox sighed. "I'm afraid I have some rather bad news for you, Captain. Perhaps you should sit down—"

"Just tell me, Phlox." He braced himself.

"Since this was our last physical before you left us for good, I undertook a more thorough examination than usual. I'm sorry to tell you this, Malcolm, but I've discovered a subtle but significant form of genetic damage to your reproductive system. Your ability to produce viable gametes has been compromised."

Reed blinked several times. It was at once better and worse than he'd feared, and it took some effort to process it. "Are you saying . . . I can't have children?"

"I'm saying it would be unwise to try."

Reed sank down onto the bed, elbows on his knees, face in his hands. It was several moments before he spoke again. "How did this happen? What caused it?"

"I'm still investigating that. It could simply be the cumulative effect of everything you've been through over the years. Space is full of odd radiations even without regular exposure to weapons fire and spatial distortions."

"So if you don't know what caused it . . . does that mean you can't fix it?"

Phlox lowered his gaze. "At the moment, no. I promise I will research the matter diligently, but for now . . ." He shook his head.

"My God." Reed took a shuddering breath. For this to happen now, just at the time of his greatest success, the peak of his career . . . it was as if the universe was punishing him for becoming too optimistic.

But then he thought about the one area where success was still elusive, and laughed bitterly at the irony. "You know . . . it's not as if I had any realistic prospect of . . . procreating in the foreseeable future anyway. I've had my share of romances, but nothing . . . nothing lasting. Never anything that had the potential for . . . that level of commitment. But still . . . family has always been important to the Reeds. And it matters to me to uphold that tradition. I've always hoped that someday, I'd meet the right woman, and . . ." He trailed off. With each passing year, that hope had grown more elusive. But now . . . even if he did find love, the Reed name and legacy might end with him.

"I understand how you feel, Malcolm," Phlox said. "You know how much we Denobulans build our lives around our families—due to the sheer size of them if nothing else. But there is always the prospect of adoption, you know."

"It wouldn't be the same."

"Not the same, but not necessarily less worthwhile. Adoptions are common in Denobulan families, since there are so many parents to go around in each one. Why, my third wife and her second husband—"

"I appreciate what you're trying to say, Phlox. But I'm . . . not ready to think about all that just yet. I'd rather you focused your efforts on finding a way to cure this—this condition."

Phlox placed a hand on his shoulder. "I'll do everything I can. You have my word on that."

October 25, 2162
Starfleet Headquarters, San Francisco, California

Jonathan Archer was pleasantly surprised when his yeoman let him know that Doctor Phlox had come for an unannounced visit. He had been in a meeting with his aide, Captain Marcus Williams, a big, square-jawed Iowan who had performed the same duty for the late Admiral Forrest, and then for his successor Samuel Gardner until he'd requested a transfer to Archer's office. Williams was a good man and a good friend, someone Archer had gotten to know well in the years leading up to *Enterprise*'s launch but had fallen out of touch with until his promotion to the admiralty. Still, their discussion of technological integration for the fleet could wait, and it sounded like Phlox was here for more than a social call.

"Doctor." Archer shook the Denobulan's hand once he arrived. "You remember Captain Williams."

"Marcus, how are you? How's the family?"

"Great, Phlox, just great." Williams had become acquainted with Phlox as well during the latter's months at Starfleet Medical. "Val's just been made armory officer on *Pioneer*, did you hear?"

"Indeed. And I'm sure you can trust Captain Reed and Lieutenant Commander Mayweather to take good care of your daughter." He sobered. "However, I'm afraid I have something sensitive to discuss with the admiral. We'll have to catch up later."

Williams glanced at Archer, who nodded. "Admiral," he said, picking up his data tablet from the desk and heading out.

Archer rested his weight on that desk and asked, "So what's this about, Phlox? Have you made any progress with Malcolm's . . . condition?"

The doctor hesitated. "I'm fairly certain I have identified the cause, Admiral."

"Well, that's good!" He studied Phlox's face. "Isn't it?"

"I am hopeful that it will point the way to a treatment, but that isn't what worries me. You see . . . what enabled me to identify the cause was a certain similarity I noticed between Captain Reed's genetic damage . . . and your own neurological damage."

Archer frowned. "What kind of similarity? What do . . . genes and neurons have to do with each other? Beyond the obvious."

"That's a very pertinent question, as a matter of fact. Both you and Captain Reed have developed your respective systemic degeneration as a result of what I'd believed to be cell replication errors—errors that manifested on a subatomic level, with particles missing or being transposed to the wrong places. I couldn't identify any radiation that could have that kind of effect, which was why I was unable to diagnose the cause of your condition until I recognized the same kind of damage in an entirely different system of the body."

"So whatever caused this, it's something Malcolm and I have in common. Something we encountered on *Enterprise*. Was it the Expanse? The spatial anomalies?"

"I considered that. But I searched Starfleet medical records for similar cases of inexplicable genetic or systemic damage, and I've found four other cases—one of whom, Warren Woods, is a former MACO who served on *Enterprise* for a time, but the other three of whom served on three different vessels. And those are just the ones who've been diagnosed so far. In some cases, as with Captain Reed, the damage is extremely subtle."

"But there is some common factor," Archer prompted. "What are you so reluctant to tell me? Is it life-threatening?"

"Not a threat to life itself," Phlox replied slowly, thoughtfully. "But it could have a significant impact on our *way* of life."

"Spit it out, Phlox!"

The Denobulan cleared his throat. "I found only one environmental or behavioral factor that all six patients have in common. The six of you are among the most active users of the transporter in all of Starfleet. In fact, since you and Captain Reed were two of the first Starfleet personnel to be transported in the line of duty, and have stayed in the service longer than the rest, I daresay you and he have been 'beamed' more than any other humans in history."

Archer stared for a long moment. Finally he rose and walked slowly to the window. "And you're saying . . . the transporter . . . put us together wrong."

"To a subtle extent, and on a subatomic scale."

"They told us it was safe," Archer said. "Emory Erickson and his team . . . they tested it for a dozen years. There were a few early casualties, but they didn't okay it for public use until they were certain it was safe. Or so they said."

"They were as certain as they could be under the circumstances, Admiral. Indeed, the transporter is perfectly safe for a single use, a dozen uses, even a hundred. The occasional bit errors are usually inconsequential, no worse than what the body would normally sustain from background radiation or replication errors in its own DNA. But transporters have been in use with increasing frequency on Starfleet vessels for over a decade now. The damage is gradual and cumulative, not something that could have been discovered until the technology had been in regular, widespread use for a number of years. After all, the odds of any single error occurring are quite low. Most transporter users are still perfectly fine, and might never suffer any damage no matter how long they use the transporter."

"But both Malcolm and I suffered damage. What are the odds of that?"

"Low, but still higher for the two of you than for anyone else. And . . . the danger might be greater if a transporter is used under less than ideal circumstances, such as when the ship is under fire or the power systems damaged. *Enterprise* certainly had more than

its share of hazardous situations over the years." He
stepped closer. "Which reminds me. The third heavi-
est user of the transporter among *Enterprise*'s crew, at
least while he was aboard, was the, ah, late, lamented
Commander Tucker. If he were still with us, it would
be in his best interest to submit to a thorough medical
examination at the earliest opportunity."

Archer almost smiled at Phlox's circumlocution.
They were alone, and it was unlikely that his office
was bugged; but Phlox had picked up some bad habits
from years of watching spy thrillers on movie night.
Still, it didn't hurt to indulge him. "I think . . . everyone . . . who might be affected by this should follow
that advice. And I'll do what I can to pass the word
along."

"Good."

"But what happens next? What are the prospects
for a cure? Or are we just going to have to give up
transporters, go back to shuttlepods again?"

"I think that decision is above my pay grade, Admiral. That's why I brought it to you."

Great, Archer thought. *Just great. Why couldn't it have
been a nice, simple Klingon invasion?*

November 1, 2162
Federation Executive Building, Paris, European Alliance

"All right, we're agreed," said Thomas Vanderbilt, running a slender, olive-skinned hand through his monk's
fringe of graying black hair. "All Starfleet services will
suspend routine use of existing transporter systems

for personnel transport immediately. For now, they're to be reserved for inanimate objects, with personnel use only in emergencies."

Across the table, the five Starfleet joint chiefs chimed in with their unanimous agreement. Archer added his voice to the chorus; although he was subordinate to the Earth fleet's chief of staff Samuel Gardner, President Vanderbilt had wanted him here as the man who'd brought the crisis to his attention. The first President of the Council of the United Federation of Planets liked to keep Archer at the forefront of the UFP's diplomatic efforts, building on his reputation as one of the key players in bringing the nation together. And this had the potential to be a diplomatic disaster for the young union.

"But what comes next?" Vanderbilt went on. "Is there some simple repair we can make?"

"It will not be simple by any means, Mister President," offered Selvok, the Commissioner for Science and Technology. The Federation Commission was essentially the cabinet of the new hybrid government, with several elected commissioners from each world, each assigned a different portfolio. "Decades of research and use of human transporter technology failed to identify this replication fault. Determining its causes and devising solutions could take years or decades further. For all we know," the middle-aged, auburn-haired Vulcan said, "there may be fundamental quantum-mechanical limits that will preclude ever making transporters completely safe."

"But other races use transporters," said the round-faced,

white-haired Gardner. "The Klingons, the Orions, the Osaarians, the Xindi."

"And the Malurians," Archer put in.

"Not exactly races known for their high standards of safety or responsibility," said Admiral Thy'lek Shran, his antennae curving forward along with his torso. Archer smiled slightly, glad that his longtime friend had agreed to come out of retirement once again to serve as chief of staff for the Andorian Guard—the division of the combined Starfleet that specialized in the defense of the Federation's borders, just as UESPA handled exploration, the Tellar Space Administration handled operational support and supply, and so forth. Shran now wore a green command tunic much like Archer's, but the division patch on his breast was the new Andorian Guard insignia, a stylized initial in Andorii script which looked to Archer like a lopsided pretzel with its upper loop tapering to a point. "Their transporters could be equally dangerous and they just don't care."

"And if we tried to obtain it from them in trade," offered the Tellarite chief of staff, Admiral Mov chim Flar, whose chest insignia resembled a stylized hoofprint, "it would take years of testing to find out if theirs were safe. Wouldn't it, Selvok?"

"Most likely," the commissioner replied.

"And nobody else in the Federation has a superior technology?" Vanderbilt asked. "Selvok, your people are so far ahead of the rest of us in so many ways."

"Not that far ahead," Shran interrupted.

Next to him, the silver-haired Vulcan Space

Council chief, Fleet Commander T'Viri, replied, "Only because you captured and reverse-engineered so much of our technology during our years in opposition."

"And improved on it!"

"Shran," Archer cautioned. The Andorian had mellowed in recent years, but he still had a temper. Yet just one word from Archer was enough to calm him.

"Vulcans have historically been more . . . cautious toward transporter usage by live personnel than humans have been, Mister President," Selvok replied. "And more patient, perhaps, with regard to our transportation needs. Although we have employed transporters for a number of years, they have not been utilized extensively enough by live personnel to allow an assessment of their long-term safety."

"And the Andorians and Tellarites didn't get transporters until they began trading with humans," T'Viri added with another glance at Shran, who mercifully restrained himself from responding.

"The bottom line is, we'll just have to get reaccustomed to traveling the old-fashioned way," Flar said. "Which is perfectly all right with me. You'd never have gotten me into one of those confounded things in the first place."

"I'm gonna miss them," said the final chief, Admiral Alexis Osman. She was a compact woman with wavy blond hair, her uniform bearing the vertical rectangular logo of the Alpha Centauri Space Research Council. So far, Alpha Centauri had few ships to contribute to Starfleet beyond a smattering of freighters and support craft; their efforts were directed more toward terraforming and settlement efforts within their own system than interstellar travel or defense. But like the Vulcans, they were a valuable partner in planetary research, as well as providing significant funding, resources, and logistical and administrative support to the combined fleet. "The sensations are extraordinary. That feeling of the world transforming around you, as if it's being dissolved instead of you. Not to mention all the hassle it saves."

"There's more at stake than that, I'm afraid, Alexis," the president said, looking glum. "Transporter tech is one of the major incentives we've been offering potential members. What will the Denobulans or the Arkenites or the Lorillians think when they find out it's dangerous? This could be a monumental embarrassment."

"We can't *not* tell people, Mister President," Archer reminded him. "Imagine how much worse we'd look if we tried to hide it."

"Of course, of course, Jonathan. I wasn't suggesting that for a moment." He sighed. "It's just that this won't make it any easier to convince other worlds to join our little club."

Archer was aware that securing new members was one of Vanderbilt's highest priorities. There were those who felt the five founding nations had rushed into unification too precipitously after the end of the war, and factions on every member world had protested the perceived surrender of their self-determination. Many on Vulcan, Andoria, Tellar, and their colonies felt the coequal Federation was just a façade for co-opting their own resources to rebuild and defend the war-damaged human worlds. But the war had proven that there were threats in the galaxy that no single government could handle alone, and the previous loose Coalition of Planets had dissolved far too easily when placed under pressure. The Federation had been formed out of a commitment to strength in numbers (though Archer liked to think that his own efforts to promote interspecies cooperation had played a role as well), and Vanderbilt, who had served as Earth's defense minister for most of the war, was devoted to that same principle.

Yet expanding the union was proving more challenging than the president had hoped. Mars had recently agreed to join as the sixth member, but others were more wary. The Denobulans, while remaining close allies, were reluctant to sign on so long as the Federation maintained its ban on genetic engineering—an Earth policy that Vanderbilt had persuaded the Federation Council as a whole to adopt, largely to avoid provoking the Klingons into retaliating against what, in the wake of the Augment crisis eight years back, they would likely perceive as bioweapons research. President Vanderbilt had backed down enough to explore relaxing the ban for lifesaving therapies, but the Denobulans, a people renowned for their patience, were in no hurry to jump on the bandwagon. The Rigelians still held a grudge over the Terra Prime violence of 2155 and were slow to trust what they saw as a human-dominated alliance. And even though the

Andorians had nominated their former subject world Arken II for Federation membership, the Arkenites were concerned that it would mean giving up their newly independent status. Vanderbilt's desire to add to the Federation's strength seemed increasingly elusive.

"Mister President," Archer put forth with deliberation, "I think it's worth considering that . . . maybe it's okay for the Federation to grow slowly. As we just saw with the Tandarans, our neighbors might feel threatened if they see us as an expansionist power. The only reason the Klingons are content to leave us be is that they don't think we pose any threat to them. But we can't guarantee that won't change if they see us getting too big too fast. And let's not forget—it was the Romulans' fear of our original coalition that drove them to launch a war on us in the first place. They're quiet for now, but I'd just as soon not risk provoking them to change their minds."

"So we should hold back our expansion out of fear?" Shran sneered. "I can't believe I'm hearing that from you."

"I'm just saying we shouldn't force things. Before we rush into making the Federation bigger, we need to settle just what kind of Federation it's going to be. What it stands for, what it has to offer."

"I hear you, Jonathan," Vanderbilt said. "And in an ideal galaxy you'd probably be right. But there are other things to consider. The potential danger of the Romulans, Klingons, or Tandarans just underlines how important it is that we *do* solidify our strength. And you never know when another unexpected threat might come out of nowhere, like the Xindi." He shook his head. "And that's assuming we can keep the members we have. I know all your governments are committed to the union," he told the joint chiefs, "but it's still tenuous, and sometimes major changes have a way of propelling the opposition into power. We need to add enough members that we can survive if we lose one or two."

Archer could tell the president's mind was made up on this issue. "Yes, Mister President," he said, and let it drop.

After the meeting adjourned, Shran sidled over to him. "I apologize for suggesting you were afraid, Jonathan. I knew that wasn't what you meant. You just took me by surprise."

He gave his old friend a smile to show there were no hard feelings. After all they'd been through in the turbulent formative years of their relationship—a spot of torture here, a severed antenna there—a few harsh words barely registered. "But you disagree."

"I'm responsible for defending the Federation's borders. The more support my fleet has at its back, the easier I'll sleep."

"And for you, with that responsibility, that attitude makes perfect sense. But the president . . ." Archer shook his head. "It just seems to me he should have a broader view. The Federation is about more than just strength in numbers. It's about . . . about hope and a common purpose. Expanding knowledge and understanding." He clasped Shran's shoulder. "What we have here—what you and I helped to create—it's not like anything the galaxy's seen before. It just has so much promise. And I don't want us to lose track of that bigger picture because we're too fixated on survival and fear."

Shran chuckled. "Sounds to me like you think you could do Vanderbilt's job better than he could. Should I expect to hear campaign slogans for President Archer?"

Archer grimaced. "Don't even joke about that. Like my current desk job isn't bad enough."

2163

2163

4

January 13, 2163
U.S.S. Endeavour

THE SHIP ON THE VIEWSCREEN had clearly been in combat recently, and come out the worse for it. The angular vessel drifted through the interstellar void at a lopsided angle, its multiple engine ports dark. Its tritanium-gray hull bore ruptures and carbon scoring across much of its surface.

"It's an Axanar ship," Lieutenant Cutler reported from the science station. "A light cruiser, normal complement of thirty." She paused. "I'm reading twenty-eight."

"Commander Sato, any response?" Captain T'Pol asked.

"Still nothing on subspace except the distress beacon."

Aranthanien ch'Revash stepped forward to stand on T'Pol's right, watching the vessel carefully. "Scan the area, Mister Kimura," he instructed, not prepared to trust its appearance of helplessness. "Identify any debris, weapon signatures, or the like."

T'Pol gave him an inquisitive look. "Commander?"

"The Andorian Guard has dealt with the Axanar before," Thanien pointed out. "They are an extremely long-lived people, and thus can be quite aggressive toward anything that might shorten their lives unduly—while being far more cavalier about ending the lives of more ephemeral species. Which, by their standards, would include even Vulcans."

"Starfleet's met them too, sir," Hoshi Sato pointed out. "We've always found them pretty friendly."

"Thanks largely to the first impression you yourself were able to make, Commander Sato," Thanien acknowledged. "But I've studied that first encounter, and I'm sure you recall that their combat vessel initially fired upon you even though you were already under attack by raiders. And once they were convinced you had a common enemy, they acted ruthlessly to destroy those raiders."

"You didn't see what the raiders did to their people, Commander. What they would've done to us. Anyone would've been outraged."

"What are you suggesting, Commander?" T'Pol asked him.

Thanien took a breath, trying to match her calm. In his six weeks as *Endeavour's* first officer, he'd found it difficult to establish a rapport with T'Pol. It wasn't for lack of trying, though. Thanien had initially had reservations about serving under a Vulcan captain, but it had been over ten years since he had faced Vulcans in combat, and Admiral Archer had convinced him that if the union of races in the Federation was to work on the large scale, it had to be achieved on the individual scale as well. Adjusting to life aboard a vessel intended more for exploration than defense was a challenge for him, a first in over three decades of service. But he admired what Archer and the humans had accomplished, and was honored that the admiral had granted him the opportunity to contribute to its further advancement. Thus, Thanien was determined to make this work.

But it wasn't easy being the newcomer in this closely knit crew. So he strove for a reasonable tone as he said, "I merely recommend that we keep our antennae wide. We don't yet know whether the Axanar were the victims or instigators here."

"I'm not picking up any debris beyond a few pieces of the Axanar's own hull, sir," Kimura reported. "There is an approaching ion trail, then some evidence of weapon discharges . . . then the trail retreats. It doesn't seem any weaker, though."

"Maybe they were damaged somewhere besides the engines," offered Pedro Ortega, the young ensign at the helm.

"But at least they could move. That puts them in better shape than the Axanar."

"And that means they could come back," Cutler added.

"I'm getting a signal," Sato announced. "It's weak, on a short-range EM band . . . Hold on."

She worked to clear up the transmission, and in moments a low-resolution image appeared on the screen, flickering with interference. *"This is Captain Edzak of the Axanar defense ship* Metsanu," said the figure on the screen, a hairless, antennaless, pinkish-gray biped with a heavily ridged, somewhat reptilian face and pale, slit-pupiled eyes. *"Thank you for responding to our distress signal. You are an Earth ship?"*

The captain rose from her seat. "Our ship is

Endeavour, representing the United Federation of Planets, of which Earth is a member. I am Captain T'Pol."

"Whatever you call yourselves, I'm glad you're here. We've had to make life support a priority and are lacking adequate components to repair our warp drive."

"We stand ready to assist you, Captain. We are unable to breathe the methane in your atmosphere, but we can send a repair crew over in environment suits."

"I'm sure we can handle the repairs on our own, once we have the parts. Your offer is appreciated, but I do not wish to inconvenience your crew unduly. More importantly, it seems likely that our attacker will return before long. Working in environment suits could slow repairs too much."

Thanien stepped forward. "Why do you believe they will return?"

"Because they've already come and gone three times. First they simply appeared in our path, sat there for a short time without responding to hails, then flew off without explanation. Must've been to get us off our guard, because the second time they appeared, they repeated the mute treatment at first, then surprised us with a powerful scanning burst that overwhelmed our systems, leaving us defenseless when they fired a moment later. Yet they left again without pressing their attack. From then on, we were on the alert, so this last time we opened fire as soon as we detected them. They fired back and knocked out our weapons and propulsion, killing two of our engineers. Then they sent a boarding party over."

T'Pol's frown had deepened as she listened to the account, and she exchanged a look of shared recognition with Sato. "Our condolences for your loss, Captain. But tell me: did the boarding party take invasive scans of your personnel?"

Edzak stared. *"Yes. Some kind of sensor beams coming directly out of their palms. We tried to stop them, but they shook off our hand weapons' fire as easily as if we were blowing on them. My quartermaster may never walk again thanks to the nerve damage they caused."*

"Allow our doctor to examine your quartermaster. He has treated this kind of damage successfully in the past."

"I take it you've faced these creatures before? Extremely thin, long-limbed, with translucent heads and some kind of feelers sticking out where their eyes should be?"

"I have encountered them once, twelve years ago. If they have followed the same pattern aboard your ship, they most likely planted a monitoring device before they left. I recommend you initiate a search at once."

"We've already found and disabled their device. You can't be too careful when strangers invade your home."

"Good. If they are unaware you have been joined by *Endeavour*, that may give us an advantage upon their return."

"Then you do expect them to return again?"

"Given that their pattern here almost exactly duplicates their actions twelve years ago, it seems likely. The next phase will probably be a demand to surrender your vessel to them."

"So they finally deigned to speak to you?"

"No. Their ultimatum was an edited playback of our own captain's speech."

Edzak nodded. *"Makes sense, in a twisted way. These things . . . they're disturbingly silent. Even when we fought them in the corridors, they didn't make a sound. No words, no cries of pain* or *effort . . . I didn't even hear footsteps as they ran. And their ships are no better, the way they sneak up on you . . ."* He trailed off, shaking his head.

"On the plus side," Sato put in, "it was over two days before they came back for that last attack."

"Yet their return was only hours after we identified and deactivated their monitoring device," T'Pol replied. "We should not lower our guard."

The captain assigned Commander Sato to work with Chief Engineer Romaine on coordinating repair efforts, due to the communications officer's prior familiarity with the Axanar. This gave Thanien time to review the logs of *Enterprise*'s initial encounter with the mysterious attackers, which he studied on the main table in the situation room alcove at the aft of the bridge. He was struck by the sensor image of the silent enemy's ship: a black, hunchbacked delta-wing craft with a notched prow and luminescent green protrusions along its flanks and rear. "Captain," he said, coming up to the alcove's forward railing and catching T'Pol's attention. "I recognize the enemy craft. An identical vessel attacked *Docana* three years ago, over a dozen light-years from here." T'Pol nodded, recognizing the name of the Andorian battle cruiser he had previously served upon. "I didn't recognize the pattern of their attacks because in our case, they only appeared twice. When they first fired upon us, we took little damage and retaliated forcefully. Their vessel was badly compromised and limped away. We did not see them again."

"*Enterprise*'s encounter was approximately sixteen

light-years from our current location," T'Pol said. "It stands to reason that the aliens' homeworld or base of operations may be somewhere in this general vicinity."

"Still, it's a huge region, much of it unknown. I'm not sure it helps us track them down."

"And the area is too large and ill-defined to make it practical to divert shipping elsewhere."

Thanien's antennae curled disapprovingly. "The last thing we should do is retreat from these aggressors. We know, from both *Enterprise*'s and *Docana*'s encounters, that they slink away when you slap them down hard enough. That's what we need to do here."

"While that might be effective in the short term, it would be preferable—"

"Captain!" Ortega called from the helm. "A ship just dropped out of warp, twelve kilometers ahead!" the lanky, tan-skinned ensign went on. "They're closing on the Axanar—no, wait, changing course toward *Endeavour*!"

"Polarize the hull plating. Raise shields," T'Pol ordered. "Weapons online."

Of course, Thanien thought as he climbed out of the situation room. *They know the Axanar pose no threat now.* He clutched the railing as the enemy vessel opened fire, its weapon ports spitting out scythelike arcs of plasma the same bright green that glowed from its flanks. *Endeavour* rocked. "Shields holding," Kimura said.

"Phase cannons," T'Pol ordered. "Target their weapons and return fire."

Endeavour's beams raked the ship's dark hull, but it

had already veered around to fire on the Axanar ship. Unexpectedly, *Metsanu* returned fire—just from a single emitter, its beam guttering like a flame in the wind, but enough to make a point. The delta-wing vessel veered off. "Intercept course!" Thanien ordered. Ortega had the ship in motion before he finished the words, and Kimura's fire did some damage to the enemy's weapon ports and raked across one of the glowing side flanges, causing its own viridian light to gutter. With both *Endeavour* and *Metsanu* closing to flank it, the vessel retreated, a green aura surrounding it before it gravity-lensed and vanished into warp.

"Pursuit course," Thanien ordered Ortega.

"Belay that," T'Pol said. "Rendezvous with *Metsanu*."

Thanien moved closer. "Captain, we have an opportunity to track them to their base."

"Have you forgotten that the Axanar still have casualties?"

"Not in critical condition."

"Nonetheless, the sooner we render aid, the better their odds of a full recovery." She met his gaze evenly. "As you pointed out, Commander, these aliens are unlikely to attack again after meeting significant resistance."

"And what of the next ship they attack?"

"This is only the third such attack we are aware of in the past dozen years. For the moment, the Axanar would seem to be the more pressing concern."

Thanien held his tongue, reminding himself yet again that he no longer served aboard a battleship. Still, he had to wonder about T'Pol. Her entire civilization seemed to be sinking into pacifism in the years since they had recovered the true writings of their great thinker Surak. He could tolerate that as a philosophy, even respect it in the abstract, so long as there were others in the Federation willing to handle the unpleasant necessities of its defense. But T'Pol was the commander of a ship of the line—a ship that, for all its nominal purpose as a research vessel, still needed to be ready to defend itself and others. Thanien had promised himself he would strive to make this work as Archer wished. But he was not yet fully convinced that he could entrust his safety, or that of his crew, to T'Pol.

Doctor Phlox and Elizabeth Cutler naturally arrived early, while Takashi Kimura was still helping Hoshi Sato set up the compact poker table. One benefit of the added hull of the *Columbia*-class was that it eased some of the crowding in the saucer section, allowing for somewhat larger senior-officer quarters, but it was still a tight squeeze, especially when trying to set out refreshments, table, and so forth with four people in the room. "Sorry, we're early again, I know," Elizabeth said. "I tried to slow Phlox down, but you know him."

"Denobula is a very crowded planet," Phlox pointed out in his defense. "We learn early in life to allow ample time to reach our destinations, in case of delays."

"You've been living with humans for over a decade, Phlox," Takashi pointed out as he pushed past Hoshi to set the dip on the table. The armory officer's own formidable bulk was responsible for more than his share of the crowding in the room, yet he maneuvered with a grace Sato had long admired.

"And with other species for more than a decade before that, in the IME," Phlox added cheerfully, referring to the Interspecies Medical Exchange of which he'd been a prominent member prior to his service on Starfleet's behalf. "But that's a considerably smaller fraction of my lifespan than yours."

"And of course Michel isn't here yet," Elizabeth said. "He'd be late to his own . . . court-martial for being late." The others stared, and she looked around sheepishly. "I figured 'funeral' was too obvious."

Hoshi chuckled, pleased that the soft-spoken, cherubic Cutler was back among the crew. After serving as an enlisted entomologist and medic on *Enterprise* for over five years, she'd been seriously injured during a battle with the Romulans and had needed a few months to recover fully. She'd been offered an honorable discharge, but her injuries had only made her determined to serve Earth more effectively, so she'd enrolled in Starfleet's officer training program, broadening her scientific knowledge and overall skills. She was a bit harder now, and a bit sadder, than she'd been when Hoshi had first met her; but then, all of them were, and Elizabeth still had much of her sweet nature. She was a welcome addition to the crew.

"Now, now," Phlox said. "Given the repairs required for both our ship and the Axanar's, Mister Romaine has good reason to be delayed. And I enjoy the extra time to sit and socialize before the game begins."

"Oh, I've been meaning to ask," Sato said. "What did Commander Thanien think of movie night?"

"He quite enjoyed it," Phlox replied. "Well . . . aspects of it. He told me he admired the respect humans had for the creative achievements and rituals of their forebears, despite the much lower technology they had at the time. He appreciated the insight into his human crewmates. But I suspect he didn't find the movie itself as entertaining. Perhaps romantic comedy was the wrong genre for him; relationships involving only two sexual partners are rather alien to the Andorians."

"Maybe we should try *Bob and Carol and Ted and Alice*," Cutler quipped.

"We should've invited him tonight," Kimura said as he laid out the poker chips. "Better yet, invite both him and the captain."

Hoshi pursed her lips. "Hmm, if you're trying to create a bonding experience for them, I don't know. Last time, Thanien was just so competitive."

"Nothing wrong with that."

"You would think so," Sato teased, punching him in his massive bicep. "But I don't think it'd help build any bridges between him and T'Pol."

"But his tells were easy to read," Cutler said. "As I recall, I cleaned up pretty well that night."

"Yeah," Sato said with a laugh. "I don't think he realizes how much his antennae give away."

"Speak for yourselves," said Kimura. "Between a linguist, an entomologist, and a xenobiologist, I'm at a disadvantage when it comes to reading antennae."

Cutler furrowed her brow. "I don't know about

that. I think Andorian antenna movements are more like cat or dog ears than insect antennae. They angle forward when they're curious, droop when they're sad, fold back when they're in fight mode . . . kind of intuitive, really."

"I'll keep that in mind for our next sparring session," Takashi said.

"You're lucky," Hoshi replied as she got out the cards. "You probably have more in common with Thanien than any of us. No problems getting along there."

Kimura hesitated. "Well . . ."

"What?"

"I don't think he's crazy about us being involved. He's asked me if it might compromise my judgment in a crisis. Or yours."

"Well, it's not exactly unheard of in the Andorian Guard," Sato protested, remembering Shran's grief years ago when his crewmate and lover Talas had been killed by a Tellarite diplomat aboard *Enterprise*. "Besides, we're equal in rank and we head different departments, so there's no ethical issue." Kimura had been a major in the MACOs, a rank corresponding to lieutenant commander, when Sato, still a lieutenant, had first become involved with him. It had been all right then since they weren't in the same chain of command. She'd caught up with him in rank by the time the services were combined, and he'd actually passed up a promotion to stay with her aboard *Endeavour*—a touching gesture, though it made her worry that she was holding him back from the career he deserved.

"I don't think he approved much when it happened

in the Guard either," Takashi said. "He's a by-the-book kind of guy." The door signaled as he spoke, and Cutler, who was closest, went to open it. "But I think he just needs to get to know us better, see what a good team we make both on and off duty."

"By watching me beat the pants off you at five-card stud?"

Phlox perked up. "Oh, are we playing strip? I've always wanted to try that."

Chief Engineer Romaine, who had chosen that moment to arrive, stared at them wide-eyed. "Umm, what did I miss?"

"Yeah, I remember those guys," Charles Tucker said. "Just about the freakiest aliens we ever met out there."

"Certainly an exception to the humanoid norm," T'Pol replied. They walked hand in hand along Sanibel Beach, clad in bathing attire. The sandy ground around them was littered with a wide variety of seashells, casting long shadows in the light of the setting sun.

In reality, T'Pol was in her quarters on *Endeavour*, engaged in her nightly meditation. It was in this state that she was at times able to contact Trip across great distances through their telepathic mating bond, mainly in times of great emotional need on his part, or, admittedly, her own. Apparently her concerns about the attack, and her disagreement with Thanien, had been sufficient to enable such a connection. Or perhaps their minds were just particularly well attuned tonight. Initially they had always perceived each other in the pure white space that T'Pol preferred to visualize when she meditated. But in recent years, Trip had convinced her to let him "spruce up the place" with vistas from his own memory. The beaches of Sanibel Island had been a favorite vacation spot for him, and he was glad of the opportunity to "bring" T'Pol here—particularly since the island, like most of Florida, was still feeling the environmental consequences of the 2153 Xindi attack and was no longer in the pristine condition that Trip's memory presented to her now.

Trip snapped his fingers. "Shroomies! That's it."

She stared at him. "I beg your pardon?"

"That's what the security guys called those aliens. 'Cause their heads looked kinda like mushrooms, you know?"

"A very juvenile slur," she observed.

"Well, they didn't show a lot of consideration for *our* feelings. And it's not like we had anything better to call 'em. Didn't seem like they could even speak."

"Perhaps you would feel differently," she observed, "if you had experienced human children addressing you as 'Miss Pointy.'"

Trip was chastened. "All right, point taken. Uhh, no pun intended." T'Pol glared, but it was just to tease him. She could feel his sincerity through the bond.

As they walked in silence, T'Pol contemplated how close this beach had come to falling victim to human folly. Many such low-lying coastal areas on Earth had been well on their way to total immersion in the previous century due to humanity's irresponsible warming of their planet's climate. Ironically, another human folly had intervened; the so-called nuclear winter following the Third World War had countered the warming process long enough for the human race, having finally discovered sanity in the wake of their near-annihilation, to stabilize their climate once and for all with assistance from Vulcan technology and expertise. The beach was a testament to humanity's ability to scrape through the worst disasters and somehow come out reasonably intact—which made it doubly appropriate that Trip favored it as his mindscape, considering how many bouts with seemingly certain death he had survived over the years. He had even managed to escape the cumulative transporter damage that had afflicted Archer and Reed, as Phlox had confirmed through a surreptitious physical some months ago. T'Pol noted a twinge of irrational hope within herself that the beach would eventually be restored to this condition once again. Perhaps one day she and Trip could even visit it in reality.

"You know," Trip said, "one attack by these aliens, I could write off as a fluke. But now you're tellin' me there've been two more in the past three years."

"That we know of," she added. "A records search has turned up several other ship disappearances in this region over the past two decades, but the rate is not sufficiently above the average to prove a pattern."

"Well, at least it's not another Delta Triangle."

She glared at him again. "The Delta Triangle is a myth."

"That's what you said about time travel." T'Pol

rolled her eyes. Rather than continuing the argument, he examined her more closely. "You're testy tonight. Thanien still gettin' to ya?"

"It is proving difficult to earn his trust," she admitted. "Our command styles and our worldviews are very different."

"As I recall," he said, "you and Captain Archer didn't get along too well at first neither. Hell, it took you a coupla years to warm up to me."

"Possibly longer."

Trip laughed. "So give it time. You're not the easiest person to get to know, but to know you is to love you."

She stopped walking and turned to him. "An interesting hypothesis. Would you care to present your evidence?"

He took her in his arms and proceeded to make his case. It may have been wholly in their imaginations, but fortunately their imaginations were quite vivid.

5

"YOU'RE CRAZY!" Valeria Williams cried. "Sir," she remembered to add as Travis Mayweather glared down at her. "You really want a different Council president every year? They'd never get anything done!"

Mayweather maneuvered around a low outcropping of basalt, working his way gingerly down the slope toward the savanna where the shuttlepod's sensors had registered the anthropoid biosigns. If he were still Val's age, he thought, he could've hopped over it like a mountain goat, as effortlessly as the taut-figured, auburn-haired tactical officer did herself. He was still in fine shape for a thirty-six-year-old, if he said so himself, but he'd still rather be a twenty-six-year-old. "Depends on how much power you give the president," he replied. "The Council's supposed to make most of the decisions, after all."

"But they only meet twice a year! Someone has to speak for them the rest of the time."

Heralded by a cascade of loose pebbles, Reynaldo Sangupta slid awkwardly past Mayweather, almost losing his footing until Val shot out an arm and caught his without even turning her head to look. "Why, thank you, my dear," the science officer said with a gallant flourish, lifting her hand toward his lips. She pulled it away, but gave him a brief smirk that was as much flirtatious as scornful. Sangupta was a good-looking young man, tall with rakish features and rich mahogany skin, and he was fully aware of his own appeal. "But what's wrong with letting the Prime Ministers' Conference make the decisions?" he went on. "The planets shouldn't have to give up too much control to the Feds."

"The ministers are too busy dealing with their own planets' problems. We need a leader for the whole Federation." Her hazel eyes darted back toward Mayweather. "And rotating between councillors isn't going to cut it, Commander."

"I see what you're saying, Val," Travis replied, testing a protruding rock with his foot and deciding it was firm enough to rest his weight on. "But I still think we need to spread the wealth more. We've got an Earth president, the capital's on Earth, the Council meets on Earth. . . ."

"We're the only ones everybody trusts as a neutral broker," Williams pointed out.

"That's just it." He hopped down to the next firm protrusion, feeling the impact more in his knees than he would have a few years ago. "The Vulcans, Andorians, and Tellarites aren't going to get over their suspicions if they don't get to see each other in action as leaders, working for the good of everyone. I'm just afraid humans could end up dominating too much."

"That's gonna happen anyway, sir," Sangupta said as he gingerly lowered himself off the same rock

Mayweather had jumped from—making the older officer feel a little better about his own condition. He paused to take a reading on his scanner, checking the position of the group of anthropoids they were tracking. Hansen's Planet had been discovered by the crew of the *E.C.S. Bjarni Herjolfsson*, who had staked a mining claim on its two dilithium-rich moons but had less interest in the planet (named in honor of the *Herjolfsson* captain's favorite prizefighter, Sven "Buttercup" Hansen), for its dilithium deposits were too deeply buried. However, Starfleet had taken an interest in their reports of a tool-using anthropoid species, and had sent *Pioneer* to investigate.

"What do you mean?" Williams challenged.

"Think about it," Sangupta went on. "With Mars in now, half the full members of the Federation are human worlds. The others, they have a few colonies and outposts here and there, but all still under their homeworld governments. But us, we're expansionists by nature. We spread out, we diversify." He pointed a little bit to the east of their current course, and they adjusted their descent accordingly. "And really, what's so bad about that? It's not like humans are all one bloc. Look at us. A Terran, a Centaurian, a space boomer," he said, gesturing to Williams, himself, and Mayweather in turn. "We're all human, but we're not all agreeing on this."

"That's a good point," Mayweather said. "I'm not sure other species would see it that way, though."

"All the more reason to give as much power as possible to the planets instead of the central government,"

Sangupta went on. "They'll be less likely to see humans as a single political unit."

"But look at what a mess the government already is," Williams countered as they reached the bottom of the slope. The savanna stretched out before them, a vast field of high, green-gold reeds flexing subtly in the breeze. It was punctuated at wide, fairly regular intervals by small copses of exotic pseudo-trees, multiple bamboo-like trunks spreading out from a common base to support wide, round photosynthetic caps like spongy chartreuse parasols. "Too much compromise, too many different institutions trying to represent every world's vision of government. The Council, the Commission, the Ministerial Conferences . . . I mean, it took them six months even to decide we should have a president at all!"

"Maybe we shouldn't," Sangupta said. "That's a relic of the days before modern communications. I say open-source the decision process. Give it to the people. For any problem, there are going to be dozens of experts out there with fresh and innovative ideas for how to fix it. Concentrate the decisions in the hands of a few politicians and those great ideas won't get heard."

"Just what I'd expect a colonial to say," Williams countered.

Sangupta bristled. "What's wrong with that?"

"Easy, Lieutenants," Mayweather cautioned. "We've got some apes to find. Anything, Rey?"

The science officer sulked for a moment before lifting his scanner. Like most Centaurians, Rey Sangupta took considerable pride in his colonial identity. Alpha Centauri III hadn't been an easy planet to tame; at first, UESPA's colonization board had written it off as too inhospitable, still suffering from a centuries-old impact winter and at too great a risk from future asteroid bombardment. That's why they'd chosen a more temperate world more than four times as distant for Earth's first extrasolar colony, Terra Nova—which had ironically fallen prey to an impact event itself after just five years. After Terra Nova had gone dark, a group whose leaders had included Zefram Cochrane himself had defied the United Earth government and founded an independent colony on Centauri III, and over the past seventy-five years had proven they were capable of taming the harsh world, though not without significant losses. By now they had large, populous cities, an active terraforming industry, outposts established on the other borderline-habitable worlds around all three of Alpha Centauri's component stars, and enough of a space infrastructure to deflect any future asteroids—plus a strong, independent spirit and intense national pride. The same pride that had made them insist on joining the Federation as a full member, rather than a UE protectorate, also made them wary of surrendering too much of their sovereignty.

"They seem to be on the move," Sangupta reported after a moment. "And there are other mammals hidden in the reeds—maybe predators lying in wait. I figure the apes generally shelter in the copses—the reeds don't grow in the shade, so they have some open ground and something they can climb if they're attacked."

Williams's hand rested on her phase pistol butt. "So we have to get close enough to get a look at them without them seeing us . . . and without getting stalked by an alien lion pride while we're at it."

The science officer pointed to their right, still studying his scanner. "That copse over there looks empty. Might make a decent observation post."

"Okay," Mayweather said. "Be on the lookout for anything coming through the reeds."

"Good thing the captain isn't here," Sangupta said as they pushed their way through the neck-high ground cover. "How could we tell him apart from the rest of the Reeds?" Mayweather and Williams both groaned, though the latter chuckled a bit despite herself. "On second thought, I know—he'd be the one that never bent."

Williams stopped laughing. "Hey, watch it. You may not like authority much, but you're an Academy graduate. You should know how to respect it."

"Hey, I didn't mean anything," Sangupta protested.

"It's okay," the first officer said. "Just let it go." He couldn't really blame either of them for their attitudes. Captain Reed had been trying his best to be accessible to his crew, but it didn't come easily to him, not with this new group. The former armory officer had hit it off easily with Val Williams, but the rest of the crew was still a work in progress.

"You've both got good points about the government," he went on, trying to change the subject. "But they're based on human experience. I'm just saying, what worked for humans won't necessarily work for everyone else. I think we should be open to other possibilities."

"Maybe," Williams said. "But I'm thinking of it from a Starfleet point of view. We need to know we have a commander-in-chief we can trust. How can that happen if we don't even know who that's going to be from one year to the next? Sure, I'd like to see presidents from the other worlds. But I don't just want to cycle through councillors. The people should elect the president. And four-year terms worked fine for the United States—the first modern democracy on Earth, remember."

"Except when they didn't," Mayweather replied, softening it with a smile. "You're not saying you want political parties back, are you?"

"No," Williams said, holding her hands out protectively. "Anything but that."

"God, no," Sangupta chorused.

As if just mentioning the idea provoked wrath from on high, it was at that moment that the first spear hurtled toward them. "Incoming!" Williams cried before Mayweather realized what the whooshing sound was, and a moment later he was on the ground with Williams's weight atop him.

"Thanks," he said as she rolled off, drew her phase pistol in a smooth, almost unconscious motion, and surveyed their surroundings. Mayweather checked to make sure Sangupta was safe; the science officer crouched to his left, and started as a second spear flew just over his head, thrown from a different direction.

"They're hemming us in!" Williams hissed. She

risked poking her head up to look around. "Must be hiding in the reeds. I can't get a shot."

"So much for clandestine observation," Sangupta moaned. "They must've smelled us coming, or something."

"Or we just made too much noise," Williams snapped at him. "Commander, I recommend retreat."

"No argument there."

Mayweather let her lead them back the way they came, but a heavy rock fell in their path, forcing them to change direction. These ape-things were small enough to hide in the reeds, but evidently quite strong. And fast; Williams fired some best-guess stun shots into the waving reeds, and one provoked a roar, but the rain of rough wooden spears and hurled stones didn't abate. "I think you're making them madder!" Sangupta said.

It soon became clear the anthropoids were herding them, but they couldn't do much about it. To Mayweather's dismay, the reeds gave way to reveal a high-walled notch in the hillside they'd just descended. They'd have to climb to get out, and that would mean exposing themselves to the anthropoids' barrage. "Cover us," he ordered Williams, and she laid down fire to try to keep the apes at bay while Mayweather drew his communicator. "Mayweather to *Pioneer*!"

U.S.S. *Pioneer* NCC-63

"*Captain!*" came Mayweather's voice over the speakers. "*We're under attack by the natives and we can't get to the shuttle.*

You know how they said the transporter's for emergencies only now? I think this qualifies!"

Malcolm Reed hesitated. *"Sir?"* Mayweather asked after a moment.

He shook himself. "Are you sure there's no other option?"

"We're boxed in, Captain, and they're too well-hidden to hit with phase pistols. The transporter's sounding pretty good right now!"

"Stand by." He paced the deck, thinking. Once this decision would have been so easy. But now they knew better. In theory, any single transport wasn't dangerous, but the effects were cumulative. How many times had Mayweather been beamed over the years?

"Sir?" Ensign Grev asked from the communications station.

Reed circled to the starboard side of the bridge. "I have a better idea. Kemal," he ordered the crewman at tactical, "target their position with a low-yield photonic torpedo, atmospheric burst. High enough to frighten off the natives without harming anyone."

The tall enlisted man worked the console for a moment. "Ready, sir."

Reed circled to where he could see the tactical readout. "Travis, all of you, on my mark, get down and cover your eyes, acknowledge!"

"Understood," Mayweather replied, though the captain could hear his skepticism and concern.

"Fire," he ordered. Kemal loosed the torpedo, and Reed watched its track toward the surface, counting down in his head until . . . "Travis, mark!"

On the main viewer, a brilliant pinprick flared for

several seconds. "Commander, report!" Reed called after a moment.

"*That did it,*" Mayweather announced, to the captain's relief. "*The apes are running for cover. I think you scorched some of the tree things, though. That was a little close for comfort.*"

"When have you ever known my aim to be off, Travis?" Reed asked with a grin. "Get back to the shuttlepod, fast as you can."

"*Gladly.*"

"What were you thinking?"

Doctor Therese Liao didn't mince words when she confronted Reed outside *Pioneer*'s decon chamber, where the landing party now waited for clearance to exit. "How are they, Doctor?" Reed asked.

"Lucky," replied the doctor. She was a small but stocky middle-aged woman whose short black hair was lightly frosted with gray. Her normally cheerful round face could become forbiddingly stern when she was upset, as she was now. "They got away with a few scrapes and bruises—plus a nasty case of sunburn. Or torpedo-burn, to be more accurate. Was setting off an antimatter warhead over their heads the best tactic you could think of? Really?"

Reed blinked. Liao's bluntness was difficult to get used to after years serving with the easygoing Phlox. "It was minimum yield, Doctor."

"But it would've been a lot faster just to beam them aboard."

"I shouldn't have to tell you the risks of that."

"What about the risks from the torpedo's radiation?

The odds of genetic damage are a wash either way. And the delay didn't do them any good, not when they were under attack from a horde of spear-throwing gorillas. There's a venerable medical principle you may have heard of that sticks and stones can break people's bones." She took a breath, continuing more softly and with strained patience. "I understand your reasons for being reluctant to use the transporter, Captain Reed." Naturally, he'd briefed the doctor on his medical condition. "But is it possible you let your personal issues get in the way of your judgment?"

In truth, he'd been asking himself that same question. But he wasn't prepared to admit that to his subordinates, except maybe Mayweather, with whom he'd probably talk about it later. Instead, he replied, "This isn't about any one person, Doctor, myself or the landing party. Starfleet's overdependence on the transporter was the cause of the larger problem in the first place. Those days are over now, and we need to get accustomed to finding more creative alternatives. I recognize there may still be emergencies where the transporter is the only solution, but in my command judgment, this was not one of them.

"Now, are the landing party cleared for duty or not, Doctor?"

Liao glared a moment longer. "They're fine. I'll tell them to get dressed and then you can debrief them to your heart's content. *Sir.*"

Liao walked back to the intercom to deliver the good news, and Reed pressed his lips together, reflecting that the conversation could have gone better. He believed he'd made the right call, but he wasn't having much success at winning his crew's trust.

February 25, 2163
Sauria (Psi Serpentis IV)

"Are you all right, Soval?" Bryce Shumar asked. "You look greener than usual."

The distinguished commissioner clutched the railing of the Saurian Global League's administrative barge and strove to keep his eyes on the horizon. "Few Vulcans are accustomed to sea travel, Captain," Soval replied tightly. "Particularly in nocturnal conditions where visible landmarks are difficult to spot."

In truth, Shumar was feeling a bit queasy himself. But before he could confess as much to the ambassador, a cool Saurian chuckle interrupted him. "And here I thought Vulcans were the strong ones in your Federation. Have we finally uncovered your weakness, Soval?"

"All races have their own unique balances of strength and weakness, Basileus," Soval replied as he turned to face the speaker, controlling himself tightly. "This is why we are all better off combining our complementary strengths for the common good."

"Or amplifying our complementary weaknesses— if the Global League is any example."

The Basileus—who by tradition was known only by his title—was the hereditary monarch of M'Tezir, the midsized kingdom that was the largest holdout to Sauria's global unity movement. He was a bit shorter than the norm for Saurians, about Shumar's height, and his smooth hide was more purplish than the pinkish or greenish-brown shades of the majority of Saurian races. As with most Saurians, his bulging eyes and the shape of his mouth and protruding snout gave him a perpetual mien of amused surprise, but Shumar had learned this was deceptive. Many Saurians were as cheerful and accessible as their appearance implied, but the Basileus was calculating, prideful, intensely competitive, and altogether too fond of pointing out the weakness of other species relative to Saurians. His people had been shaped by the excesses of their planet—gravity a fifth above Earth's, a hot climate producing intense weather and forcing most higher life-forms to be nocturnal, active vulcanism that spewed toxic gases in the air and triggered unpredictable shifts in temperature. It made them an extremely robust species that could survive in conditions that would kill most humanoids. Even natural aging took a couple of centuries to overcome them.

Their one weakness, however, was a sensitivity to bright light, requiring negotiations with them to be conducted in relative darkness; hence the nighttime conferences aboard the administrative barge, which had the added bonus of quieter weather and calmer seas than daytime would bring. Shumar, Soval, and the other Federation representatives had night-vision eyepieces if they proved necessary, but the Saurians had obliged them to the extent that their own huge, dark-adapted eyes could tolerate, festooning the barge with larger-than-usual quantities of the dim, bioluminescent lanterns and wall paints they used to light their dwellings—based on microbes the Saurians had bred to glow in a rich variety of colors, making the barge quite a beautiful sight. And that was even without the insect tamers whose trained and selectively bred firewasps danced overhead in choreographed, multihued patterns.

"The League has brought prosperity to all Lyaksti'kton," came another voice. Shumar turned to see Presider Moxat of the Global League's Executive Council—an elderly female whose green-bronze hide was weathered with age but who was still quite strong and vital. "And it could do the same for the people of M'Tezir if you would only allow it, Basileus."

"Perhaps it has eluded your attention that M'Tezir is now the richest kingdom on N'Ragolar," the monarch countered, pointedly using his own people's name for the planet.

"I spoke of the people, not the kingdom. We do not allow ours to starve so that the privileged few can live in luxury."

"My people are deprived because of the way your nations have oppressed and marginalized us for centuries! You've always dismissed us as worthless and weak. Little did you know of the vast trove of precious metals and crystals beneath our feet."

"Don't talk as though you were hoarding some great secret," Moxat chided. "That dilithium and tritanium were as useless to you as to us."

"But they are of immense value to the galaxy, Presider. More value than your decadent art and music and liquor."

"Don't be so sure," Shumar put in. "Saurian brandy is already in demand throughout the Federation." Shumar had been sure to purchase a few cases of the horn-shaped brandy bottles on each of his visits here over the past few months. It had lived up to the *Silk Road* crew's hype, a potent spirit with a superb flavor balance and an impressively long, complex finish. Even without M'Tezir's mineral riches, Sauria would surely become wealthy in trade from their spirits alone.

"And Saurian music has gained much admiration among the Vulcans and Andorians," Soval added. "Not to mention the rich pharmaceutical resources of your tropical rain forests. All the nations of your world have much to offer in trade."

Shumar appreciated Soval's efforts to shore up the Federation's egalitarian stance toward Sauria's nations, but it wasn't easy in the face of the intense rivalry between the Global League and M'Tezir. Before contact, most Saurians had considered the M'Tezir a largely irrelevant throwback to an era of warring monarchies, a people too aggressive in their values and customs to fit into modern civilized society, but too small and poor as a nation to pose any real threat. But once it had been discovered that the rare minerals crucial to interstellar technology had been concentrated primarily on M'Tezir's small continent, suddenly the weak, backward kingdom had become a power player, possessing a commanding advantage that the Basileus had not hesitated to parlay into a seat at the negotiating table. It had been a challenge for Soval to avoid any sign of favoritism in his negotiations for mining rights.

"Your commitment to fair inclusion is admirable, Commissioner Soval," said Moxat. "It is a value we of the Global League cherish as well."

The Basileus scoffed. "Do not believe them, Commissioner. Their 'inclusion' is a sham. Lyaksti has been the dominant empire on Sauria for three millennia. Their so-called equal partners in the League are puppet states, too afraid to defy it."

"We have left the Lyaksti Empire in the past," Moxat countered. "We are the Global League now, and the League is dedicated to even-handedness. It is why our seat of government is here in neutral seas, traveling from land mass to land mass, favoring no one nation."

"So they claim," the Basileus said to Soval. "But they still call the whole planet Lyaksti'kton, as if claiming it for their own. And these barges were used by the Lyaksti royal court as well. A court that had to travel from subject land to subject land for they kept draining each one dry to feed its excesses. Only M'Tezir was strong enough to drive them off."

"You seem satisfied enough now to treat the barge as neutral ground."

"An unavoidable compromise. I came because I know I am indispensable to the Federation. They need my mineral rights, and would no doubt be quite vengeful should any harm befall me at your hands."

Moxat hissed and shook her head. "Paranoid relic. If you will excuse me, Commissioner, Captain, I see a legislator I need to speak to."

Not wishing to be upstaged by the Presider's exit,

the Basileus made his farewells also, leaving the human and Vulcan alone.

"This is just what I warned you about in the first place, Captain," Soval said. "Our arrival has shifted the balance of power and destabilized the political situation. The M'Tezir nation's bellicose isolation was rendering it irrelevant in a growing era of global co-operation. Left alone, this planet might have been unified in a few generations. Now, the M'Tezir are more powerful than ever. I still question whether we should enable them by trading for their minerals at all."

"You're always looking for the direst consequences, Soval," Shumar replied. "Yes, they snipe at each other quite enthusiastically, but the key is, they're *talking*. They're here, together, to pursue a common cause: partnership with the Federation. We have the opportunity to be a unifying force—to bring them together far sooner than they could've achieved without an outside catalyst."

"Take caution, Captain," Soval said. "Such an activist attitude toward pre-warp cultures can have destructive consequences. At least one Earth cargo ship has been known to provoke a holy war on one of the planets it contacted. Early Vulcan spacefarers three centuries ago tried to bring logic to the Andorians, but they resented what they saw as an attempt to pacify them, and the result was centuries of enmity."

"The same thing happened when you first contacted the Klingons half a century later," Shumar pointed out, "and they were already warp-capable. How many decades were you at war with them again?"

"The Klingons," Soval replied with poorly masked irritation, "are a textbook case of the disruption alien contact can cause. The invasions by the Hur'q not only left them with a heightened sense of hostility toward outsiders, but gave them warp technology and advanced weaponry before they had the sophistication to wield them responsibly. It was these experiences that led us to adopt our policy of noninterference."

"But who's to say those aren't the exceptions? My point is, maybe it's not a civilization's level of space technology that should be the dividing line. Maybe there are other factors that make the difference. There have certainly been pre-warp contacts that didn't turn out disastrously, like the Denebians or Valakians. There must surely be races out there that we can reach out to as neighbors and partners without disrupting their societies, that we can elevate to membership in a prosperous interstellar community. Maybe it's simply a matter of carefully assessing which pre-warp cultures are safe to approach and which ones are best to avoid."

Soval studied him. "Perhaps," he said. Then he directed his gaze outward to take in the Basileus, who'd gotten into another argument with a League official. "But are we wise enough to know which is which?"

6

March 5, 2163
U.S.S. Endeavour, **orbiting Wolf 46-III**

COMMANDER THANIEN FIDGETED as he watched the probe data come in on the situation table's screen along with Captain T'Pol and Lieutenant Cutler. "This is frustrating," he said. "I was looking forward to the new experience of serving on an exploratory vessel. But I expected that to mean actually visiting the planets we explored. Not staring at probe image feeds from orbit."

"Commander, if you can come up with a way for us to move around in four Earth gravities," Cutler told him with a wistful smile, "I'll be the first to go down with you. I'd love to look at these guys up close."

"These guys," as Cutler called them, were the native life-forms of the superterrestrial planet they currently orbited, a rocky world with nearly ten times the mass of Earth or Vulcan and an atmosphere so dense that even its oxygen existed in concentrations toxic to most humanoids. Starfleet-issue EV suits were designed for low-pressure environments, not hyperpressurized ones, and would require the addition of some form of motorized armature to enable anyone to move freely in that gravity. "Your curiosity is commendable," T'Pol told Thanien. "But exploration often requires patient observation and contemplation. Particularly in a case like this, we have no idea how disruptive our presence might be to the natives' worldview."

That worldview seemed to be relatively two-dimensional, from what the probes could see. The indigenes were wide and flat-bodied, with muscular, flexible underbellies that let them undulate forward in a manner with similarities to both Terran snails and serpents. Two forward pincers and a complex prolapsing jaw gave them manipulative capability which they employed to construct crude, single-level dwellings with walls of mud brick and roofs of hide or rough canvas—since in their planet's gravity, being underneath anything solid could be quite deadly if it collapsed upon them. Their atmospheric density and chemistry meant that fires would not burn, only smolder, which had limited their technological growth. But indications were that they had found some intriguing ways to adapt, and T'Pol looked forward to studying them over the days ahead.

"Captain?" Sato's voice interrupted T'Pol's contemplation. "We're receiving a transmission." She worked her console as T'Pol came forward. "It's Admiral Archer, for you."

"In my ready room," she instructed. "Mister Thanien, continue monitoring the probe telemetry. Observe carefully," she added with a quirk of her brow.

Once in private and seated at her desk, she opened the channel on her monitor. "Admiral. It's good to see you."

Archer smiled. *"You too, T'Pol. And we'll be seeing more of each other pretty soon."*

"You're recalling us to Earth?" It was not unexpected; as Archer's personal flagship, *Endeavour*'s time was not always its own. The admiral preferred to let it spend as much time exploring as was feasible, in order to set an example for what he felt Starfleet's priorities should be, but that had to be balanced with the need to keep the ship reasonably near Earth and ready to change plans at a moment's notice if Archer needed it. Fortunately, space was vast, and even in "local" space, there was still much unexplored or little-explored territory.

"That's right. I need you to take me and an Earth delegation to a ministerial conference on Deneva."

T'Pol was surprised. Ministerial conferences were one of the organs of the Federation government; when a particular issue of importance to the entire Federation arose, the member worlds' respective ministers with the relevant portfolios would gather to address the issue and devise policy. That was clear enough, but the venue was unexpected. "The Deneva colony is still rebuilding in the wake of the war," she said. "It seems an odd place for a conference."

"Well, it's not just Federation worlds that are involved." He paused. *"You remember that attack on the Axanar ship in January?"*

"Naturally. Has there been another such incident?"

"It looks like there may have been quite a few. I was approached by emissaries representing several nonaligned worlds——Axanar, Rigelians, Ithenites, Xarantine. They'd heard about your encounter

and compared notes. According to them, a number of their ships have either been attacked by the same aliens or disappeared mysteriously in that region. And the frequency of the attacks has been increasing lately. These silent aliens—they call them Mutes—seem to be getting more aggressive. The unaligned worlds are worried, and they've asked us for help."

T'Pol absorbed his words. It was no surprise the alien emissaries had sought out Archer, given his reputation. "I assume they mean military intervention?"

"Yes, and that's what the defense ministers are getting together to debate. On the one hand, we don't want to rush into another war. But if these Mutes are becoming more of a threat, it's better to deal with it sooner than later. On top of which," Archer went on in wry tones, *"President Vanderbilt sees this as an opportunity."*

"He hopes a partnership with these worlds will help convince them to join the Federation."

"That's right. After the transporter debacle, we could use a chance to rebuild our neighbors' trust, to show the rest of the galaxy what the Federation can really do. So this could be a pretty important conference. You'll be escorting me, the Earth defense secretary, and Defense Commissioner Noar to Deneva. Admiral Shran will be joining us." His lips tensed. *"If there is a military action, the Andorian fleet will be doing most of the heavy lifting."*

"Understood. I'll have Ortega set course for Earth immediately."

Archer studied her. *"You sound disappointed. I hope I'm not taking you away from anything too urgent."*

Had anyone else noted her disappointment, she would have been concerned at her failure of control. But Archer knew her better than . . . almost anyone. "There is a matter of some . . . gravity," she deadpanned, "but nothing that can't wait. Indeed, I was just discussing the value of patience with Commander Thanien." At least the probes were still sending telemetry which *Endeavour* could continue to monitor for some time after departing. And perhaps later they could return with the right equipment for a landing party.

Assuming, she thought, *that the Federation doesn't get embroiled in another war.*

March 12, 2163
U.S.S. *Pioneer*, orbiting Earth

"I'm sorry Admiral Archer couldn't be here to meet you in person," Captain Marcus Williams said when Malcolm Reed met him at the entrance to *Pioneer*'s engine room. "It meant a lot to him to keep these upgrade trials in the family, as he put it."

"We're honored to participate, Marc," Reed replied. "Finally reconciling human-made systems with alien tech would be a major advance for Starfleet. Frankly it's been something of an embarrassment for the Earth fleet that we can't use shields at warp without one or both systems suffering. Call it parochial if you like," he added *sotto voce*, "but I'd rather not place the Federation's defense solely in Andorian hands."

"Careful, Captain, your guests are here," the big, square-jawed man murmured back. Coming down the corridor behind him was the engineering team that would be performing the upgrades, a mix of Vulcan, Andorian, and Tellarite engineers. But at their head was a man belonging to a species Reed didn't recognize. The small, stringy-haired man had seemed human at first, but as he drew closer, the captain realized he had a series of leopard-like spots running from his temples down the sides of his face and neck. His diffident manner, downturned gaze, and chewed fingernails suggested he wasn't the type to go in for tattoos, so the spots must be a species trait.

"Doctor Dax," Williams greeted him, "I'd like to introduce Captain Malcolm Reed. Captain, this is Doctor Tobin Dax of the Cochrane Institute."

"Pleased to meet you, Doctor Dax," Reed said, extending a hand.

The engineer offered a perfunctory, slightly sweaty handshake in return. "Captain," he said in a tight, nasal voice. "Umm, these are, are my team," whom he proceeded to introduce, stumbling over one or two of the names. "Sorry. Ahh . . . could we see your engine? Please? If it wouldn't be too much trouble."

"Of course," Reed said, leading them through the heavy, submarine-style hatch into the engine room beyond. It was much the same as the engine rooms on *Enterprise* and *Endeavour*, but a bit roomier due to the slightly more compact warp reactor at its heart.

"Oh, she's a beauty," Dax sighed, smiling for the first time. He climbed the ladder to the raised control station mounted on the reactor; Reed saw that though he appeared to be relatively young, perhaps in his early thirties in human terms, he already had a sizable bald spot.

Reed noted that a few of his engineers reacted warily to the entrance of the multispecies team, their body language becoming territorial, defensive. The captain could understand their embarrassment at not being able to solve the problem without external assistance; but he hoped that was all he was seeing.

But *Pioneer*'s chief engineer, Alan Sheehan, would have none of that. "Doctor Dax," the big, red-haired man said in his booming voice, extending a hand as the Trill arrived beside him at the control station. "Welcome aboard, welcome! It's a privilege to meet you at last. We're going to have a lot of fun on this project, I know it!"

Dax seemed cowed by Sheehan's garrulous presence, offering a timid handshake in return. "Th-thank you. That's very . . . um. Can you show me your current specifications and status?"

"Certainly," Sheehan said, calling up the information on the screen. Reed noted that the other engineers had eased their stance, following Sheehan's example. A few even engaged the other visiting engineers in conversation.

Dax studied the readouts for a few moments and operated some of the controls on the panel, smiling. He seemed to connect far more easily with the console than with the man beside him. "Hmm. Okay. We'll have to recalibrate that . . . and. . . . Hmm, that might be a bit of a problem."

"What?" Sheehan asked.

"Oh, sorry. Just muttering to myself. I do that. I'm sure we can figure it out."

"You've worked with Earth technology before, Doctor Dax?" Reed asked.

"Hm? Oh, yes. I led a warp coil calibration team aboard *Columbia* . . . ahh, just before she was lost. Terrible waste, that."

Reed softened. "It certainly was."

"Yes . . . I did some of my best work on those coils." He went back to studying the warp controls.

"Doctor Dax also worked for Captain Stillwell on the telecapture countermeasure project during the war," Williams put in, trying to move past the awkward moment.

"Oh, let's not talk about that," Dax said, shaking his head. "Sorry, but . . . not a happy time for me." Reed wondered if this nervous little man even knew what happiness felt like.

Sheehan wasn't giving up on being friendly. "You're from Trill, right? You're the first one of your people I've had the pleasure of meeting."

"Oh. Well, I'm afraid the Trill . . . tend to keep to themselves. Very private. Sorry."

"Not your fault," Sheehan laughed, clapping him on the back and making him jump. "So how did you come to be associated with the Cochrane Institute?"

"I like to travel," he said, eyes still on the engine. "My first—um, my mother, Lela, she was one of the first Trill to visit other worlds, like Vulcan. I guess I . . . inherited that from her."

"So why Earth rather than Vulcan, then?" Reed asked.

"Vulcan technology is more mature. Yours . . . well, you still have so many problems to solve. That's more interesting."

"And you think you've found the solution to our current problem?"

"Well, that's what we're here to find out," Dax said with an awkward, breathy laugh. "And, uh, really, the sooner we can, ah, get started—"

"Of course," Reed said. "Alan, I'll leave them in your capable hands."

"No worries, sir," Sheehan said with his usual confident grin. "We'll have the recalibrations done in no time!"

"Give or take," Dax added.

Once they were back in the corridor, Williams studied Reed, noting the look on his face. "Something bothering you, Captain?"

"It's probably nothing. I'm sure Doctor Dax is good at what he does. But he is a little . . . shifty. And nervous, like he was hiding something."

"For what it's worth, he worked on one of Starfleet's most sensitive projects during the war."

"Which went on for years and amounted to little."

"And if he'd been responsible for any kind of sabotage, Stillwell would've found out." Williams lowered his voice. "Between you and me, he can be a little paranoid about those things."

Reed sighed. "Well . . . I suppose I'm the last person who should judge someone for being socially awkward. Just my old armory officer's reflexes kicking in, I suppose."

"Speaking of which," Williams asked, "how's your current armory officer working out?"

"Your daughter's a fine officer, Marc. Perhaps a

little impetuous at times, but she respects the chain of command."

Williams smirked. "If only that had been true when she was a teenager."

"Well, she speaks highly of you now."

"Who said I was the one in command? You've obviously never been married."

Don't remind me. "Anyway, she's conducting inventory in the armory now, if you'd care to drop by for a visit."

"I appreciate it," Williams said. "Lead the way." As they headed down the corridor, he continued. "The impetuousness . . . I'm afraid it runs in the family. Lord knows, I'd be happier if she'd gone into engineering or, or linguistics than security."

"She's never given me cause to doubt her judgment."

"Easy for her captain to say. I'm her father. Worrying comes with the job."

Reed studied him. "Well, then maybe I'm better off not having children."

His fellow captain thought it over. "No way. You don't know what you're missing."

It wasn't the answer Malcolm Reed had hoped to hear.

March 13, 2163
Deneva Colony, Kappa Fornacis III

Deneva was a testament to human perseverance. The colony, established in the late 2140s as a support base for asteroid miners in the Kappa Fornacis system, had been conquered by the Romulans in the first year of the war; upon its liberation the following year, not a single survivor was found. Earth Starfleet had established a base to defend the system's resource-rich asteroids, but had no expectation that another civilian colony would ever be established after the massacre that had occurred. Yet thousands of new settlers had come nonetheless, drawn by the asteroids' riches, by Deneva Prime's natural beauty, and most of all by the determination not to let the Romulans cow humanity into submission. When the Romulans retook the system three years after its liberation, resettlement had seemed a terrible mistake; but this time, all the colonists had been evacuated or gone to ground in the asteroid mines, waging a guerrilla campaign to redirect small asteroids onto impact trajectories with the planet in hopes of driving the Romulans off. The occupying forces had deflected most of the asteroids, but enough small ones had gotten through to keep the Romulans from solidifying their gains until the war came to an end some eight months later. In the nearly three years since, the colonists had returned and rebuilt their home settlements better than before, and the resurgent mining operation had continued to draw new colonists seeking to make their fortunes.

Though a fair-sized impact crater remained a few kilometers away, the heart of the capital city had been fully restored—including the government center where the ministerial conference would be held. The center was an architecturally simple, glass-walled structure that had originally been part of the Starfleet base, but had since been extensively adorned with murals and sculptures reflecting the brief, turbulent history and cultural fervor of the Denevan settlers. The initial reception was held outdoors in its sculpture garden to take advantage of the lovely local weather at this time of year—though it was still a bit cooler than normal due to some residual asteroid dust in the upper atmosphere.

The attendees at the conference were even more diverse than the group who had initially approached Archer. Since the conference had been announced, other governments had come forward to report known or suspected Mute attacks. The Xyrillians had lost more than one ship in the region, and the Tesnians, alarmingly, reported that an entire colony of theirs had disappeared. Search parties had found all ninety-three settlers missing, along with most of their technology, their belongings, and even their buildings. There was no sign of Mute habitation on the planet, leaving their motives as mysterious as ever. But if they had now escalated to attacking planetary habitations, there was no telling how far they might go next.

"Admiral Archer, there you are!" Archer recognized the female who approached him as Boda Jahlet, the Rigelian ambassador, whom he had first met during the initial Coalition of Planets negotiations eight years ago, and who had been one of the emissaries to approach him about arranging this conference. Her craggy, marble-colored face was adorned with horizontal green stripes, while a pair of black lines arced from her hairline to the corners of her mouth, bisecting her eyes and outlining a darker-hued section on either side of her nose. Archer had never been sure if they were natural coloration, tattoos, or makeup, but the elaborate beads that hung from her multihued hair and across her chest indicated she was no stranger to self-decoration. "And Admiral Shran. A pleasure to see you again."

"Ambassador," Archer said, and Shran nodded greetings beside him.

Another figure moved up beside Jahlet—a heavyset, purple-robed humanoid male with a yellow face mottled with dark spots, a protruding brow, no nose, and a high, hairless cranium. Archer had first encountered his species at the Rigel X trading post during *Enterprise*'s maiden voyage. "And you remember the Xarantine representative, Orav Penap," said Jahlet.

"Of course. Good to see you again."

Penap clasped his hand warmly. "A pleasure, a pleasure. We're so glad you could make it, my friends. I hope these talks will be fruitful for us all."

"They'd better be," came a gruff voice from behind Archer. "I'd hate to have come to this dismally bright place for nothing, so you'd better not be wasting my time."

Archer smirked, having grown accustomed to this sort of comment during the journey. "Ambassadors, this is Min glasch Noar, the Federation Defense Commissioner. You'll have to forgive him for having the bad taste to be born a Tellarite."

Noar barked a laugh, appreciating Archer's mastery of Tellarite Civil Conversation. The ambassadors took it in stride, having dealt with Tellarite representatives before and understanding their fondness for argument.

"Rest assured," came a new, resonant voice, "the threat we are here to address is genuine and imminent."

The speaker came forward, and Archer was startled to see his gray reptilian features. He turned to Jahlet. "I wasn't aware the Malurians were part of this conference," he said, his voice tightly controlled.

The Malurian stepped closer. "I can't blame you for your hostility, Admiral," he went on in his polished, rich baritone. "Certainly you've been given little reason to trust my people, and I confess I've played a part in that myself."

Archer felt a shock of recognition. He'd never seen the man's true face before, but he remembered that voice, a voice that had come from a Malurian disguised as an Akaali merchant. The reptilian face before him now had much the same structure as the false Akaali face he remembered, rounded features that hovered somewhere between babyish and thuggish. "Garos, wasn't it?"

The Malurian bowed. "Dular Garos is my full name."

"You've got a lot of nerve showing yourself here." He turned to Jahlet and Penap. "Ambassadors, do you know this man is a criminal and a killer?"

Garos held out his hands. "I confess, I made some tragic mistakes in my past. Mistakes I'm still paying for to this day."

"Funny. I don't see any prison bars here."

A heavy breath. "Such things can be subjective, Admiral. I am an exile from my people. We Malurians tend to stay close to home. Indeed, we must, for our females rarely leave Malur. My alignment believes we must nonetheless reach out into space."

"Alignment?" Commissioner Noar asked.

"A social and political grouping . . . you might call it a corporate state, though in many ways it is more of a family. My alignment, Raldul, believes that expanding beyond Malur is the only way our people can survive in an increasingly crowded and competitive galaxy. The majority alignments disagree—vehemently. The Raldul are treated like criminals for our interest in space . . . and we have been forced to act as such, which is what led to the circumstances where we met, Admiral."

"But you say you're in exile," Archer challenged.

"Thanks to you," Garos said without evident rancor. "Or rather, thanks to my own actions on the Akaali homeworld."

"Because you killed all those people? Or because you failed in your mission for your . . . alignment?"

"As far as my judges were concerned, they were the same offense. If I had simply used a less toxic drill lubricant, you never would have discovered my operation." He lowered his scaled head. "And ever since, I have had to live out here, cut off from my home and my mate, and try to make amends for my negligence by serving Raldul to the best of my ability."

Archer found his show of remorse unconvincing. "And what about the attack on the Tandarans a few months back? Did your alignment have anything to do with that?"

Garos shrugged. "I'm afraid you'd have to take that up with them, Admiral. I am no longer central in their confidences. They tell me what they need me to know."

Shran's antennae twisted skeptically. "But you say they're the only alignment that's actively involved in space."

"An excellent point, Admiral Shran," Garos replied as lightly as if they were enjoying an abstract philosophical discussion. "I concede that my people have not been the best neighbors in the past. But surely you of all people," he said, gesturing to all the UFP representatives, "appreciate that former rivals can unite in their common interest."

"Indeed, indeed," said Penap, coming up beside Archer and Garos and spreading his fat arms to symbolically encompass them both. "Many of our peoples have had our clashes in the past—even we Xarantine, who try our best to help everyone obtain what they need. But these Mutes. . . ." He shook his mottled yellow head. "These Mutes are a threat unlike any we've faced before. How can we deal or negotiate with beings who won't even speak to us? Whose intentions and actions we can't understand, whose needs we can't define? Who attack all of us indiscriminately, not caring who we are?"

"They are as mysterious and intractable a foe as the Romulans," Jahlet added, beads rattling as she shook her head. "Maybe more so. We may not know what the Romulans look like, but at least we have talked with them, negotiated a cease-fire."

"You mean we *made* them accept a cease-fire," Commissioner Noar boasted. "Rest assured, the Federation is not a power to be trifled with. We simply have to show these Mutes who's got the power."

"That is why we approached the Federation for help," Jahlet said. "If anyone can defeat them, you can."

"Indeed," Garos intoned. "While it is true that you have yet to surmount certain . . . technological obstacles," he went on, making Archer wince, "one thing you have successfully proven is the strength that lies in unity. We are all better off working together . . . setting aside old grudges."

His brown eyes held Archer's as he spoke. But the admiral offered no words in return. Garos had a point that the current crisis outweighed past disputes. But he still had that same smarminess that Archer remembered from the Akaali planet. Archer would negotiate with him for the good of all the represented worlds— but he wasn't about to lower his guard.

March 14, 2163
U.S.S. Endeavour, Deneva orbit

"You have to admit," Shran said to Archer as they dined with T'Pol in the captain's mess after the first day of the talks, "so far Garos seems to be on the level."

"Granted," Archer replied. "The evidence of the Mute attacks on Malurian ships was pretty compelling. I'm willing to concede that they're as genuinely concerned about this threat as the rest of us. It's just . . . I'd feel better if they'd sent a different representative."

"Perhaps," T'Pol suggested, "you should set aside your personal history with the man and consider the matter more objectively."

"T'Pol's right, Jonathan," Shran said after taking a sip of pale blue Andorian ale, which to this day he could handle far more easily than Archer could. "I more than anyone should know that if there's one thing you're good at, it's putting past grudges behind you—and convincing others to do the same."

Archer sighed, feeling embarrassed. "You're right. What matters is solving the current problem. And the joint task force that Garos is pushing for isn't that different from the one we organized to find that first Romulan stealth ship all those years ago. And that was the first step toward the Federation."

"And we all know that wasn't without its turbulent moments," Shran said, his voice solemn as he remembered the fatal consequences of the Andorian-Tellarite feuding that had almost derailed the alliance before it began. He shook off the moment of melancholy with a puff of breath and another swig of ale. "Any group like this, there are going to be people with their own agendas, their own contentious histories. The trick is finding common ground, and the Mutes certainly provide that. If we combine our ships with the unaligned fleets, we'll have a large enough force to patrol the region, locate the Mute pirates before they strike defenseless ships, and track them to their homeworld."

T'Pol's gaze swept between the two males. "What would we do once we located that world? As yet we have no way of communicating with these aliens."

"Once they see their homeworld surrounded by enemy ships, they'll have to talk," Shran said.

"And what will we do if they do not?"

Archer interposed. "I doubt it'll come to a planetary bombardment, if that's what you're worried about. We've seen how these aliens behave. Weird as they are, they're still just common bullies. They harass you until you show you can give them a bloody nose, then they run away. A show of force should be all we need to bring them to the table."

The *Endeavour*'s captain set her tableware down and pondered. "Not long ago, in this very room, you said that our strength was not an asset if it made others afraid of us."

"I meant neighbors like the Tandarans or Arkonians. Not pirates like the Mutes."

"You meant species that might be provoked into a more aggressive response. The principle is the same." She regarded Archer. "Consider. Why did the Xindi launch their initial attack against Earth itself? Why not test their prototype on some remote planet so humanity would have remained completely unaware that the main attack was imminent?"

That was something Archer had wondered himself from time to time. "I guess . . . they wanted to demoralize us. Break our spirits."

"Make you afraid of their power."

"Yes."

"And did humanity cower in terror, too frightened to fight back?"

Archer realized where the captain was going. "No. We stood up to defend our own and took the fight to them."

"Exactly," T'Pol said. "Surak wrote of this in the *Kir'Shara.* 'Aggression in the name of defense provokes its own reflection.' Employing intimidation as a means to subdue an enemy usually backfires, making them more aggressive rather than less."

"Come now, T'Pol," Shran said. "I've lived with the Aenar long enough to understand a thing or two about pacifism. Well, a little, anyway. But what's the alternative here? We can't just lie back and let the Mutes attack ships and settlements with impunity. Their raids grow more numerous by the year. How long before they attack someone's homeworld?"

"Space travel in this region has also grown more frequent in recent years," T'Pol pointed out. "The peace between formerly hostile worlds has promoted an increase in trade and civilian travel throughout the region. Increasing prosperity and technology have promoted expansion to found colonies or locate new resources. Conversely, groups preferring to operate on the borderline of civilization, such as the Malurians and many Xarantine traders, have been pushed farther out by the emergence of the Coalition and now the Federation. Perhaps it is not the aliens' aggression that has grown, but merely the number of available targets."

"Targets they haven't hesitated to go after. Either way, they're ramping up their attacks, and once they get used to more active raiding, they'll want more, believe me."

"Shran's right, T'Pol," Archer told his old friend. "We need to nip this threat in the bud. Hopefully once we find their homeworld and get them to talk to us, we can find common ground, negotiate a resolution. If we can't . . . if they're just too alien . . . then maybe we can figure out how to stay out of each other's way.

"But this is just the sort of thing the Federation is for. We have the strength to do something together that nobody could do alone. I mean, we have all these ships now, this whole great big combined Starfleet. Should we just let it go to waste patrolling our borders? Or should we use it to make a difference for everyone?"

"Is that what this is really about, Admiral?" she asked. "Would this task force truly be a necessary response to an otherwise intractable crisis . . . or simply an attempt to find a justification for the continued existence of our warfleet? Are we solving a problem, or manufacturing a problem to fit our solution?"

While Archer pondered her words, Shran threw her a look. "We haven't manufactured anything, T'Pol. They came to us for help. Would you have us turn them away?"

"It is not their request for our aid that concerns me, but the type of aid they requested. Do we want the Federation to become known primarily as a military power? As, to use a human expression, a hired gun that others can recruit to fight their battles for them?

What precedent would that set? And what reactions would it trigger? The Malurians were almost able to provoke the Tandarans into war out of fear that we had aggressive designs on them. And while the Klingons have withdrawn to deal with their internal strife, they have done so only because they do not believe the Federation poses a threat to them. If they decided that we did, then all of our combined forces would not be enough to defeat the Imperial warfleet."

"Not yet, anyway," was the most Shran would concede.

Archer realized, though, that T'Pol's words echoed his own advice to President Vanderbilt about the risks of expanding too aggressively. Surely military adventurism would be even more provocative.

But their neighbors had asked for their help, and the foe they faced was very real and very ruthless. What, then, was the alternative? Where was the balance between standing up for the Federation's values . . . and compromising them?

7

COMMISSIONER MIN GLASCH NOAR was pleasantly hoarse and weary after a lively day of debate. Admiral Archer had made things interesting with his new proposal, sparking enjoyably intense disagreements among the Federation defense ministers as well as the unaligned delegates. He had argued in favor of a smaller, less provocative task force in conjunction with an extensive communication and detection grid so that any ship in distress could quickly summon help, and so the movements of the Mute ships could be more safely and effectively tracked. Noar had found the reduced element of risk in his proposal inviting, especially once Kunas, Vulcan's minister of external security, had pointed out that the larger Starfleet contingent the unaligned worlds were requesting would weaken the Federation's ability to deter smuggling and raiding activities along its borders by Orions, Nausicaans, Klingon privateers, and the like. After all, Noar had argued, what made these Mutes a worse threat than the others?

Admiral Shran had pointed out the increasing frequency of their attacks, and argued that so long as their motives and resources remained a mystery, there was no way to know whether they were just petty raiders out to hijack ships or aspiring galactic conquerors testing their neighbors' weaknesses. The Centaurian defense minister had backed him up, pointing out that the worst threats the region had faced in recent years had come from unknown foes—first the Xindi, then the Romulans. Noar privately conceded they had a point; what kept him up at night was his inability to prepare against those threats he had no knowledge of. But the prospect of letting pirates and criminal networks infiltrate deeper into the Federation's backyard disturbed him too, and Archer's more judicious plan seemed to strike a good balance.

Earth's defense minister, Althea Knowlton, had countered that the Mutes were known to destroy communications beacons in their territory, and had been unconvinced by Archer's technical explanation of how the beacons would overlap and provide redundancy, so that any outage could be quickly tracked down before the network could be further compromised. She added that the Federation had a moral duty to help its neighbors in need, to discover the fate of the crews the Mutes had taken, and to liberate them if they were still alive. This was not a time for half measures, she insisted. Noar had enjoyed the dyspeptic look on Kunav's face when Knowlton had argued that if the Vulcans had fully committed their fleet to the defense of the Coalition of Planets to begin with rather than settling for the halfhearted, passive response of a detection grid, the Romulans would have been defeated much sooner.

But that struck Noar as "fighting the last war," as the humans said. It wasn't yet known if the Mutes were anywhere near as great a threat as the Romulans or warranted an equivalent response. Perhaps it was wiser to start with Archer's more cautious plan and only escalate if circumstances warranted.

As the conference members filed out of the hall, Dular Garos took note of their fatigue, and of the tension of those delegates who didn't take to a lively argument as readily as a Tellarite. "My friends," the Malurian intoned, "we have made you weary, so the least we can do is offer you our hospitality and refreshment. Please, join us tonight in our encampment."

"Yes," added Orav Penap, spreading his mottled yellow arms. "I have been remiss in my honor as a Xarantine not to offer you succor and ease sooner. Please, come so we may express our gratitude to the noble Federation."

Archer looked as though he'd rather return to his ship, but diplomacy demanded accepting their invitation, so the group allowed the unaligned delegates to escort them to their encampment on the edge of the compact city. Though it was spartan, the encampment was made lively by the diversity of its occupants. The Axanar mostly stayed in their ship, the one place on the methane-poor planet where they could remove their atmosphere suits, but the compound was otherwise rife with beaded Rigelians, garrulous Xarantine, diminutive copper-skinned Ithenites, lanky, gray-scaled Malurians, and bulbous-browed Tesnians, all interacting peacefully, though not without the occasional verbal clash to keep life interesting. *They could already be well on their way to joining the Federation,* Noar thought with pleasure.

But there were others here, he registered as the group neared Penap's section of the compound. In keeping with the Xarantine's promises of hospitality, servitors of several species, all scantily clad and more than half female, presented themselves invitingly to passersby, offering their wares and services. Noar spotted several Risians and Nuvians, along with a pair of Klimasz butterfly dancers, one covered in red body paint, the other gold. "Please," Penap said, "feel free to partake of our service providers. We have someone to fulfill every possible need."

Noar watched the females with considerable interest, but Archer reacted with unease. "I . . . appreciate the gesture," he said, "but it's not necessary."

"Ahh, perhaps you simply prefer a more . . . specialized service." He clapped his hands, and four more "providers" emerged—stunning, graceful females whose vivid green flesh was barely concealed by their garments.

Noar found these the most fascinating sights yet, but Archer reacted with anger. "You've got Orion women? Don't you know how dangerous they are? They give off a powerful pheromone that can control people's minds, even cause psychosis!"

Penap laughed. "I see you have encountered members of the Orions' elite lineages, Admiral."

"Elite lineages?"

"Females whose pheromones are exceptionally potent,

able to make males do whatever they wish. Yes, I know that they effectively rule from behind the throne. But it is a trait that runs only in certain genetic lineages. Most Orion females' pheromones are not nearly as potent, and they serve the males as the males serve the elites. Otherwise why would anyone risk buying Orion slave women once they knew the truth?"

Minister Knowlton frowned and said, "You must know that the Federation does not approve of slavery." Nonetheless, her gaze was fixed on the Orions as intently as Noar's was.

"Nor do we, Madame Minister," Penap assured her. "These ladies are all escaped or manumitted slaves. I assure you they work for me voluntarily and are paid a generous wage for their services as dancers, masseuses, or . . . whatever other talents they may choose to offer you of their own free will."

"No, thank you," Archer said. "I think I really need to be getting back to my ship."

"Your loss. But as you will."

Shran departed just behind the human admiral, muttering about his mates back home. The Vulcan and Centauri ministers left with them. But Noar and Knowlton remained, as did the Andorian secretary of war. The Andorian opted for one of the Nuvians, while Knowlton went off with a buxom Orion with wild, dark auburn hair and rich emerald skin. But Noar found himself drawn to a different Orion. While the other two posed and preened and offered themselves to him bluntly, this one stood silently on the threshold, her deep green eyes gazing up demurely from beneath a mane of thick, straight hair as profoundly black as the goddess Phinda's eyes. Under its brief, diaphanous robe, her slender body was the lightest shade of green he had ever seen on an Orion. Though she was not as curvaceous or obvious in her allure as the others, she possessed an innocent, submissive sensuality that enticed him greatly.

"Ahh, you like the quiet ones, do you?" Penap said knowingly.

Noar grunted. "She's awfully scrawny," he countered, just to be polite. "Pale, too. Doesn't she get any sun? And what kind of a massage could she give me with hands that delicate?"

Penap grinned, recognizing that he wouldn't put up such resistance if he weren't genuinely interested. But it was the Orion herself who answered, slinking forward with sinuous grace. "Clearly your ignorance about Orions is as expansive as your gut," she purred in a soft, breathy voice that brushed against his ears like silk. "But I'd be willing to teach you a lesson . . . providing you're not as cowardly as you look."

He returned her smile. "We'll see about that," he told her. "Let's go."

She turned and slinked away, glancing invitingly over her shoulder. He came up behind her—though not alongside her, since he was enjoying the rear view too much. "Do you have a name?"

"I am Devna."

Once they were in her chamber, Devna bade him to disrobe for his massage. She let her own robe fall as well, revealing what little hadn't already been evident through it. And "little" was the word for her endowments, which he pointed out as a playful insult, though actually he found her shape quite lovely. Noar laid on his belly and soon found that the daintiness of Devna's hands was deceptive; they kneaded his muscles expertly, imparting both relaxation and pleasure. "You've worked hard today," her honeyed voice went on. "You must have had much to debate."

"There are many complex issues to discuss—no doubt above your little head. And the talks are confidential."

"Anything we say—or do—in here does not leave this room," Devna assured him. "And I do so love a good debate." Her words were as slow, smooth, and methodically sensual as the strokes of her fingers.

"Mmm, well, I suppose it can't hurt." He outlined Archer's new proposal and the ensuing arguments, the rehearsal of a lively debate soothing him almost as much as did her superb caresses and breathy voice.

"It sounds like Archer's case was most convincing," Devna finally said.

Noar scoffed. "I said it would be over your head. The debate is still ongoing, with much to be decided. It could go on for days," he chortled.

"But the Vulcan was right, don't you think?" He felt a tremor in her fingers. "I can't blame them for fearing the Orion Syndicate. The things they do to the ones in their power. . . ."

He sat up and turned to face her. "Fear has nothing to do with it! We're hardly helpless, frail things like you. We have nothing to fear from the Orions or anyone else." He cupped her cheek in his hand. "And neither do you, as long as you're under Federation protection."

She stroked his hand with her own, her dark, dewy eyes gazing up at him through long lashes. "I wish I had your courage. I've been afraid most of my life. I was always so small, so pale, so underdeveloped . . . even the other females pushed me around." Her hands roved across his hirsute chest.

"Well, it's your own fault for being weak, you know. If you want to be taken seriously, you have to stand up for what you want and not let others push you around! Ah, a bit lower. No, to the left . . . bit more . . . aahhhh!"

"You're so commanding. How I envy you."

"As well you should, little one."

"Still," she went on, "don't you think you should use that strength to defend your own? The only way I survived so long was by taking care of myself first. It was always me or them."

"The way of the coward, of the weakling. The Federation is the strongest power in the region. That's why they came to *us*. They see we have the power. How do we prove that to the galaxy if we don't use it? Yes," he went on as her fingers dug into his flesh more eagerly, as her breaths came faster, "if we really want to scare off your former masters and all the rest, that's the way to do it. Not by cowering behind our borders, but by showing everyone that the Federation won't back down from a fight!"

"Ohh, yes!" Devna threw herself against him, and they needed no more words.

March 16, 2163
U.S.S. Pioneer

As soon as Valeria Williams was alone in the turbolift with Rey Sangupta, his hands were all over her. She made the most of the first kiss, and the second, then pushed him away. "Come on, Rey, not here."

"Let's have dinner together," he said, oblivious.

"Don't be ridiculous. Flaunting it in front of everybody? Besides, you know I'm having dinner with Grev and the doc." The startlingly gregarious Tellarite communications officer had already gone ahead to haul Doctor Liao away from her work. Williams suspected Grev already knew about her and Sangupta, and had deliberately given them a moment of privacy. "Come on, I promise I'll drop by your quarters after."

"I'll be waiting." His seductive smile didn't quite mask his frustration at having to keep their fling private. Knowing Rey, he probably hated not getting to boast about it; Williams was aware that she was considered one of the most desirable women on the ship. She wasn't particularly bothered by that fact; Rey was one of the most alluring men aboard, and she wouldn't mind some boasting privileges herself.

Williams headed to sickbay to meet with Grev and Liao, giving Sangupta time to pick up something in the mess hall separately. When she arrived with them a few minutes later, he'd evidently been and gone, taking his meal back to his quarters. Since the command crew had been kept working late by an overlong combat simulation, the hall was mostly empty. The Trill engineer, Tobin Dax, sat by himself reviewing a data tablet and picking at a largely uneaten salad. The only other people in the room were the ship's anthropology and archaeology officer, Ensign Henry Polanski, and the ship's historian, a sandy-haired man whose name Williams couldn't quite remember. Stan? Sam? The soft-spoken, bookish man hadn't left much of an impression on her; she was more attracted to brash, confident types like Rey Sangupta.

The two antiquarians had taken a table near the opposite end of the room from Doctor Dax, and by unspoken agreement, Williams and Liao gravitated in that direction as well once they'd collected their precooked meals from the compartments along the wall. "Maybe we should sit with Doctor Dax instead," Grev suggested in soft tones.

"He seems quite satisfied to be by himself," Therese Liao said. "I'm content to let him stay that way."

"Oh, Doctor," the chubby young Tellarite said, shaking his shaggy blond head. "I thought you'd overcome your xenophobia issues."

"I'm not xenophobic!" Liao protested. "I'm just . . . not used to interacting with aliens. I didn't encounter many, living on a low-warp cargo ship. The only times it happened, usually, were when I had to deal with an alien infection that got aboard. Some of those did nasty things to my crew, my family."

"I assure you, we're not all diseased," Grev taunted playfully.

Liao blushed. "That's not what I meant to imply. But the thing is, with Dax, I can't even tell. He refuses to let me perform a physical—just gave me a pre-cooked medical scan result and a note from his personal doctor."

Grev snorted. "So you think he's hiding something?"

"Honestly, Grev," Williams said, "I do get that vibe. He's very guarded. Secretive."

"Come on, Val, just look at the man. He's *shy*." Polanski and the historian left, nodding at the three of them but not so much as glancing toward Dax. "And we haven't been doing much to make him feel welcome," Grev went on. "We're treating him and his team like intruders in our home."

Williams thought it over, studying the quiet little Trill's hunched shoulders, his rapt attention on his work. "Maybe you're right," she said, standing and picking up her plate. "Maybe we should try to be more friendly."

"That's the spirit!" Grev said, rising to join her.

"I think I'll stay here, if you don't mind," Liao said. Grev gave her a moue of disappointment but didn't argue—which, by Tellarite standards, meant he was seriously unhappy with her. "Look, I've been on my feet all day, and I'm not as young as you. Let me know if he turns out to be a great guy, and we'll see where it goes."

They made their way across the mess hall. "Doctor Dax?" Grev asked.

Even the communications officer's gentle voice startled the Trill. "May we join you?" Williams asked, putting the same careful, soothing tones in her own voice that she'd use to calm a panicked gunman holding hostages.

"Oh. Umm . . . I guess so. If you want."

"Thank you," Grev said, and they sat themselves down. They had to push a couple of Dax's tablets aside, for which he apologized reflexively.

Williams picked up one of the tablets and took a look at it, skimming through a few screens. There were starship schematics on it: a saucer-shaped ship with an integrated cylindrical section running through the center; a vessel with a spherical main hull like the *Daedalus* class but with three nacelles; a *Columbia*-type saucer squared off in back with a small secondary module above and nacelles mounted below. "These look like Earth designs," she said. "But I don't recognize them."

"That's . . . because they don't exist yet. They're just concepts."

"I thought the plan was to integrate the fleets eventually," Grev said. "For new designs to incorporate the best from every species' tech—like a continuation of what your team is doing here."

"That's what Commodore Jefferies wants," he said. "But . . . I think the best thing Earth contributes is the overall shape and structure of their ships."

"What do you mean?" Williams asked.

Talking about engineering was clearly the right way to get Dax to open up. "Well, Vulcan and Andorian ships are . . . they're great if you want a combat vessel. Their hulls are long and thin—minimizes the forward profile you present to an enemy. Makes you a harder target to hit. But Earth ships, with your spherical or lenticular hulls, have a more efficient internal arrangement. It's easier to get personnel or resources from one part of the ship to another. It's better for a multipurpose ship, or a science ship where you need smooth communication between departments, not so much a top-down organization.

"And the engines, too—Vulcan ring drives are powerful and efficient, but not as easy to adjust in flight as Cochrane-style outrigger nacelles. Again, not as good for flexible mission profiles. And Andorian inboard nacelles are well-shielded, good for combat, but there's a trade-off in longevity and power consumption. Not so great for long-term or open-ended missions like deep space exploration."

"What about Tellarite ships?" Grev asked. Dax just stared, as did Williams. The Tellarites had never been much for starship engineering, preferring to buy their ships from outside contractors. "Okay, just trying to do my part."

Williams frowned. "But Doctor, why are you assuming that these science ships or multipurpose ships are Starfleet's future? Surely we've learned that we need a strong combat fleet. If the Deneva Conference goes the way it's looking, that's going to be proved yet again."

Dax looked down at his salad. "I do have colleagues who favor that thinking. They're pushing for a unified fleet design that's closer to Vulcan or Andorian." The Trill shrugged. "But I think it's better to be . . . able to change identity as you need to, not stuck with just one. Your Earth ships adapted pretty well to combat when they had to. But they can run rings around everyone else when it comes to exploring.

"Don't misunderstand—there's certainly room for improvement. I think getting the different species' technologies to work together is just the first step. Once you've all pooled your understanding, combined the best of all your stuff, it'll synergize, and Starfleet ships will get even better." He tilted his head. "But I think that from the outside, at least, they'll still look basically like Earth ships."

"*If* you're right, Doctor," the armory officer said. "If we have the luxury of being explorers or diplomats. But if this Mute thing erupts, or if the Klingons go on the rampage, then the Federation is going to need ships specialized for war. I hope you're prepared for that eventuality as well."

The Trill sighed heavily. "I've had my fill of wartime projects. If it comes to that, I'll probably go home. Or back to Vulcan, at least. I have a friend or two there."

You have a friend? she thought. *On Vulcan?*

"Well, I think your designs are very nice," Grev said. "So let's just hope it doesn't come to that."

"Yes," Dax said. "Let's hope."

March 17, 2163
U.S.S. Endeavour

When the conference voted to approve the full task force, Minister Kunas was the only dissenter. Archer was surprised; he'd thought that Commissioner Noar had been coming around to his point of view at first, but over the past two days, the commissioner had been one of the most emphatic voices in favor of the more aggressive plan. Once it had become clear the task force would be approved, it had become a matter of hashing out the details—the number of ships, the relative contribution of each member, the location for the command base, and so forth. On the last point, Ambassador Jahlet invited the Federation to establish its command post in her native system, Raij'hl—a name which humans tended to hear and spell as "Rigel," like the far more distant star in the Orion constellation, so the star was sometimes called Beta Rigel to avoid confusion. The local Rigel was a regional hub of commerce and diplomacy, home to immigrants of many species including Xarantine and Ithenites, and it was closer than any Federation world to the territory the task force would be patrolling. The conference, in consultation with the joint chiefs, had agreed with these rationales for accepting the invitation—though Archer had noted that Commissioner Noar had become more enthusiastic in his support upon learning that Penap and his camp followers, including the Orion women, would be accompanying them.

Archer tried to remember that it wasn't his place to judge the commissioner's personal habits. Maybe he was just letting his own experience with Orion women—or, rather, with one elite family thereof—color his perceptions. He'd asked Sato to look into

Penap's claims about the differing levels of phero-monal potency among Orion females, and accord-ing to her, it seemed to be true. The whammy that the Orion woman Navaar and her sisters, D'Nesh and Maras, had inflicted on the *Enterprise* crew in late 2154—rendering the men hyperaggressive and suggestible, inducing headaches and irritability in the women, and triggering a premature sleep cycle in Phlox—had been anomalous among reports of encounters with Orion females. Certainly many of them had a considerable sexual allure that seemed as much a function of their pheromones as their physical beauty and innate passion, but to all in-dications, most of the humanoids who owned or otherwise interacted with Orion women retained their self-control (up to a point, anyway) and ran no evident risk of delusional or psychotic behav-ior. It seemed true that the pheromones exuded by Navaar's family had been exceptionally strong—and having all three sisters aboard *Enterprise* at once, per-meating that closed environment with a triple dose of their chemistry, must have intensified the effect. In any case, Archer had no reason to suspect that Noar's judgment was being compromised by the Orion he'd been spending so much time with over the past few days. After all, it wasn't exactly out of character for a Tellarite defense official to favor a show of aggression.

"Shran's selecting the ships to be pulled from the border patrol fleet," Archer reported to T'Pol, Thanien, Sato, and Kimura as they stood around the situation table. "They're mostly going to be from the Andorian Guard contingents patrolling in the Carina and Cetus border regions."

"The Denebians won't like that," Kimura said, reacting to the latter name. "With the Vulcan fleet in mothballs, they've been depending on the Andorians for protection." The Vulcans had maintained a trading partnership with the Deneb Kaitos system for decades, a relationship the Federation had now inherited.

"Shran says there hasn't been much trouble in that sector recently," Archer told him. "Now that Deneb is a Federation protectorate, that seems to have scared off most of the criminals and pirates.

"*Endeavour* will escort Shran, Noar, and myself to Rigel," he went on. "They'll be overseeing the fleet, and I'm going along as liaison to the unaligned nations. But once the fleet's assembled, you'll be going with them."

"Sir?" T'Pol asked.

He set his jaw. "I don't underestimate the threat these so-called Mutes pose. I remember what they did to *Enterprise*, to my crew. But I don't want to get dragged into another war either, not if there's an alternative. Your job," he said, his eyes taking in T'Pol and Sato, "is to try to find that alternative. The Andorians are soldiers—the best we've got," he said with a nod to Thanien. "But you're explorers. Scientists. Experts in first contact. Use that. Learn everything you can about these Mutes. If you can figure out what they want, how they think, how they communicate, then maybe

we can find a way to head off an armed conflict . . . or
at least end it as quickly and cleanly as possible."

"Understood." T'Pol's voice was level, but he could
see in her eyes how much she shared his hope for a
peaceful resolution.

"You can count on us, Admiral," Sato added.

Archer smiled at her. "I always have."

8

"VERIN, A PLEASURE to see you again!" Thy'lek Shran clasped arms with his old colleague, then turned to introduce him. "Admiral Jonathan Archer, this is Commodore Nisverin th'Menchal. He'll be leading the task force aboard *Vinakthen.*" Shran gestured to the transparent aluminum wall of the spaceport's visitors' lounge, beyond which *Vinakthen* floated, a beautiful, strong *Kumari*-class battleship—newer than his own long-lost *Kumari,* the first ship of the class, but enough like her to give Shran a pang of nostalgia when he looked out the port.

Archer shook the other Andorian's hand in the human manner. "Commodore. Good to meet you at last."

"And you, Admiral. An honor to meet you."

Archer gestured to T'Pol. "This is Captain T'Pol of *Endeavour.*"

The captain nodded, and the elderly, stout th'Menchal gave a similarly reserved greeting. "Captain," he said. "Your *assistance* is appreciated."

"Indeed, indeed," came a new, booming voice. Shran turned to see Dular Garos approaching, as smarmily gregarious as ever. "On behalf of the unaligned members of this joint operation," the Malurian went on, "I must express what a great reassurance it is that Admiral Archer has assigned his own flagship, and his own trusted right hand," he went on, nodding at T'Pol, "to stand beside us in our time of need."

Th'Menchal tensed, but T'Pol faced the commodore and spoke with humility. "It is our privilege to serve."

"And ours as well," Garos said, gesturing to the view outside. "As you can see, we have contributed one of our most powerful warships to the effort: the *Rivgor*."

The vessel he gestured to was a sleek gray warship contoured like some great sea beast, its warp engines ensconced in heavily armored cowlings along the sides. Rows of tiny windows on its flanks gave testament to the sheer massiveness of the vessel, which dwarfed even the *Kumari*-class cruisers in the task force. "I recognize the class," T'Pol said. "Is this the same vessel that engaged *Enterprise* above the Akaali homeworld twelve years ago?"

"A sister ship," Garos replied. "The Raldul alignment owns a number of these vessels."

"Interesting," Archer said, an edge in his voice. "And why do the Malurians need so many gigantic warships?"

Garos spread his hands. "Most of their volume is cargo space, Admiral. We often deal in large quantities of valuable trade goods. Goods which raiders or competitors might wish to steal for themselves. It's only reasonable to transport those goods within vessels capable of fending off any assault."

"Do its origins matter, Admiral?" th'Menchal asked. "Mister Garos, I am grateful for the addition of such a powerful ship to our task force. The greater the show of strength we can display, the more we will cow our enemies and reassure those they threaten."

"True enough, Commodore," Archer said. "But it's important to be able to trust that the ones wielding that strength will use it responsibly."

Th'Menchal's antennae curved forward aggressively. "And how is it your place to determine what is responsible here? Are you leading this task force, or is Admiral Shran?"

"Verin, a word?" Shran said. He drew his friend aside. "Verin, you're being rude."

Th'Menchal stared. "And you've been too softened living with Aenar and humans. I have cause to be concerned, with Archer here. See how everyone bows at his feet."

"Verin, *I'm* the one who'll be giving you your orders. Archer is just here as liaison with the unaligned worlds."

"Does he know that?"

"Don't worry. Jonathan does have a tendency to meddle, and a self-righteous streak as wide as Fesoan's rings, but he's no glory seeker. He respects my authority."

"I hope so," his old friend said. "These humans . . . they're too soft, too careful. Oh, they held their own against the Romulans, true, but war isn't in their nature—they'd rather be exploring and negotiating. We could've ended the war for them in months if we'd chosen to get involved sooner. If this Federation is to survive, it'll be because Andoria leads its defense."

"We already do, Verin."

"Oh, they use our ships, our crews, yes. But under a human commander-in-chief, a council that's half-human, a Vulcan in control of our foreign policy . . . and Archer held up as the guiding prophet of it all, with T'Pol as his chief disciple." The commodore grabbed Shran's arm. "Promise me that if it comes down to a fight, you won't let them hold my Guardsmen back from doing what's needed."

Shran brushed his hand away and glared up at him, speaking through clenched teeth. "I will exercise the same command judgment you've always known me to have, without needing to solicit either Archer's approval *or* yours—*Commodore.*" Th'Menchal backed down. "Yes, Andoria is the backbone of the Federation's defense. But it takes more than a backbone to make a living, breathing organism. We're part of something bigger now, and I expect you to remember that."

"Yes, Admiral."

"Good." Shran took a breath to gather himself. "Now let's get back to the buffet table before the redbat runs out."

March 20, 2163
U.S.S. Thejal AGC-6-38, orbiting Rigel V

It was a pleasure, Thanien thought, to be aboard an Andorian Guard vessel again—even if it was one of the smaller *Sevaijen*-class cruisers instead of a *Kumari*-class ship like *Docana* had been. Several of the larger battlecruisers formed the heart of the joint task force, but the nostalgia that had brought Thanien to *Thejal* was rooted far more deeply.

"Hello, cousin!" the cruiser's captain greeted him warmly when he stepped through the docking port from *Endeavour*.

"Kanshent," he replied, taking her into his arms. Captain Shelav's return embrace was as crushing as ever; she had always been big and strong even for a *shen*. "It's been too long."

"It has indeed. And look at you! You're getting scrawny! Don't they feed you aboard that human ship? We need to get a proper meal into you."

Thanien looked forward to that, but he insisted on a tour of the ship first. It was comforting to be back aboard a starship that didn't have handholds everywhere, a constant reminder of the unreliability of human gravity plating. Not to mention the more efficient and sensible bridge layout—all the consoles facing outward, since the captain needed to see their displays more than their operators' faces, and the helm officer working side by side with a dedicated navigator who performed continuous real-time charting of shifting subspace geodesics, ion storms, rogue planetoids, and the like so that the vessel would not be at the mercy of outdated charts. It was Thanien's hope that as Starfleet became more integrated, its designers could be persuaded to adopt a more Andorian bridge configuration fleetwide.

A "proper" meal naturally meant Dreshna cuisine. Kanshent Shelav's branch of the family had always been more traditionalist than Thanien's, which was why she insisted on using her native Dreshna name even though the Guard officially registered her by her Imperial name Trenkanshent sh'Lavan. Thanien himself answered just as readily to Aranthanien ch'Revash as to Thanien Cherev, although living among humans had given him a new perspective on the necessity for a global nomenclatural standard.

Thejal was too small to have a chef in its complement, but Kanshent was glad to fill that role herself, and roped Thanien into chopping the vegetables just like old times. They caught up on family while they cooked. Kanshent spoke enthusiastically of how her eldest *chei* had won acceptance into the Guard Academy, and of the accolades her *zh'yi* had won for her latest concert. Thanien had little to tell in kind; he had not stayed close to his bondmates after he had discharged his reproductive duties, never finding the secret to balancing career and family the way Kanshent had. He had always felt most at home aboard starships, and as a fellow officer, Kanshent was the family member who understood that the best, and the one he could relate to the most easily.

Yet her response was more guarded when he spoke of his experiences aboard *Endeavour*. As always, she was more comfortable with tradition, though she never judged his greater willingness to embrace novelty. Yet her expression hardened, her antennae drawing subtly back, as he spoke of his difficulties finding common ground with T'Pol. "I don't know why you even try," she said, stabbing at her *chirini* roast. "Of all the Earth ships you could have signed aboard, why the one with the Vulcan captain?"

"Admiral Archer himself requested it. He has great admiration for Captain T'Pol."

"Archer has not fought the Vulcans as we have. As *you* have, or have you forgotten?"

He took her hand. "I will never forget the loss of my *shreya*, nor your *charan*. But both happened long ago, under a different Vulcan regime, a different Vulcan culture. T'Pol was not responsible for our parents' deaths."

"I know the rhetoric, cousin. I have heard enough of it since we agreed to integrate the fleets." She took a bite of her sauteed *hlad* root, washing it down with a sip of ale. "And I understand it. The Federation makes sense. We're better off working with the Vulcans, and the others, than against them. But T'Pol is not just any Vulcan. She was in the High Command for over fifteen years. Before that she was with the Ministry of Security, a spy!"

"Only briefly. And her later service was with the Science Directorate."

"She was still with their military. Who can say what war crimes she may have been complicit in?"

Thanien shook his head, antennae drooping. "Kanshent, you've got to stop living in the past. Whatever her superiors might have required of the captain in her younger days, she's more than proven her trustworthiness over the past dozen years serving with Archer, helping him build the peace."

"Maybe. But how can that ever be enough if she hasn't been brought to account for her prior misdeeds?" Her fist struck the table.

"Cousin . . ."

"I understand the value of the Federation, Thanien. I want it to work as much as you do. But before our worlds can truly move forward in trust, we all must make amends for past mistakes. Have the Vulcans *ever* apologized for their actions in the war? For taking our parents from us?"

He picked at his food, not grateful to her for stirring up old wounds. The attention to his plate hardly helped, for the meal was too much like the ones his *shreya* had prepared. He pushed it away. "There's nothing we can do about the past, Kanshent. Our responsibility is to focus on the dangers that face us today. Like the Mutes. We need to stand together if we're to defeat them."

"The past anchors us, cousin. It gives us a *place* to stand. You can't hide from it because it hurts. That pain tells you who you are. It demands recognition."

He couldn't think of anything to say; he only sat there stiffly. After a moment, Kanshent came around behind him and put a strong arm around his shoulders, brushing her head against his. "I'm sorry. We shouldn't be at odds. I know you'll do what's right."

The conversation moved to other, safer matters. But the ease with which they moved past their argument only highlighted the void that remained between T'Pol and himself. Was it possible that what separated them was more intractable than he had been willing to admit? Was it possible that T'Pol had reason not to let him into her confidence?

March 23, 2163
U.S.S. Pioneer

"Shields holding at maximum," Val Williams reported. "Target locked."

Captain Reed nodded. "Fire."

"Firing."

On the screen, a bright orange beam lashed out and began slicing through its target. "Target severed clean through," Rey Sangupta announced moments later from the science station. "Great shooting, Val!" He grinned across the bridge at her, but an alert signal beeped from his console, drawing his attention back. "Uh, the severed portion's fragmented. Debris incoming on a collision course."

"Tractor beam," Travis Mayweather ordered.

The lieutenant operated the controls. The beam shot out . . . but the debris kept coming. "No effect, sir! I don't understand . . ."

"It's the shields," said Sangupta. "They're scattering the tractor beam!"

"Tallarico, steer us clear," Reed ordered.

"Too late, sir!" the helmswoman cried. "Brace for impact . . ."

The ship trembled as the shield generators absorbed the impact of the cometary chunks. The loosely packed clumps of rock and ice shattered easily against the force barrier, rendering Regina Tallarico's warning somewhat unnecessary. "No damage," Williams said a moment later. "Shields holding."

"Yes, they're holding fine," Reed groused, "but what are they doing to the tractor beam? Doctor Dax, what happened?"

The nervous little Trill made noncommittal noises as he studied the telemetry. "Just a moment . . . Um. That shouldn't have happened. Perhaps Lieutenant Williams miscalibrated the beam?"

"Hey, Val knows what she's doing," the science officer barked. "The problem's with whatever you did to the shields!"

"Thanks, Rey, but I can defend myself," Val shot back.

"That's enough," Reed told them both. "Doctor, report."

"Hmm . . . there does seem to be a problem with the gravimetric gradient . . . an unanticipated lensing effect at tractor frequencies. Sorry."

"How long will it take to fix it?"

"Uh, I don't know yet. We'll have to review these results . . . build new models, run simulations . . ."

"So not anytime soon, you're saying," Mayweather interpreted.

"Sorry. No."

Reed sighed in frustration. The sound almost kept Mayweather from hearing what Tallarico muttered under her breath—something about how Starfleet had been better off without all this alien junk.

He saw that the captain had heard it too and was about to confront the helmswoman about her impolitic remark. Mayweather didn't think it would help matters if that happened in front of Doctor Dax, so he moved forward and said, "Captain . . . it's been a long shift. We're all on edge and probably not thinking clearly." He threw Tallarico a look as if to say, *Right?* She blushed and gave a chastened nod. "So why don't we all call it a night and get back to this in the morning?"

Reed gave him a look of gratitude and nodded. "All right. Alpha shift, you're relieved for today." The regular bridge crew started securing their stations and briefing their reliefs as they arrived. Tobin Dax left the bridge in a hurry to review his findings with his team.

Before Mayweather could leave, though, the captain caught his eye. "It's time," he said, casting glances toward Sangupta and Williams.

Mayweather nodded reluctantly. Given Sangupta's proclivities—both of their proclivities, really—he'd been hoping their fling would prove ephemeral and resolve itself. But the science officer's outburst of inappropriate chivalry proved that it was still a going concern, and possibly starting to affect the lieutenants' work. As he and the captain had planned if it came to this, Mayweather came up to Sangupta while Reed approached Williams and asked her to join him in his ready room. "Lieutenant," Mayweather said to the science officer, "would you come with me for a minute, please?"

Sangupta looked at him in puzzlement but simply said, "Yes, sir."

It was a short ride in the lift to Mayweather's quarters. Once inside, he said, "Rey, it's about you and Val."

Sangupta blinked, playing dumb. "What about us?"

"Don't try to kid a kidder, Rey. It's a small ship, and you two aren't very good at being discreet."

"Okay," Sangupta said, "granted, we've been having a little . . . thing going on lately. But with all due respect, sir, what's the problem? We're equal in rank, we're in different departments . . ."

"And you just almost bit Doctor Dax's head off because he suggested Val made a mistake. Not to mention that you've been fatigued when you come on shift in the morning, even been late a couple of times. Val hides it better than you."

"All right, sir, maybe we've gotten a little carried away with each other. I mean, can you blame me? She's really—"

"That's enough, Lieutenant."

"Yes, sir."

"Rey, the captain wants it to stop. He doesn't think that kind of relationship is appropriate on a ship this small. He's telling Lieutenant Williams right now, and I'm telling you."

Sangupta tried to mask his irritation, with little success. "Why couldn't he tell us both?"

"We thought this would be less . . . awkward. So far you're not giving me reason to doubt that."

The younger man clenched his fist by his side. "And of course Val will do whatever he orders."

"He is the captain."

The science officer sighed. "Understood, sir. It ends now."

"Good." He patted Sangupta's shoulder. "Look at it this way: She's the daughter of Admiral Archer's right-hand man. Do you really want to risk what might happen to your career if you screwed things up with her?"

Sangupta paled. "You . . . have a point, sir."

Of course, Mayweather knew Archer would never be less than scrupulously fair, but his words seemed to make Rey feel better about ending the relationship—and maybe reduced the chance of a relapse.

Once he'd dismissed Sangupta, he headed back to the bridge, passing Val Williams on her way out of the ready room. She seemed perfectly cool and collected as she acknowledged him, but he could hear the resignation in her voice.

"How did it go with Sangupta?" Reed asked once the ready-room door closed behind Mayweather.

"It took a little convincing, but he accepted it. Val?"

"No problems. She understood my position and accepted my orders."

"Well, that makes one of them." He sighed. "Did we really have to crack down on them so hard? I mean, Hoshi and Takashi—"

"Hoshi and Takashi don't serve aboard my ship. You know I've always preferred a more by-the-book approach to discipline than Admiral Archer employed aboard *Enterprise*. I can't blame T'Pol for continuing that tradition aboard *Endeavour*, at least with those two. They've proven they're able to balance their professional and personal lives in a mature way. And I can understand T'Pol being sympathetic to their desire not to be separated." Mayweather nodded. It had been something of an open secret that she had grown close to Trip Tucker before his untimely death eight years before. "But the community we had aboard those ships had its own particular alchemy, and Jonathan Archer was the one who made it work. I have no illusions about my own ability to anchor that kind of community. But that's why we have Starfleet discipline and regulations."

"I understand that, Malcolm. But you're not exactly making many friends among the crew."

"I'm not here to be their friend, Travis. I'm their commanding officer. That calls for their respect, not their friendship."

"Funny. I thought the reason you asked me to be your first officer was because of our friendship."

"Because I trust you. Professionally speaking, that's what matters. Our trust and respect for each other as officers, and for the chain of command. Not just us, but the whole crew."

Mayweather leaned against the wall. "I guess so. But it'd be easier for the crew to trust you if they knew you well enough to have faith that you have their best interests at heart."

"They should respect the rank. The position."

"I'm sure they do. But that only goes so far." He stepped closer. "Malcolm, you're a much easier guy to like than you give yourself credit for. Let them see that. Don't keep sending me to do all the talking with everyone you can't compare armory stories with."

Reed was quiet for a moment. "I'll try, Travis."

"All right." That seemed to be the best he could get for now. But Mayweather clung to his optimism. Maybe once they got through this upgrade problem and tensions eased, Malcolm would be willing to loosen up a little more.

That is, if they could ever actually get the upgrades to work.

March 24, 2163
Federation Executive Building, Paris, European Alliance

Thomas Vanderbilt found Admiral Gardner and Li Meilen, his security advisor, waiting in his outer office once he emerged. "Sorry, folks, the briefing's going to have to be on the run. I'm just about to leave for Vega Colony and I'm already running late."

"Don't worry, Mister President," Gardner said. "*Starfleet One* won't leave without you."

"Very kind of you, Sam," he went on as he led them out into the corridor. "It's just that I don't want to keep the Saurians waiting now that we're so close to working out a deal for their mining rights. That monarch of theirs, the Basilisk?"

"Basileus," said Li.

"Right, he insists he won't make any deal unless he meets personally with the ruler of the Federation. Hopefully I can convince him that I approximate that description in some small way."

"Speaking of which," the Centaurian security advisor went on, "the election results are finally in on the Alrond colony. Lecheb sh'Makesh won."

Vanderbilt grimaced. "And did she . . ."

"Just as she promised. She's called for the colony to secede from the Federation and declare itself the seat of the true Andorian Empire in exile. And she has the Alrondian defense fleet commanders on her side."

"Samuel, do we need to worry?"

"It's no more than a dozen ships, sir, and only one outdated battlecruiser," the white-haired chief of staff assured him. "They have no aggressive intent—they just want their colony left alone."

"But the election was very close," Li added. "There's not enough of a popular mandate to guarantee secession, and there's no legal recourse for permitting a branch of the fleet to go renegade. This seems to be just an extreme case of an anti-Federation protest movement blowing off steam."

Vanderbilt shook his head. "They're coming out of the woodwork lately, it seems."

"We did come together pretty fast after the war ended. Now that the initial excitement's worn off and people are seeing the messy business of making it work, it's given the anti-Federation voices more ammunition."

"And some of it's in response to the Mute task force, sir," Gardner said. "There are protests on Vulcan and Mars against imperialism and military adventurism."

"Amazing. Just a decade ago, the Vulcans were the ones with the massive armed fleet policing the region.

One ancient text gets uncovered and they're suddenly pacifists."

"Not all of them," Li replied. "The anti-imperialist protestors had a clash with some Anti-revisionists. Just a very lively debate for the most part, but a few of the Anti-revisionists almost got violent."

Vanderbilt searched his memory, snapping his fingers. "Those are the guys who insist the *Kir'Shara* was a Syrannite forgery to undermine the High Command, right? They want the old regime put back in power?"

"Yes, sir, and put in charge of the Federation— whereupon they'd kick the Andorians out."

"Oh, sh'Makesh would like them."

"Well, except for the part where they hate each other with a passion."

Vanderbilt sighed. "How many protests on Tellar this week?"

"About fifty."

"Well, at least something's normal."

They entered the lift. "Samuel, speaking of the Mute task force, any word?"

"They picked up a distress call last night from an Ithenite ship, but when they reached the coordinates, there was no sign of it."

The president frowned. "One of the task force ships?"

"No, a cargo freighter. It does look like the Mutes got it. The task force is combing the area now."

"Okay, keep me posted."

The lift deposited them on the ground floor. "Anything else I need to know before I leave?"

"There's been a recent upswing in Nausicaan and Nalori raider activity along the border," Gardner replied.

Vanderbilt furrowed his brow. "Because of the ships we pulled off for the task force?"

The admiral shook his head. "Different sectors. Mostly near the Tandar Sector and Orion space."

"Can we spare a few more ships to send that way?"

"As long as things stay quiet around Deneb, it might be doable. And nothing's going on there except the Denebian fever outbreak, which the Denobulans are treating. I'm reluctant to weaken any other border regions, though."

"Well, keep an eye on the situation for now. Let's see if it gets worse."

"Yes, Mister President."

"Anything else?"

"Not for the moment," Gardner said.

"No, sir," Li said. "Have a good trip."

"What's the weather like on Vega Colony this time of year? No, never mind, I'll ask the ship's captain. You can go back to work now, Sam, Meilen. Thank you."

"Thank you, Mister President."

9

March 26, 2163
U.S.S. Thejal

THE BLACK-AND-GREEN DELTA-WING VESSEL sat silently in *Thejal*'s path, hanging in the viewscreen like a *f'sherr*-beetle before it struck. "Here we go," Kanshent Shelav muttered under her breath before ordering her comm officer to open a channel. "Alien vessel, this is the Federation battleship *Thejal*. Identify yourself and declare your intentions." The response was only silence, as expected. "Your vessels have been identified as the responsible parties in a series of unprovoked attacks in this region and are suspected in several ship disappearances. I am authorized by Starfleet Command to require you to submit your vessel and crew to inspection. If you do not cooperate, we will use all necessary force to disable—"

A burst of feedback erupted over the comm channel, and the lights and status displays flickered on the edge of overload. "The scanning beam," tactical officer ch'Refel called. "Brace for impact!"

Even as emerald fire erupted from the Mute ship and lashed against *Thejal*'s shields, Kanshent ordered, "Return fire! Disable their vessel!"

But the enemy was already on the move. The first beam only grazed a corner of their ship, the rest missing cleanly. With a green blaze, the ship disappeared into warp. "Damage report," Kanshent called.

"Two of our forward shield emitters are offline," ch'Refel replied. "Inertial damper grid is depolarized, and one of the atmosphere processors took damage. We'll need a few hours for repairs."

"Notify the rest of the task force, and send a message to Rigel command post. Let them know the Mutes may be adopting a more aggressive stance. They fired upon us in their first encounter rather than the second." Ch'Refel's antennae bent skeptically. "You disagree?" Kanshent asked.

"With respect, Captain—we know they have encountered an Andorian vessel before. Perhaps they felt they could skip the preliminaries this time."

"Possibly. But it's still worth alerting the rest of the task force that the Mutes' strategies are adaptable."

"Understood."

"Captain!" It was zh'Vansh, the communications officer. "We're receiving a hail," she said. "It's *Rivgor*. The Malurian ship."

"Onscreen."

The broad, gray-scaled face of Dular Garos appeared on the monitor. *"Captain. We were patrolling nearby and detected your encounter. Are you in need of assistance? We can rendezvous within two hours."*

"Thank you, Mister Garos, but our damage is manageable." Kanshent considered. "Still, it's safe to say the Mutes will be back for us. And they seem to be willing to skip a step or two where our vessel is concerned. Their next attack may be decisive."

"We stand ready to assist Starfleet in any way you require."

"And Starfleet appreciates it." She saw ch'Refel's antennae folding back in irritation but let it go for now. "Tell me, have you had any indication that the Mutes detected your vessel?"

"We've registered no scanning beams. And my ship's engines are designed to be . . . low-emitting." No doubt, Kanshent reflected, for the sake of smuggling operations. But for now, Garos was an ally, however questionable his ethics.

Indeed, that ethical flexibility might come in handy now. Garos gave her a devious smile. *"Are you proposing we orchestrate an ambush, Captain?"*

"Yes, I am."

"I like the way you think. I'll be there in a couple of hours and we can work out the details."

"Have you ever tried Andorian cuisine, Mister Garos?"

The Malurian smiled again, more amiably this time. *"I'm always open to sampling new cultures."*

"Excellent. Then we'll discuss plans over dinner."

"I look forward to it."

"Thejal out."

Once the viewer was dark, Kanshent stepped over to the tactical station. "Mister ch'Refel. I'd appreciate it if you'd keep your attitudes toward Starfleet to yourself when we have an open comm channel on the bridge. Don't assume other races can't read your reactions just because they lack antennae."

Those antennae curled downward in abashment. "Apologies, Captain."

"And if you can't handle being part of Starfleet, perhaps you should consider a career change."

"With respect, Captain, it's not that. I just . . ."

"Yes?"

"Why 'Starfleet'? Why did they have to use the Earth name when they combined the fleets? Why not . . . 'the Federation Guard'?"

"Or 'the High Command'?" Kanshent riposted, chastening him. "It's a fleet of starships, Veni. Can you think of a more generic name than 'Starfleet'?"

"Generic or not, it is identified with the humans."

"And that is its virtue," she told him. "It was Earth's Starfleet that won the trust and respect of the unaligned worlds. It was Earth's Starfleet that proved its strength to them by winning the Romulan War."

The tactical officer scoffed. "Only because we saved their hides at Cheron."

"We and others, yes. But it was their reputation that won our support. And their reputation, and Archer's, that leads others to seek our help now. Why not take advantage of that? It's only a name."

"It just feels sometimes like the humans are running everything."

"Would you rather the Vulcans still were?" They shared a grimace at the thought. "The humans are useful as a buffer between the rest of us, and as a genial face to put forward to our neighbors. And their ambition is taking them far. I'm willing to ride in their wake as long as it benefits Andoria."

He gave her a sidelong look. "And if it stops benefitting us? Do we go live on Alrond?"

Kanshent chuckled. "We will do what benefits our people, always. But that is a decision for another day. Today, we have an ambush to plan."

"Yes, Captain."

And a dinner menu, she thought as she returned to her command chair and began a computer search for Malurian dietary requirements.

March 27 to 28, 2163

Kanshent found Garos to be a courteous and entertaining dinner guest—even bringing a gift, a rather entertaining bottle of Malurian mead. He also proved to be, unsurprisingly, quite devious when it came to concocting ambushes. The two commanders worked out their plan with much laughter over dinner, then put it into action with all seriousness the next morning.

The site Garos chose for the ambush was a rogue ice giant less than a light-year from the site of the Mute attack, an almost featureless gray orb floating in perpetual shadow, accompanied only by the few moons that had survived its ejection from its birth system or been captured in the intervening eons. *Thejal* took up a tight orbit around the innermost and rockiest of those moons, which possessed sufficient mineral resources to make it convincing that they were mining it for repair materials. They took enough of their systems offline or into low-power mode that they would appear convincingly defenseless—enough to give Kanshent cause for concern, even with the assurances of ch'Refel and the chief engineer that the weapons and shields could be brought up to full power on short notice. *"Do not worry, Captain,"* Garos told her from aboard *Rivgor* as they made their final preparations. *"We will be concealed nearby at full power, able to occupy the Mutes until you are at full strength."*

"If all goes perfectly," Kanshent replied. "I don't like to rely on luck."

Garos gave a confident smile. *"I prefer to make events play out in my favor."*

Thejal sat in orbit, playing lame, for over a day before sensors detected a warp egress nearby. The Mute ship closed quickly on their position, and for the first time it broadcast a hail. Kanshent was unsurprised to see her own image appear on the screen, hear her own challenge to the Mutes edited to serve their script. *"You—are—disable—d. Require you to submit your vessel."* The message repeated on a loop.

Kanshent's antennae twitched in annoyance that she'd given them such perfect material. "Shut that off."

"Do you want to issue a challenge, Captain?" zh'Vansh asked.

"Why? To get it hurled back in my face? No."

The vessel closed slowly, relentlessly, but did not open fire. Kanshent stepped over to ch'Refel's station. "Fire a weak burst from the 'working' cannon. Try to miss slightly."

"I never learned how to miss, ma'am."

She chuckled. "Expand your horizons. Or at least your target lock."

"Yes, Captain." He fired. "Imagine that. I missed slightly."

"Really."

"And the Mutes still approach. No change. No return fire." Ch'Refel paused. "They're coming to take possession," he said. "They intend to board, probably kill the crew, then take their prize home."

"Are we so sure?" Kanshent asked the young tactical officer, adopting the tone of the Guard instructor she had once been. "Consider: If they capture ships as prizes . . . why do they never use them?" She nodded at the screen. "All we see are those ships. Fire again."

"Yes, ma'am." He missed a little less this time, but still did no damage. "But . . . there's never any sign of debris or bodies. If they don't use the ships, what purpose do they put them to?"

"Perhaps they dissect the captives and their ships to study potential enemies. Learn their technology, their weaknesses. Decrypt their databases. By this point they could have accumulated data on half a dozen neighboring races or more."

"Readying for a mass invasion?"

"Perhaps." She smirked. "And maybe they're saving some of the captured ships for then. Maybe to use as false-flag decoys. And so we come back around to where we began with the Romulans."

Ch'Refel checked his console. "Five thousand *zhihal.*"

"That's close enough," Kanshent said. "Power up shields and weapons. Let's hit them for real. Zh'Vansh, invite *Rivgor* to the party."

The Mute ship slowed its approach as it detected *Thejal*'s power surge, but that was its only response. The first barrage weakened its shields, but still the

Mutes did not return fire. "What are they waiting for?" ch'Refel asked.

The black vessel hung above the moon's surface for a few moments and then began to thrust into a higher orbit. "They're retreating."

But just then, a torpedo sailed upward from the ice giant and struck the vessel's flank. The Malurian ship rose from the clouds where it had been hiding, looking like an aquatic predator breaching the surface of a dark ocean, and continued to bombard the enemy. "Flank them," Kanshent ordered, and *Thejal* came around to block their path, firing. Two ships were normally not enough to hem in another, but maneuvering around a giant planet with a tight moon system was more constraining than maneuvering in open space, as Garos had wisely realized. They had the Mutes cornered.

And like any cornered prey, the Mutes struck back. Spreading arcs of green energy lashed against *Thejal*'s shields. "The forward emitters are damaged again!" ch'Refel reported.

"Compensate."

The helm officer tried to turn the ship away, but those spreading bolts were tricky, and some of their energy splashed around the edge of the lateral shield and dug into the exposed hull. "Return fire! Take out their weapons!" Kanshent called. *What is Garos waiting for?*

Their return fire struck true; ch'Refel lived up to his assertions. *Rivgor* fired at the same time, striking the same flank. "Their shields are failing!" ch'Refel called.

"*Thejal* to *Rivgor*. Target their engines. Fire to disable."

Both ships struck at the glowing modules on

the ship's aft, whose green light flickered and faded. "Cease fire."

But *Rivgor* kept on firing. "Its weapons are at full strength!" ch'Refel exclaimed—just before the Mute ship erupted in a blinding flash, leaving only an expanding cloud of debris.

"Get me Garos!" Kanshent demanded. A moment later, the Malurian's gray face appeared on the screen. "What happened? We needed prisoners to interrogate!"

"Forgive my overzealous weapons officer, Captain. We were only concerned for your safety."

"I appreciate that, but as you see, we can handle ourselves."

"But not without damage. You seem rather vulnerable at the moment."

"Perhaps if your weapons officer had shown more zeal a few moments earlier, we would not be so vulnerable."

"Hm," Garos replied. *"Well, perhaps we should correct that imbalance."*

His face vanished from the screen, replaced by an image of the massive Malurian warship bringing its weapon ports to bear on *Thejal.* "Garos, what are you doing?" Kanshent cried.

But the only response was fire.

Rivgor

"The Andorian warship was completely destroyed," Dular Garos reported to his partners over the private viewscreen in his quarters. "My weapons officer was successfully able to replicate the energy signature and firing pattern of the Mute ships."

"Up to your old tricks again, I see," his benefactor purred, a finger twirling her long black hair. *"Using impersonation to turn your enemies against each other. I have tried to teach you more original forms of deception, you know."*

"And your methods have been effective up to a point. But your . . . operatives have not been able to insinuate themselves into every Federation official's bedchamber. There is still considerable pressure for a peaceful solution from some quarters—especially Archer and his pet Vulcan. The loss of a Starfleet ship of the line at Mute hands should inflame passions nicely."

"Do not presume to lecture us about passion, Garos!" Navaar leaned forward as if to offer him a better view of her assets, letting just enough anger into her expression and voice to enhance rather than undermine the sensual way she presented herself. *"We are the masters of that particular weapon."* Behind Navaar, her junior sisters, D'Nesh and Maras, stepped closer toward the pickup to reinforce their visual impact, emphasizing the abundant quantities of green skin that they habitually left exposed.

"Then you might try to remember," Garos told the Orion merchant princess in a bored voice, "that my own passions are unmoved by your rather crass attempts at seduction, Navaar." Not only was he biochemically bonded to his mate back home, just as monogamously devoted to her as were her other seven husbands, but Malurian males had no sexual interest in females who were less than half again their height and three times their weight. "That's why you chose me, remember? You need an ally who can think for himself, not a pheromone-addled slave."

"Don't overestimate your importance," D'Nesh told him. The middle sister by age, only slightly younger than Navaar, the curly-haired D'Nesh nonetheless fancied herself the "cutest" of the trio and generally acted accordingly. But beneath that bright, innocent smile, she was perhaps the most vicious-minded of the three. *"Even you don't know how many assets we have in play. You're a small piece in a much bigger game."*

"Now, now, sister," Navaar chided. *"Garos and the Raldul alignment are an invaluable part of our stratagem. Their mastery of disguise has let us penetrate deeper into Vulcan, Axanar, and other places where our sisters cannot easily spread their influence."*

Ah, Axanar. Garos was particularly proud of that one. Designing facial prosthetics that actually filtered methane and supplied oxygen to the wearer had been a challenge even for Raldul's master maskwrights. But it had paid off; his agents had successfully bribed or blackmailed enough Axanar defense officials to persuade them to cooperate with the other unaligned worlds in seeking Starfleet aid. At the same time, dozens of Orion slave women in service to Navaar and the Syndicate had employed their own subtler forms of persuasion—including pheromones rather milder than the elites' but still stronger than their sellers and pimps admitted—on the Rigelians, Ithenites, and

Tesnians, and, subsequently, on a few of the Federation delegates to the Deneva Conference.

"And now he's given us an incident that we can use to inflame more rage and conflict," Navaar went on. *"We should be grateful to him for that."*

"True," D'Nesh conceded. *"The chaos should be quite entertaining."* Maras just smiled and stroked her sides. The youngest and least intelligent of the three sisters by a significant margin, Maras spoke little, preferring to communicate with her body, which she tended to keep even more exposed than her sisters did. But then, apparently, her sisters were starting to approach the age when their beauty would begin to decline (not that Garos could tell the difference), which was perhaps why Navaar and D'Nesh were so determined to secure their power and legacy within the Syndicate while they still could. They were fortunate that Maras lacked their cunning and ambition, or she might have overthrown them by now. Although perhaps Garos was being too cynical. Orion sisters of the elite lineages were close to one another by necessity. Their intense pheromones tended to repel other females, excepting close relations. Their sisters or first cousins were often the only true allies they could have.

"I appreciate your confidence," Garos told the Orions. "But I confess, I have my reservations about pushing Starfleet too far. A handy enemy to distract them from policing their borders is certainly of value; business has suffered badly since this interstellar peace took hold. But it's a delicate balance to strike. Push the Federation too far in a warlike direction and it could backfire. If they truly were to embrace the idea that they had a responsibility to police the galaxy . . . they could become an empire as dangerous as the Romulans or the Klingons. And then they wouldn't hesitate to crack down on both of our people's business endeavors far harder than they already have."

Navaar gave him a sultry smile. *"Trust us, Garos. I assure you, we've considered all the angles."*

"I hope so, Navaar. I joined you because you promised me we could destroy the Federation—not make it stronger."

"Oh, but Garos. Why do you think we prefer to rule from the bedroom instead of the throne?" She put her arms around her sisters' shoulders, and they posed for him as a group. It was so reflexive to them that they didn't even care whether they had a receptive audience. *"Because we know that, sometimes, one of the best ways to destroy someone is to give him the power he wants."*

She slipped free and stepped closer to the camera, twirling a strand of her hair. *"Why do you think we've had your operatives infiltrate Vulcan to stir up anti-war protests? Merely as another distraction? Think about it: Do you imagine the Vulcans would tolerate being part of such an aggressive Federation as you describe?"*

He considered it. "Given what cowards they've become since the Syrannites took over, no, I suppose not."

"And how long would the Tellarites stay comfortable as part of the Federation," D'Nesh added, *"if the Vulcans weren't there to balance out the Andorians? Especially with our friends on Alrond making the Andorians look hungry for conquest."*

"I can see that. But it would still leave a powerful

human-Andorian union, with plenty of warships and plenty of will to use them."

"*But with less support and less trust from those around them,*" Navaar said. "*We can hate their kindly benevolence all we want, but the fact is that it's one of the most effective scams ever invented—even when they actually believe it. Archer brought the Federation together by reaching out and winning his neighbors' trust. He and his allies have been working to spread that trust further, to gain more allies who could come to the Federation's aid in its times of need—and maybe even join them, make it bigger and harder for entrepreneurs like ourselves to stand up against.*"

Maras laughed. "*Bigger and harder.*"

Navaar threw her an affectionate glare. "*Without that trust, the might of what remained of the Federation would provoke fear. And we could play on that fear, as you tried to do with the Tandarans, Garos.*" She smiled. "*Though I think we could select a more effective mark. We do a lively business in slave girls with the Klingon Empire.*"

"I understand now," Garos said. "Instead of trying to weaken them, you harden them until they become brittle."

Navaar laughed. "*Yes! And then . . . we apply the necessary force to shatter them.*"

March 29, 2163
U.S.S. *Endeavour*

Thanien had refused to believe that Kanshent and *Thejal* were gone. The whole time that *Endeavour* had spent en route to the rogue giant, he had clung to the hope that Garos's transmission had been a deception or a mistake. When Cutler and Kimura confirmed that the cloud of debris orbiting the inner moon did indeed include Andorian hull alloys and organic remains, enough to account for a whole *Sevaijen*-class cruiser, his hope vanished in a torrent of despair and rage. He struggled to hold in his emotions, remembering that he was on a human ship . . . a Federation ship . . . and such displays were inappropriate here.

It was not so much that his cousin and her beloved crew had died. That was a risk every Guard member lived with every day, and Thanien had lost his share of colleagues and friends over the years . . . often to the Vulcans. But he had seen her so recently, and she had been so vital, so challenging, so proud of her family back home. And she had been taken by a nameless, voiceless foe, one he could not even face and demand answers from.

"I'm truly sorry that we were unable to bring them down faster," Garos told T'Pol and Thanien over the bridge viewscreen, speaking from his own bridge aboard *Rivgor*. *"But Captain Shelav and her crew battled fearlessly to the end, weakening the Mutes enough that we were able to deliver the final blow before we too were destroyed. They have our eternal gratitude for that."*

"No doubt," T'Pol replied. "It is regrettable that you were unable to capture any of their crew alive, or retrieve any viable data stores from the remains."

"Yes," Thanien said through clenched teeth. "It is more urgent than ever now that we track them down to where they live."

"Perhaps next time," Garos said.

"Thank you for your assistance, Mister Garos," the captain said. "*Endeavour* out." She turned to face her first officer. "Mister Thanien . . ."

"Captain?" Lieutenant Cutler interposed. "Could you take a look at these sensor readings? Something's not quite adding up."

T'Pol circled around the science console to study the readouts Cutler showed her. "There, you see?" the younger woman said. "The weapon signature . . . it's a little bit off from what we've seen in other Mute attacks."

"Perhaps an individual variance in this particular vessel. Or an interaction with the radiation field of the giant."

"Maybe, but there's also this." Cutler called up another readout. "See the debris distribution? The way the fragments are interacting? . . ."

"Yes, I see," T'Pol said after a moment. "The displacement pattern is not entirely consistent with *Thejal* exploding first. Although there are factors it is difficult to account for. *Rivgor* could have flown through the debris cloud, disrupting it. Or the gravitational interactions of the moons could have altered debris trajectories chaotically."

"Could be, sure," Kimura said from the other side of the bridge. "But what's bothering me, Captain, is this firing pattern." He called up a simulation on the main viewscreen, showing his reconstruction of the killing blow. Even in these simplified graphics, it was painful for Thanien to watch. Yet he bore witness gravely, refusing to look away. "In the past, the Mutes have always fired to disable. They want to capture ships intact. But *Thejal's* destruction was no accident. Their firing pattern deliberately targeted the exposed sections; then when the rest of the shields failed, they targeted the engines specifically. This was no accident—they fired to destroy."

"They were under attack on two fronts," Thanien countered, "bracketed in. They struck out of self-preservation, obviously."

"Perhaps," T'Pol said. "But while each of these anomalies alone is easily explained, in combination they create room for doubt. Garos has not always been trustworthy."

"Garos is on our side!" Thanien objected. "Whatever his past, we fight a common enemy, and that must be our focus." He peered at her. "I thought the Federation was about forgiving others' past crimes, setting aside differences. Are you not ready to set the past aside after all?" *And was I too quick to set your past aside? Too quick to dismiss my cousin's questions about it?*

The captain met his gaze with that infuriating calm of the Vulcans—hiding her true reactions, as they always strove to do. If anything, he realized, the Surakian teachings that had swept Vulcan in recent years had made them better at such concealment than ever before. "I am simply pointing out how many unknowns still remain in this situation. We should seek to answer some of those outstanding questions before we act."

"Think that way and we will never act! What we *do* know is that the Mutes are a menace, and that knowledge demands action! We must take the battle to these demons and force them to submit once and for all!"

T'Pol studied him for a moment, then moved closer. "You are grieving," she said. "I should grant you the time to process your anger, and not force you to confront its cause any longer. Please take the rest of the shift off. We can handle the investigation." She tilted her head. "You might consider talking to Doctor Phlox. His advice can be quite . . . comforting."

In other words, you don't trust me, Thanien thought. Her attempt to mimic human compassion was risible. She simply didn't trust the judgment of an emotional Andorian.

How, then, could he trust her to do what was necessary now?

"You're right not to trust this Garos guy," Trip told T'Pol as they met in meditation space. The beach was not comforting her tonight, so Trip had consented to let the space revert to the empty white void she preferred. "I've looked into his record. Exile or not, he's still got pretty strong ties to the Malurian syndicate."

"They call it an alignment," T'Pol replied.

"A mob by any other name would smell as rotten."

She gave him a quizzical look. "I would not have expected you to paraphrase Shakespeare—even in so mangled a fashion."

"Well, I've had to broaden my horizons a lot these past few years." He kept quiet about the specifics: the cover identity he'd assumed the year before that had required adopting a more literate persona; the days of harrowing, drug-assisted crash learning; the infiltration of a resurgent Terra Prime cell capitalizing on fears of Earth losing its identity within the Federation; the pretense of befriending a man he loathed in order to set him up for a fall; the unexpected sense of guilt once that man was discredited, broken, and turned on by his own followers.

Still, he could tell that T'Pol sensed his sudden melancholy, so he covered by shifting his focus to the more positive potentials of what he did. "If you're not having any luck finding out whether Garos was on the level about *Thejal*, I could do some digging. My sources may know more—"

"That's not necessary," she said sharply.

"Look. I know you're not crazy about our methods. But—"

"Methods that your compatriots claim are justified under extreme or existential threat. At this time, we have no reason to believe the threat posed by these aliens is nearly so drastic. There is no reason for your involvement."

"I'm just talkin' about gathering some information."

"Starfleet can handle it," she insisted. "We can't be effective at defending the Federation if we need to turn to others for help at every turn."

"Where's the sense in turning away help when it's available?"

"I don't like the precedent it sets."

Trip sighed, recognizing her resolve. "All right. But

if I should just . . . happen to stumble on something useful . . ."

"Trip."

"Okay, okay." He said no more about it. After studying him a moment longer, T'Pol let it go, satisfied that he would respect her wishes on the matter.

And once again, Trip hated how good he'd become at lying to the people who trusted him.

10

April 2, 2163
U.S.S. Pioneer

"Engineering to bridge," Alan Sheehan's voice came over the intercom. *"We've completed the coil calibrations and the reactor's warming up. We'll be ready for warp within two minutes."*

Finally, Malcolm Reed thought, though he kept it out of his voice as he said, "Thank you, Commander. Stand by." He turned to the engineering station. "Doctor Dax, I hope you're confident it will actually work this time."

"Well, it should, Captain," the diffident Trill replied. "Most likely. I think we're getting the hang of your coils now." He shrugged. "We'll see, anyway."

Coming from Dax, Reed reflected, that was a vote of high confidence. At least he sincerely hoped it was. It had been a frustrating few weeks as Dax and his team had gone through multiple failed attempts to balance the warp drive with the shields. No matter how many simulations they had run, the actual results had failed to match. Dax had attributed it to the "idiosyncratic" warp coil—manufacturing process used by Earth engineers; each individual coil was subtly different, with its own "personality," and calibrating them to work together was a trial-and-error process—especially when they were required to perform in a way they hadn't been designed to. Apparently Cochrane-style warp fields were too finely tuned, too sensitive to the gravimetric interference of a deflector envelope; other species' drives produced warp fields that could more easily compensate for the effect through some sort of built-in cushion in their spacetime geometry. Dax had been trying to add similar compensatory layers to *Pioneer*'s warp field, but aligning the coils to produce the necessary interference patterns had proved challenging. If anything, the required geometry was even more sensitive to fluctuations than a normal Cochrane field. But Dax's team was confident that once they found the right balance, it could be "locked in" and more easily replicated in other ships, or at least be a starting point for future refinements.

In his darker hours of fatigue and frustration, Reed had wondered if Starfleet would be better off ditching Cochrane drives altogether and building their future ships around Andorian nacelles. But while Dax was open to a hybrid design, he still felt (and Commodore Jefferies agreed) that the twin-outrigger Cochrane drive was the most versatile warp configuration around—though he confessed that the same lability that made it so adaptable also made it difficult to lock the changes down now.

At the helm, Mayweather finished his discussion with Ensign Tallarico and rose to address the captain. "We've got the course laid in," he said. "Should be as smooth a ride as we can manage—no major masses or energy sources within two light-years, no significant subspace density gradients that we know of." They were starting in interstellar space already to minimize the influence of stellar gravity and radiation on the warp field, giving Dax the purest baseline possible with which to work.

The Trill scientist jumped a bit as the engineering console gave off a signal tone. "Um . . . engineering reports ready, sir."

Reed waited a moment, then asked, "So are we good to go?"

"Oh! Yes, of course, Captain. Sorry. We're, ah, go for warp at your discretion."

This time he did say it aloud, though only for Mayweather to hear: "Finally." His first officer smiled, eyes gleaming with anticipation. "Tallarico," Reed ordered, "take us to warp two."

Reed could feel the vibration in the deck plating as the compact ship's engines drove it into warp. After a flash of light and distortion, the viewscreen showed the usual streaks of prismatic light. "Warp two, sir," the slim blond helmswoman reported a few moments later.

"Lieutenant Williams, stand by to activate deflector shields."

"Aye, sir," the armory officer replied.

"Doctor, are you ready to compensate?"

"It should be automatic, Captain," Dax answered. "But I'll be monitoring."

"All right. Lieutenant—activate shields."

"Shields activated."

Almost immediately, the tone of the warp engines

changed. "Losing speed, sir," Tallarico said. "But only twelve percent."

"So close!" Dax muttered. "Hang on, I just need to tweak the intermix formula a bit . . . no . . . no, no, not like that!"

Before Reed could demand an explanation, the ship began to tremble—and something bizarre happened on the main screen. The orderly streaks of starlight gave way to a twisting, spiraling web of interference patterns, making it look like the ship was speeding through a tunnel of light. "What the hell . . . ?"

Dax worked his console frenetically as alarms sounded. "Some kind of field imbalance!"

"Ensign, drop to impulse!" Mayweather ordered.

"Negative helm control, sir!"

Now the bridge lights seemed to be blurring, stretching out before Reed's eyes. The trembling was getting worse. "Engineering! Shut down the engines!"

"*We're . . . trying . . . , sir!*" Sheehan's response seemed slowed down, as though there were some kind of time dilation effect operating *inside* the ship, between the bridge and the engine room. "*But it'll . . . take . . . some . . . time!*"

"Doctor Dax, is there anything we can do?"

"Hold . . . on. Let . . . me . . . an-al-yze . . . these . . . rea-dings."

Time dilation across the width of the bridge? How severe did the spacetime distortion have to be to cause that? The light distortion was worsening too, along with the trembling. The captain was starting to feel lighter—was the gravity plating going offline too? But that was the least of their problems. The hull began to groan from the gravimetric shear. If this continued much longer, *Pioneer* could be torn apart.

It took a few moments, sorting through the sensory distortion, before he realized Sheehan was speaking again. *"Shut . . . down . . . in . . . five . . . fourrr . . . three-ee-ee . . ."* The intervals grew longer with each nominal second. The gravity was gone now; Reed clung to his chair, and he saw Mayweather holding on to the helm console by its safety handle. *"Two-oo-oo . . . onnnnnne . . ."*

The swirling vortex on the screen collapsed in on itself. The ship heaved and groaned, circuits crackled and burned out, and the viewscreen flared white as Reed felt himself flung to the deck.

Malcolm Reed sat up, years of training letting him shake off his disorientation and pain and take in the situation quickly. The ship hadn't blown up; that was something. But alarms were sounding, and one stood out in his attention above all the others: a radiation alarm.

"Status!" he called, looking around for Mayweather. He spotted him motionless on the deck, his head bleeding. Blood on the edge of the helm console. He rushed over, felt for a pulse . . . thank God, there was one. "Get a medical team up here!" he cried.

"Captain," Rey Sangupta reported breathlessly. "We're . . . sensors show we're in proximity to a super-Jovian planet. We're deep in its radiation belts."

"Get us out of here," he ordered Tallarico.

She tried, shook her head. "Engines aren't responding. No warp or impulse."

Reed hit the intercom. "Engineering, status." Nothing. "Engineering, report!"

"This is T'Venri," a voice came after a moment—it was one of Dax's engineers. *"Commander Sheehan is badly injured and being taken to sickbay. The engines are . . . not in substantially better shape. The coils are offline, at least three of the dilithium crystals are burned out, and the impulse reactors are not responding. Still assessing time for repairs."*

"We don't *have* any time," the science officer reported with unwonted gravity. "The radiation is too intense. We need to get out of it within twenty minutes or we're fried."

"We, we can't move that far in time," Dax said, "even on thrusters. We're stuck here." He wrung his sweaty hands.

"We could try getting everyone to sickbay," Williams proposed. "It's the most shielded part of the ship."

Reed realized he'd been in a similar situation once before, back on *Enterprise.* "There's one place more shielded: the catwalks in the warp nacelles. With the engines down, they should cool enough to be habitable."

"But, but, but you can't," Dax sputtered. "We, we can't fix the engines from inside the nacelles! We'd be stuck here!"

"Sir, we're in a decaying orbit," Tallarico said. "We have at most four days."

Reed addressed them all forcefully. "We'll deal with those problems later. For now, I'm ordering everyone to the starboard catwalk, best possible speed. Alert Doctor Liao to bring everything she'll need to treat her patients." He picked up Mayweather, struggling to carry the taller man. Williams moved in and took the first officer's other arm, making it look effortless. "All right, let's go!"

U.S.S. Endeavour

"Firing," Takashi Kimura announced. Phased energy beams raked the flanks of the black ship on the screen, causing their green light to flicker out. "Engines are down."

But arcs of plasma tore out from the ship's bow, and *Endeavour* rocked. "Continue fire," T'Pol ordered. "Neutralize their weapons."

She spoke not only to her own tactical officer but his counterparts on the two Rigelian scout ships that flew behind the alien raider as *Endeavour* flew in front of it. A Xarantine task force ship had been the first to encounter this particular vessel. The aliens had made no attempt to retaliate for the destruction of another of their vessels, perhaps not realizing the Xarantine's connection to its destroyers. The Xarantine had fired first, driving the ship into retreat, and reported its trajectory to the nearby Rigelian scouts, which had intercepted and harried it, knocking it to impulse before *Endeavour* arrived. The Starfleet vessel had positioned itself ahead of the enigmatic ship, catching it in the crossfire that had now neutralized its propulsion—though of course its momentum still carried it forward at a fifth the speed of light, the other ships coasting with it at equal velocity.

The aliens' weapons inflicted significant damage on one of the Rigelian scouts, tearing through one of the stout wings of the slender, conical gray vessel and coming dangerously close to its starboard warp nacelle. The scout veered off, decelerating. "Their navigational deflector's taken damage," Sato relayed. "They can't maintain this speed."

"Understood," T'Pol said. "How long until reinforcements arrive?"

"*Vinakthen* should be four minutes away. *Rivgor* . . . probably not much longer. I can't get a precise estimate."

The ship rocked again. "Mister Kimura."

He remained unflappable. "Almost there, Captain." Another two efficient shots from him took out the last of the hostile vessel's weapon ports.

The Rigelians fired one more sustained burst. "That took out their main power," Cutler reported. "They're helpless."

T'Pol turned to Sato. "Open a channel." At the other woman's nod, she said, "Attention, hostile vessel. This is Captain T'Pol of the Federation vessel *Endeavour*. Your propulsion and weapons have been neutralized. I advise you to surrender peacefully. If you cooperate, we might be able to resolve this conflict without further violence." She waited, but no reply came. "Our reinforcements should arrive shortly. You cannot escape. Communication is your only logical recourse."

Nothing. Even in total defeat, the aliens maintained their resolute silence. "Even making the offer was a waste of time," Thanien said after a few moments.

"Commodore th'Menchal is hailing," Sato said.

"Open a channel."

The aged Andorian appeared on the screen. *"I've been monitoring. Clearly they won't cooperate. Once Vinakthen and Rivgor arrive, we'll board their ship, take the crew prisoner."*

"Very well," T'Pol said. "We will prepare a boarding party in EV suits."

"If I may, Commodore," Thanien interposed. "Why not simply transport them aboard? We know a single isolated use of the transporter isn't dangerous. And even if it were—they're the enemy. They've killed hundreds, maybe thousands of good people."

"They are an enemy we need to understand," T'Pol countered. "Their biology and neurology are different from ours in ways we cannot predict. If the transporter's rematerialization process lacks complete fidelity, it may obscure some vital piece of information on a molecular or genetic level."

Thanien was taken aback. He leaned closer, lowering his voice. "Is that . . . a realistic concern, Captain? This is not a matter for science to resolve. This is a military conflict."

"He's right, Captain," th'Menchal said. *"Who knows how fiercely the Mutes will fight on their own territory? Consider the danger to our crews."*

"I am, Commodore. If the aliens are brought aboard before we can secure them and place them in restraints, they could endanger the safety of our vessels and their personnel.

"Not to mention," she went on, "that their atmospheric and environmental needs evidently differ from ours. If they aren't in protective suits when beamed aboard, they could suffer brain damage or death before we could gain any useful information from them. I think we can all agree that would be . . . counterproductive."

After a moment, th'Menchal nodded. *"Very well. We shall prepare a boarding party of our own. Vinakthen out."*

Thanien turned to T'Pol. "I volunteer to lead our team."

"Commander, if you seek to exact revenge . . ."

"I will obey Starfleet rules of engagement to the letter," he replied tightly. "I just . . . want to look them in the eye."

T'Pol restrained herself from pointing out that they did not appear to have eyes in the conventional sense. It wouldn't help resolve whatever tension had arisen between the two of them. She simply nodded and said, "Very well. And Commander—be careful."

"Mute" ship

The capital ships used tractor beams to slow the alien vessel to a safer velocity before launching the boarding shuttles. The vessel presented no evident docking ports, so the shuttles had to blast through the hangar-bay hatch on the vessel's dorsal spine. The bay proved to be unoccupied when it was blown open to space, though it would have made little difference to Thanien if it had been otherwise.

Commander Kimura brought *Endeavour*'s shuttle-pod to rest between two of the Mutes' piscine black shuttles, with its sister shuttle and the two from *Vinakthen* landing close behind. The Malurians from *Rivgor*, satisfied with the safety of their own transporters, would beam across once the Starfleet teams had secured a position.

The boarding teams poured out of their shuttles, particle rifles at the ready. The humans wore the bronze suits of Earth Starfleet, while Thanien wore his own silver suit, whose boxy, high-domed helmet gave his antennae room to move. Only the UESPA and *Endeavour* patches on his suit distinguished it from those worn by *Vinakthen*'s party.

The *Vinakthen* team found an airlock hatch and forced it open, leading the others into a vestibule containing a rack of the Mutes' carapace-like EV garments, which reportedly generated some form of force-field helmet around their heads. The vestibule automatically repressurized with air that read substantially denser than Andoria or Earth normal, with lethal levels of carbon dioxide. Once the environment was stabilized, Thanien cued the Malurians to beam over.

The teams split up as they made their way into the interior of the ship. It reminded Thanien of an ice-borer warren, a maze of narrow tunnels with no light sources beyond the team's helmet lamps.

"Are they blind as well as deaf?" Kimura mused.

"They sense something," Thanien replied, his antennae twitching at what they perceived. "There are electromagnetic variances as we move through the corridors, in some sort of ordered pattern. I think it's how they navigate. Perhaps they 'see' EM fields."

They reached a node where the corridor widened, with new tunnels branching from it in three dimensions, sloping to connect to higher and lower levels. Some form of consoles adorned the walls, and a pyramidal protrusion on the ceiling was giving off shifting magnetic fields that Thanien could sense but not interpret.

"Sir!"

Even as Kimura spoke, Thanien registered soft swishing, tapping sounds from all around them, and he spun to bring his lights to bear, as did the others. Two of the aliens dropped from the upper shafts, two more from side tunnels, surrounding the party. The descriptions hadn't done justice to their strangeness—tall, unnaturally lanky beings with extra joints on their limbs and hideous gray-green heads with small antenna-like stalks in place of eyes and horrific vertical slits for mouths. The party was momentarily shocked by their emergence from the darkness. Crewman Money recovered quickly, but before she could finish raising her rifle, one of the creatures had downed her, moving too fast for Thanien to see how, and knelt to pull at her helmet. Thanien fired his own rifle, bothering the creature only a little. It wore a simple gray and brown jumpsuit, with no carapace; evidently their resistance to energy weapons was due to more than the shielding alone. Were their nervous systems so alien that it gave them an immunity?

Kimura added his fire, while Teska and Curry fired at the others. The Mute finally fell before it could breach Money's helmet seal, but Teska fell before a second creature, which staggered under his fire but was relentless in its approach. Thanien brought it down, then turned his fire to the other two, joined by Kimura, Curry, and the dazed but recovering Teska.

Outmatched, the other two Mutes retreated down one of the downsloping passages, one too narrow for the EV suits to fit through. "We'll have to mop them up later," Thanien said. "For now let's get Money and these captives back to the hangar bay."

U.S.S. Endeavour

"Securing the ship is proving more difficult than we thought," Thanien reported. *"The Mutes are relentless. They refuse to surrender or communicate in any way. More, there doesn't seem to be a single command center, just stations distributed throughout the ship. I can't imagine what kind of command structure they have. We may have to take down every Mute aboard before we can secure the ship. And three of our teams have already sustained casualties, though none fatal so far. The Malurians have already retreated. They beamed back to Rivgor with three captive Mutes."*

"Captain?" Cutler said, drawing T'Pol's gaze to the science station. "It's worse than that. I'm reading power starting to return to engines and weapons systems."

"That's not all," Sato added. "I'm getting subspace emissions . . . I think they're sending a distress signal."

"At least they'll talk to someone," Cutler muttered.

On the main screen, Commodore th'Menchal stepped forward. *"Taking the ship would be too costly. The Malurians have the right idea——let's secure the prisoners we have and withdraw. That'll give us leverage and an opportunity to study these creatures. Hm, I would have liked to study their weapons and drives at our leisure, but the boarding parties' scans will have to suffice. Captain, get your team out of there, and quickly, before reinforcements arrive."* He sighed. *"As much as I hate to withdraw from a fight,* Endeavour *and the Rigelians are too badly damaged for another engagement so soon, and we don't know how many reinforcements may be coming. As soon as your people are aboard, go to warp. We'll regroup at Zeta Fornacis."*

"Acknowledged," T'Pol said.

"At least we finally have our hands on a few of the ghik-kiths. Let's see how long they hold their silence now."

U.S.S. Pioneer

"I've got Travis and Alan stabilized," Therese Liao reported to the captain. They stood at the threshold of the makeshift medical tent her orderlies had erected around her in the catwalk even as she and her medics had performed emergency surgery on the two men. Now the medics were taking care of the other, thankfully more minor injuries. "Travis should make a full recovery, but under these conditions, that's only going to happen if he stays sedated for a few days to let his body heal." She sighed heavily. "Alan's a different matter. He's stable for now, but he's in a coma and there's only so much I can do for him in here. Ideally we need to get him back to civilization so he can get the long-term treatment he's going to need."

Reed appreciated how much it took for the space-boomer CMO to confess there were limits to what she could do aboard ship. Sheehan's condition must be grave indeed. "Unfortunately that may not be an option," he told her. "According to Grev, communications are one of the many nonfunctional systems. Whatever happened to us, it's burned out every subspace field coil on the ship—even the distress beacon. Worse, it's sent us considerably off course. We weren't supposed to go anywhere near a planetary system. So Starfleet won't know where to look for us."

The doctor stared at him. "That means our only hope is to get our engines up and running—or at least the thrusters. But that would mean leaving the catwalk . . . and even the EV suits would only give an hour's protection against this radiation at most. What are our odds of getting the repairs done before we spiral down into the planet?"

"Just focus on taking care of your patients, Doctor," Reed said, wishing he could come up with something more reassuring to say. Unfortunately, the person who was good at that was lying unconscious behind her.

He left the medical tent, climbed upon the raised metal walkway that ran down the center of the long cylindrical space, and passed through the door into the next catwalk segment, where most of the crew was housed. It was easier to fit *Pioneer*'s forty-six-person complement, plus the six-person engineering team, into the nacelle than it had been with *Enterprise*'s eighty-three a decade before, but things were still hectic as the crew strove to set up usable equipment, food and water distribution, waste reclamation, and the like using what few resources they'd managed to scrounge together in the rush. It didn't help that the surfaces within the catwalk, along with the air itself, were still uncomfortably hot so soon after coil shutdown. Reed had almost burned his fingertip activating the door control.

Members of the crew gathered around him as he entered the compartment. "Captain! How's the chief? And Mister Mayweather?" Reed recognized the burly, florid-faced speaker as Alex Tatopolous, one of the junior engineering crewmen.

"The doctor has them stabilized," Reed told them. "We'll know more later."

"How are we going to get out of here, sir?" asked Adeola Osunwoke from life support. "Without the chief, how are we going to fix the engines?"

"Doctor Dax's team are evaluating the problem even now."

"Them?" Tatopolous protested. "Sir, we wouldn't be in this mess if it weren't for them tampering with our technology."

"That's enough of that," Reed barked. "We're still investigating what happened, and at this point we need whatever expertise we can bring to bear. I expect you to treat our guests with all due respect, is that clear?"

"Yes, sir," a chastened Tatopolous murmured.

"What was that, Crewman?"

"Yes, *sir!*"

"Very well. I assume you have duties to attend."

The crewmen went back to their tasks, obedient but hardly reassured. Reed found himself longing for Mayweather's expertise as much as they longed for Sheehan's.

Finally he reached the nacelle monitor station at the forward end of the catwalk, where the bridge crew was attempting to set up a workable control interface with the bridge and main engineering—a difficult thing to achieve when they hadn't had time to prepare from the other end. "How's it coming?" he asked.

"We've managed to tap into sensors, sir," Sangupta told him, "but there's a lot of interference from the radiation. I'm pretty sure I know where we are—just a couple of parsecs off course, really, but it's an uncharted system, no habitable planets. Nobody here to help us, and slim odds of anyone finding us."

"Any luck regaining thruster control?"

"Sorry, sir, nothing." Tallarico sighed, brushing back a blond strand that had come loose from her ponytail. "We've established a command interface, but all we're getting are error messages. I think the radiation has damaged the RCS quads."

"Well, better them than us," Grev ventured, trying to put a positive spin on things.

"Without them, we're doomed anyway," the helm officer countered.

"Does anyone have any good news?" Reed asked.

Tobin Dax lifted a tentative hand. "Um, I think we've figured out what happened."

"Go on."

"Well, I'm still not quite sure *how* it happened. I mean, yes, theoretically, that kind of metric transformation is possible, but the coil configuration shouldn't have been able—"

Sensing the captain's building impatience, Sangupta interposed, "We fell through a wormhole, sir."

Reed stared. "A wormhole? You mean one of those shortcuts through space, like a Xindi vortex?"

"Well, no, sir, those subspace vortices . . . well, they were a side effect of the altered physics of the Delphic Expanse, which is why the Xindi can't use them anymore now that, well, you know. No, this was a good old-fashioned Einstein-Rosen bridge." He shook his head and laughed. "Which is pretty remarkable, sir, when you think about it. We're the first humans—and Trill, et cetera—ever to create an artificial wormhole and pass through it!"

"He, he's right," Dax said. "If, if we can figure out how this happened, learn to duplicate the effect . . . and stabilize it . . . it could revolutionize space travel."

"That's all well and good, but does any of this help us get out of here now?"

Dax and Sangupta traded a look. "Ahh, no, I'm afraid not," the Trill said. "Sorry. As it is, we're lucky the wormhole exited in normal space, instead of terminating in some subspace domain whose physical laws would disintegrate us in seconds. Or just collapsing in on itself and crushing us. Or—"

"I get the idea, Doctor. In that case, I suggest you

set the wormhole theory aside for now and focus on getting our impulse engines up and running."

"Yes, sir," a chastened Dax replied. "But from up here, it's hard even to diagnose what's wrong with them, let alone fix them. And with Mister Sheehan injured, there's only so much we can do. . . ."

"Doctor Dax. When you came aboard, you were given command authorization second only to Mister Sheehan in order to perform the necessary engine modifications. Modifications that you and your team know better than anyone else on this crew. Under the circumstances, that makes you my chief engineer. And I'm ordering you to fix the engines. Understood?"

Dax bowed his head. "Understood. Sorry."

"And stop apologizing!"

"Sor— Yes, sir."

Wonderful, Reed thought. *Our lives are in the hands of this terrified little sad sack.* He turned and gazed at the wall, imagining the people and the lost opportunities that lay beyond. *Well, it's not as if I was going to leave much of a legacy anyway.*

U.S.S. Endeavour

"I've succeeded at replicating the aliens' environmental needs," Phlox reported to the captain and Thanien as they stood in sickbay along with Hoshi Sato. "I've coordinated with the other ships to ensure they use the same environmental settings for their, ah, guests." The main monitor displayed a night-vision image of the two captive aliens in the darkened decon chamber, which Phlox had configured based on the boarding party's scans of the environment aboard the alien ship. Alongside the live feed was a computer reconstruction of the aliens' anatomy, which T'Pol studied with some fascination. They were neither entirely vertebrate nor invertebrate. Their body surface was a transparent layer of flexible chitinous material, thinnest where it covered the eyestalks and fingers, thickest and most rigid over the head and torso. Beneath it was a layer of wrinkled, gray-green tissue that was itself faintly translucent, with the shadows of internal organs barely visible within. It suggested the dark was their natural environment; they did not need an opaque skin to protect their internal organs from solar radiation.

The captives had been placed in force-field carapaces for transport back to the ship but had been divested of them once secured in decon, then allowed to revive on their own. "Their atmosphere is not dissimilar to ours in chemistry," Phlox went on, "but it's much denser, with levels of carbon dioxide that would be quickly fatal for most humanoids—while our own atmosphere would be too low in oxygen and humidity to sustain them for long. I imagine that's why they like it so dark—their homeworld must be far from its sun in order to avoid a runaway greenhouse effect."

"Wouldn't a dense atmosphere carry sound better?" Sato asked.

"Perhaps too well," T'Pol suggested. "Silence may have been their best defense against detection by predators."

"Or perhaps there's simply too much competing noise in their environment, so they found another way to communicate," Phlox added. "They are apparently sensitive to infrared radiation, as well as the magnetic fields you sensed aboard their ship, Commander. Normal lighting includes enough of an infrared component to obscure their vision."

"What are they doing?" Thanien asked, leaning forward. On the monitor, the aliens were moving around the decon chamber, probing its surfaces with the palms of their four-fingered hands held centimeters away from them.

"Much of their magnetic and thermal sensitivity seems to be concentrated in their hands," Phlox replied. "I've removed their gloves, which appear to contain an array of more powerful sensors and transmit their readings directly through the palms."

The aliens came together in the center of the room, reaching their palms toward each other, standing still briefly before resuming their examination. "I think they're talking to each other," Sato said.

"Yes, I noticed that before," Phlox said. "They're exchanging infrared and magnetic pulses. That must be how they communicate. However, as you can see, their moments of loquacity are brief. And they haven't, ah, *said* a word to me or to the guards outside—only to one another."

T'Pol turned to her communications officer. "Commander, do whatever you can to establish communication. Coordinate with the other ships. We need to find a way to open a dialogue with these beings."

Thanien stepped in front of her. "They have no trouble composing ultimatums from our own words. If we speak, they will understand."

"Some of them might, but we don't know if these two will," Sato replied. "And they don't seem to want to talk back. Until they do, I won't have enough of a baseline to build a translation from." She shook her head. "If I even can, with something so alien."

"Then we must make them talk," Thanien said. "Stop trying to make them comfortable. Brighten the lights. Thin out the atmosphere. Deafen them with intense magnetic fields. *Force* them to ask for mercy."

His antennae were swept back, T'Pol noted. He was not merely being emphatic, but barely controlling his rage. "Commander. The Federation does not engage in torture."

"Even if it's the only way to find their homeworld before they destroy more of our ships, invade our worlds?"

"Your premise is flawed, Commander. Torture has never been a reliable means of extracting accurate information. Countless studies over the centuries have shown that it actually works against that goal. Either the victims lie to give the torturers what they want, or the neurological stress actually impairs the accuracy of their recall."

"Besides, Thanien," Sato said, "if you were tortured for the location of your homeworld, wouldn't you die before giving it up? What makes you think they'd react any differently?"

"You keep telling us how profoundly alien these

beings are," the first officer riposted. "How do we know how they would react until we try? The Andorian Guard *has* used coercive methods before with some efficacy."

T'Pol moved in, her face close to his. "I remember their methods quite well, Commander," she declared, recalling how Shran's men had beaten Jonathan Archer and threatened her sexually at the P'Jem monastery a dozen years before. "I do not recall them being particularly efficacious."

"In any case," Phlox interposed at volume, "this is a moot discussion. As long as I have any medical authority on this ship, there will be no torture of anyone in my care!"

T'Pol watched Thanien closely, hoping that he would relent and accept his place in the chain of command.

However, her hopes were not fulfilled. "Fortunately," the Andorian said, "those aboard this ship are not the highest authorities in this task force."

Rigel V

Archer arrived in the middle of a lively debate over the disposition of the prisoners. Shran and Commissioner Noar were with him in the Rigel command center, while attending via the multiple screens on the wall were T'Pol and Thanien aboard *Endeavour*, th'Menchal on *Vinakthen*, and Garos aboard *Rivgor*. To Archer's dismay, just about everyone was backing Commander Thanien's proposal to "coerce" the prisoners into

talking—all except T'Pol, who spoke against it, and
Shran, who'd offered no comment so far, just hearing
out the arguments. "You all make good points," Shran
finally said. "Commander, Commodore, I understand
how deeply the loss of *Thejal* enrages you both. I agree
the Mutes must be made to pay."

Alarmed, Archer moved up to speak in Shran's ear.
"Admiral, if I could have a word with you?"

"Not now, Jonathan," Shran hissed.

"I'd just like to offer an opinion—"

"That's not your place."

After a tense moment, Archer subsided. Shran
turned back to the monitors. "However," he went on
more loudly, making Archer's ears perk up, "I've seen
what Lieutenant Commander Sato is capable of when
it comes to deciphering alien languages. We'd be fools
not to take advantage of that resource when we have
it. We'll consider more extreme methods if they become necessary, but for now, we're going with Captain
T'Pol's recommendation."

"*Yes, Admiral,*" an unhappy th'Menchal conceded.

"*Admiral,*" Garos interposed, "*I admire your discretion,
but given the time factor involved—*"

"I have made my decision, Mister Garos. Your
crews agreed to abide by Starfleet authority while
they're part of this task force."

"*Understood,*" Garos said after a moment, not hiding
his irritation as well as he probably thought he was.

"You have your orders, all of you. Shran out."

The screens went dark, and Noar stepped forward. "You may command the task force, Admiral,

but remember, you still answer to the Federation. If this . . . diplomatic venture doesn't work, I expect you to pursue more forceful methods, is that clear?"

"Commissioner," Archer began.

But Shran interrupted, keeping the Tellarite's attention firmly on him. "I don't need you to remind me of my responsibilities, Commissioner. I will do whatever the situation demands, and I don't need a civilian kibitzing my every move."

Noar stared down the shorter Andorian for a moment, but his body language was much less dominating than Shran's. The commissioner huffed and said, "Very well. As long as I've made myself clear." He retreated as hastily as decorum allowed.

Shran whirled on Archer, not relaxing his belligerence. "And you! You were the one who talked me into coming out of retirement again. You said I was the person you trusted most to represent the Guard within Starfleet, to be the bridge between Andorians and other races."

"I . . . do remember saying that."

"Then why are you trying to second-guess my authority? Those are my ships out there, my colleagues, my friends. Their safety and their success are my responsibility, not yours. Or are those lunatics on Alrond right after all? Is the Federation really just a front for a pink-skin empire?"

Archer held up his hands. "You're right, Shran. I'm sorry. I didn't mean to undermine your authority. And I should've trusted you to make the right decision."

"Yes, well . . ." He looked away, abashed. "I'm

not as comfortable with torture as I used to be. I've found it . . . unnecessary and regrettable too often after the fact. If I can't make up for those mistakes, at least I can try to spare others from having to make the same ones."

Archer smiled and clasped his friend on the shoulder. After a moment, he went on. "It's just . . . I'm worried about what's going on out there. If we get too . . . aggressive . . . toward the Mutes, we may end up starting a war we could've avoided."

Shran stared at him. "You don't think the war's already begun?"

"I don't think we know enough about the Mutes to understand the purpose behind their attacks. Maybe these ships are pirates or renegades, did you consider that? Maybe, if we can locate their home government, they might even be willing to help us *stop* the raids."

Shran's antennae curled down as he contemplated his old friend's words. It was a few moments before he replied. "It's a constant source of amazement to me that you humans ever managed to survive being so relentlessly optimistic."

"Look at our history, Shran. The only reason we survived our own darker side is because we *learned* to be optimistic. To believe in a better world and work hard to make it happen."

"All right, all right, I've heard the speeches." Shran crossed the room, coming to a pause before the monitor that showed the current deployment of the task force ships. "I'm not looking for a fight, Jonathan. I'm not that man anymore."

"I know."

"But if there's one thing that hasn't changed—that will never change—it's my determination to protect the lives I'm responsible for by whatever means necessary. And now I'm responsible for the defense of the entire Federation." He let out a self-deprecating huff of breath. "It's a big responsibility."

"I can only imagine."

"I hope there is a way to protect all those lives without having to sacrifice more of my officers. But if war is the only way, I won't hesitate to do what must be done."

Archer was silent for a time, reflecting on the grim necessities of war. But after a moment, Shran punched him in the shoulder. "Where's that optimism you were just talking about, Jonathan? *Endeavour's* still out there. I may not be convinced there's a peaceful way out of this, but your crew has a history of finding ways to make peace when nobody else thought it was possible. If anyone can pull it off, they can." He leaned forward. "And they can do it without you second-guessing their every move. You taught them well."

Archer gave a sighing laugh of resignation. "You're right. It's just . . . I don't have much else to do around here."

Shran tilted his head. "There's a very good Xarantine restaurant a couple of blocks from here. Dinner?"

"If you're buying." They headed for the door.

"Are you kidding? By my count, you still owe me at least three favors. . . ."

April 3, 2163

"It's that T'Pol," Commissioner Noar groused as he lay in bed with Devna. "I knew it was a mistake to let Archer put her on the task force. She has Syrannite leanings—practically a pacifist! No surprise she doesn't have the guts to do what has to be done."

Devna sat up and positioned herself to face him, making sure to give him a good view of her slender body as she stroked his chest. "But she's not in command of the task force, is she? The Andorian fleet commander can override her."

"If Shran lets him! The problem is that she carries Archer's mystique with her. They all bend over backward for him. And he's grown complacent! Thinks that just because the Romulans are beaten, we can relax and go back to exploring like a bunch of inquisitive children."

"I see," Devna replied. "Well, Admiral Shran is the ranking military officer. I guess there's not much you can do to override him."

Noar harrumphed loudly, propping himself up on his elbows. "That shows how much you understand about how the Federation is organized, you silly creature. This is not a military dictatorship. I'm the voice of the Federation government here, and if Shran misbehaves, it's well within my power to put him in his place!" He glanced ceilingward. "That is, once I convince the ministers to join me in forming a united bloc."

She leaned forward, letting her chest brush ever

so gently against the coarse hairs of his. She sped her breathing by just the right amount, willed herself to become more aroused so as to secrete more phero-mones. "I've never been with a man so powerful," she lied. "A man whose word could shape the destiny of armies, of whole worlds. It's intoxicating."

"Now, now, Devna. It's . . . a grave responsibil-ity . . . on behalf of my people." She leaned in closer. "I take that very . . . very seriously. But . . . I'll grant, it does come with . . . considerable rewards."

He pulled her against him, and Devna let her body function on autopilot, withdrawing to a quieter place within herself. She'd been trained in the erotic arts for nearly half her life now, had put that training into practice for more than a third of it, and the moves came to her effortlessly, by reflex, like a dance. Some-times she enjoyed it, with a desirable enough mark or with a friend, but this was strictly work. She found little worth desiring in Tellarites as a rule, either in their porcine bodies or their blustering personalities. She'd been with enough of their kind to know that the bombast and aggression were usually just a cover for insecurity and fear. Why else would such a confronta-tional people have been willing to subsume themselves within the Federation—and be such a minor partici-pant in Starfleet? They put up a tough front, but ul-timately they were happier to have others protecting them.

Granted, she'd been with one or two Tellarites who were self-assured and generous of spirit, who only played at the customary arguments of their people to be sociable and didn't mind letting others win. But as a rule, it was the more insecure, defensive ones who felt driven to compensate by pursuing power and authority. And of course it was the ones in power that Devna and her slave sisters got assigned to most of the time: the ones who held valuable secrets that they could be coaxed into boasting about to a helpless slave girl; the ones who would agree to anything to keep their illicit dalliances from being exposed to their spouses or their constituents; or the ones who could be sweet-talked into policy choices that helped the Orion Syndicate, with some subtle assistance from the moderately potent pheromones that rank-and-file slave women were purported not to have.

Min glasch Noar was a classic example of that kind of Tellarite, and it was pathetically easy to play on his fears to goad him into favoring a more aggressive military policy, whether it was his fear of monstrous alien invaders or his fear of irrelevancy. If anything, she felt a little sorry for him. In the middle of the night as they lay together, when he lowered his guard as he would with no one else and professed his undying love for her, she sometimes felt like she was taking advantage of a frightened child. That, far more than his physical ugliness or his ham-fisted lovemaking, was what drove her to withdraw inside her quiet place at times like this. Sometimes she wished she could find a quiet, peaceful place for real, a place far away from the intrigues and appetites and aggressions of the universe, and live out her life there, free to be who she chose to be.

But that would never be. No Orion was truly free; there were only layers upon layers of ownership and submission. Noar was in her thrall, just as she was enthralled to her slavemaster Parrec-Sut, who in turn was chattel to the Three Sisters. Devna sometimes mused that even that powerful triumfeminate were trapped by their own overwhelming chemistry, never able to bond with anyone outside their own family, always having to battle for dominance with other elite lineages. But maybe that was just an attempt to delude herself, to assuage her envy at those females whom biology had blessed with greater pheromonal power and the higher status that came with it.

Such envy was fleeting, however, and it embarrassed Devna to feel it, as much as it embarrassed her to feel pity for marks like Noar. This was the role she had been born into, the role imposed on her by biology, tradition, and fate. This was her life, and the best she could achieve in that life came from serving her masters and mistresses well and taking pride in the quality of her service.

So if the Three Sisters wanted a war, Devna would use all her wiles to ensure they got one.

11

April 4, 2163
Vega Colony, Alpha Lyrae IX

CAPTAIN BRYCE SHUMAR and Commander Caroline Paris stood together in the Vega Museum of Antiquities, examining the twisted, pitted shapes of metal and composite that filled its atrium. Through the skylight overhead, Vega was a blinding white dot, its light casting strange, stark shadows on the artifacts and making it harder to discern their purpose. "Does that look like a tractor beam generator to you?" Paris asked, gesturing at one blackened piece.

"It could be a waste reclamator for all I can tell," Shumar replied. "Hardly any of these fragments are intact enough to let us do more than guess."

Paris gave a cocky grin. "Oh, but that's the fun of it! It's like those old Rorschach tests. Or looking at clouds."

Vega was one of Earth's oldest successful colonies, founded around the turn of the century, not long after the Alpha Centauri settlements had proven viable. It was also one of the most unlikely places imaginable for a colony. Vega was a hot, short-lived star; by all rights it shouldn't even possess habitable planets at its tender age of less than half a billion years. Yet its ninth planet, a watery world in the heart of the habitable zone at seven AU, was home to an unlikely Minshara-class biosphere. The Vulcans who had first surveyed the system a century before had determined that the planet had been terraformed by an advanced civilization, one that had evidently been wiped out centuries earlier in a civil war so devastating that it had torn apart dwarf planets in the system's outer reaches, creating the enormous debris disk that now surrounded the star. The mass extinction had affected most of Vega IX's biosphere, not just its sentient inhabitants; but the plants and small animal forms had since recovered, and the lack of larger fauna made it an amiable world for human settlement. The Vulcans had been satisfied with a cursory survey of the ruins, finding no immediate practical interest in them. But humans had been irresistibly drawn to the mystery of the Vegans—and to the hope that they might have left some caches of advanced technology behind when they were destroyed. Nothing had yet been found beyond these bits of wreckage, but Vega Colony had thrived and become one of Earth's most important outposts.

It also happened to be the closest Federation world to Sauria, so it was here that the summit meeting between President Vanderbilt, Presider Moxat, and the Basileus of M'Tezir was taking place—the final step, so Shumar hoped, in the long negotiations for a trade agreement with the Saurians. But as usual, it was proving difficult to get the Global League and the Basileus to agree on anything more than where to hold the next round of their ongoing argument. "I'm glad you talked me into taking a break from all the bickering," Shumar told his first officer.

"Yeah," Paris said. "I figured the ruins of a cataclysmic, world-destroying civil war would be a refreshing change." Shumar rolled his eyes.

Unfortunately, the change of pace didn't last long. Shumar was surprised to see the Basileus himself approaching the two officers, accompanied by a pair of royal guards, their skin much the same lavender hue as his own. They all wore bulbous, somewhat comical dark goggles to shield their sensitive eyes from Vega's actinic light. "Captain Shumar," the Basileus said. "And Commander Paris. I have decided to take Governor Maggin up on his invitation to experience the culture of his colony."

"Good, good," Shumar said noncommittally. "What's your impression of it so far?"

"It is . . . a quaint achievement. Rather unambitious in size and scale."

Paris threw him a glare. "Well, considering we've only had sixty-some years to work on it, I'd say we've done pretty well."

"You may be right," the monarch conceded. "Perhaps it only seems minor in comparison to the achievements of the civilization that preceded it."

Paris glanced over at the remains. "You know, we don't really know that much about what they actually did achieve."

The Basileus spread his arms. "They had the power to remake this entire world—and destroy others," he added, his eyes seeming to flash even through the goggles. "That is the kind of achievement I would expect from those with the power to travel among the stars. I can easily imagine what they could have done with such power."

"I just bet."

He tensed, controlling his irritation. "Captain Shumar, I wonder if we could converse in private—and out of the sun. I have a matter I would like to discuss with you."

Shumar exchanged a look with Paris, whose expression said, *Better you than me, pal.* "Very well," he said. "There's a private meeting room over here."

Once inside, Shumar dimmed the lights to a bearable medium, for which the Basileus thanked him, although the Saurian did not remove his goggles. "I would have taken this to your president, but he insists on having all parties present for any policy discussion. I felt it would be better to make this overture to you, as one military man to another, so that you could relay it to your president."

"I'm not sure that would be . . ."

"Understand, I wish only to bypass the Global League's obstructionism. Their unreasonable demands are making it impossible to arrive at a satisfactory resolution."

Shumar spoke with care: "They're not the only ones who've made demands, sir."

"But theirs are not commensurate with their value! Your commissioner clings to his pretense of even-handedness, but we all know it is M'Tezir's mineral wealth that the Federation desperately craves." Shumar gave no answer. The Basileus took it as agreement and continued, stepping closer. "As for the rest, the brandy and drugs and art, well, you could obtain those too . . . if you were dealing with a single broker. One government in control of all N'Ragolar's trade."

"Are you telling me," Shumar replied with the sardonic dryness that was his heritage as an Englishman, "that you intend to join the Global League at last?"

The Saurian monarch peered at him, inasmuch as eyes that huge could peer. "I am learning to recognize human sarcasm, Captain. We both know that is not my proposal at all. M'Tezir will never submit to Lyaksti tyranny." Again, he sidled a step closer. "However . . . given access to the right . . . resources, M'Tezir could take action to free N'Ragolar's other nations from that tyranny. Whereupon we could build a genuinely fair, global coalition which would grant generous terms of trade to our benefactors."

Shumar let the monstrousness of the proposal sink in before replying with the same dryness. "In other words, you're asking for weapons you can use to conquer Sauria yourself."

"For the good of all—including your own."

"Apologies, Basileus, but to me it sounds more like you're nursing a historical grudge and asking us to help you indulge it. That's not going to happen, sir. The Federation has no intention of taking sides in any local conflict, and we certainly won't help you start a war."

The Basileus's lips pulled back, exposing sharp teeth. He paced around the table in the center of the room, then turned to face the captain. "I do not understand your recalcitrance. I know you do not share Commissioner Soval's beliefs in noninterference."

"I believe the Federation has a responsibility to help people where it can. Improve their standard of living, encourage equality and peace, save them from diseases or famines. Not arm aspiring conquerors."

"But you need our resources in order to do all those noble, benevolent things." The Saurian leaned forward, placing his hands on the table. "I am grateful to the Federation for bringing knowledge of the greater universe to my world. But that includes the knowledge that there are other powers besides the Federation. Powers that would also be eager to acquire our mineral reserves. If the Federation will not accept my proposal, I may be forced to take it to the Klingons, or the Orions. All our dilithium, our tritanium, our rare earths would fall into their hands, not yours."

Shumar smiled, letting the monarch know he had made a mistake. "Basileus . . . I can say with confidence that if you take your proposal to the Klingons, or the Orions, they will most likely just come in and take your dilithium, your tritanium, and all the rest by force—and take your people as slaves in the bargain. Far from extoling you as their liberator, the people of Sauria will damn your name down through the ages for bringing such devastation upon them.

"At least with the Federation," he went on, "your nation will be treated as fairly as everyone else, and it will surely prosper as a result. Especially since we will protect you from the Klingons, the Orions . . . and any others who would aspire to conquer your world."

Those large, veiled eyes stared at him unblinkingly for a long moment. "I see you are firm in your position. You argue persuasively, Captain. Very well." He headed for the exit. "I shall see you at tomorrow's session, then."

"Tomorrow," Shumar agreed.

Paris was waiting for him when he exited the meeting room. "What was that all about?" He filled her in. "Damn," she said. "I knew that guy gave me the creeps. Talk about your Napoleonic complexes."

"I'm afraid you'll have to finish the tour without me, Caroline," he told her. "I think I need to have a talk with the commissioner."

"This is exactly what I have been warning you about all along, Captain," Soval said once Shumar had briefed him—along with President Vanderbilt, who had been meeting with the commissioner at the time. "Our contact has already destabilized the political situation on Sauria in a potentially cataclysmic way."

"I have to admit, Soval, I'm starting to see your point," Shumar replied. "But Mister President, this simply makes it more imperative that we stay engaged with the Saurians. We can't undo what's already happened, but walking away at this point, leaving things so unstable, would only do more harm. We've seen what happens when we wash our hands of the problems we've already caused for pre-warp civilizations." He reminded them of what he considered a particularly egregious example from Jonathan Archer's career: When an *Enterprise* officer had left his communicator behind on a pre-contact planet on the brink of war, the discovery of the device had sparked a military panic. Archer had been captured while attempting to recover the communicator, and his attempts to avoid confessing he was from space—even after his captors' own scientists had deduced that truth themselves—had only made things worse, convincing the inhabitants that their enemies had superior technology and genetically engineered soldiers. "Our last survey probe showed that those people are still at war, over a decade later. If Archer had simply told them who we were, managed the consequences of the accidental contact instead of retreating and leaving them to their own paranoia, countless lives could have been saved."

He turned to Soval. "Yes, first contact carries the potential of dangerous mistakes. But walking away after our mistakes have already done harm is a far greater mistake, leading to far greater harm. We have destabilized the Saurian situation, and that is why it is imperative that we stay engaged with the Saurians and help them resolve the tensions we have provoked."

"How do we know such further engagement won't simply exacerbate the tensions even more?" Soval challenged.

"We have to try, Commissioner. We can't just run from our responsibilities the way Archer did."

"Watch it there, Bryce," Vanderbilt said. "Jonathan Archer is a man I count as a friend, and I have no doubt he was doing what he believed was necessary."

"I'm sure he was. But it proved to be the wrong decision. I don't want to see us repeat it."

The president sighed. "I have to agree with Bryce here, Soval. This isn't like that thing with the communicator. The Saurians know us already. We have a relationship. There's no worry about secrecy here, no reason not to stay engaged and do what we can to clean up our messes."

"With all due respect, Mister President," Soval asked, "would you feel the same way if it were not for the potential political and economic gain for the Federation?"

"I don't know, Soval. But it's my job to consider the political and economic good of the Federation. Whatever our concerns for the Saurians' well-being, I have to think about the well-being of the billions of Federation citizens whose lives would be a lot worse off if the Klingons got Sauria's wealth.

"So it's decided. We stay engaged, we keep an eye on the Basileus and do what we can to placate him . . . and we hope it doesn't blow up in our faces."

U.S.S. Endeavour

Hoshi Sato closed her eyes, reaching out to feel her way along the corridor wall with her hands as she and Takashi Kimura made their way toward the decon chamber. It was only moments before she tripped over a wall protrusion, but Kimura caught her deftly. "What are you doing?" he asked.

"Trying to get into the aliens' heads," she said.

"What's it like to perceive the world as much through your hands as your eyes? If I can understand that way of seeing the world, maybe it'll help me figure out the concepts their language is built around."

"Okay, but could you do it someplace where you won't bump into people and things?"

"I was trying to—"

An alert klaxon interrupted her. Kimura recognized it immediately. "Breach in decon!" he cried, racing around the corner ahead of Sato. She realized the lights were out in that part of the corridor and raced after him. Before she even reached the corner, his voice cried out briefly and was cut off.

"Takashi!" she cried, picking up the pace.

The Mutes were out of their cell, crouching over the limp forms of Kimura and the crewman who'd been guarding the chamber. "Get away from him!" Sato cried, forgetting everything she'd observed or deduced about these beings' communication. Realizing she was armed, she grabbed for her phase pistol, drew it, and fired at the creature whose hands were roving over Kimura's head. It barely seemed fazed, shifting easily out of the line of fire.

Then the other one was moving toward her incredibly fast, and its hands reached for her, and—

Hoshi Sato awoke to see Doctor Phlox's comforting visage, and she recognized the sounds and smells of the menagerie of strange and medicinally useful creatures Phlox maintained in sickbay. "Takashi. Is he . . ."

"I'm fine," she heard him say, and she turned to see

him sitting up in the adjacent bed. The guard from before—it was Teska—lay unconscious in the third bed.

Sato sat up as well, finding herself reasonably intact and strong. Captain T'Pol and Commander Thanien stood near the foot of her bed. "What happened? Did the Mutes escape?"

"Oddly, no," T'Pol told her. "When the security team arrived, they found that the aliens had moved Commander Kimura and yourself back into the decon chamber."

"As hostages?"

"No. If anything, they seemed to be examining you. They were . . . removing your clothing." Sato shivered. "Fortunately the team was able to stun them and retrieve you before you fell prey to hypercapnia."

"To what?"

"Carbon dioxide poisoning," Phlox clarified. "But you should be fine now. The CO_2 levels were already diminished in the chamber because of the open door. Apparently the aliens can withstand a greater range of atmospheric variations than we thought, at least for brief periods."

"But why would they do it?" Kimura mused. "They were right next to the launch bay. They could've made a run for it."

"In a sub-warp shuttlepod?" Thanien asked.

"They could've fired on us to damage our engines, then sent out a distress signal."

"Clearly they preferred to attack the crew," the first officer countered. "Most likely they hoped to hijack *Endeavour* itself."

Sato had been pondering what she'd been told. "I don't think so, Commander. Phlox, do we have surveillance video of the attack?"

"We certainly do."

She was able to regain her footing with little difficulty, and spent some time reviewing the playback on the main sickbay monitor. It was disquieting seeing herself dragged unconscious into the decon chamber, poked at and partly undressed by these eldritch creatures with faces like Munch's *The Scream* as interpreted by H. P. Lovecraft. But she found herself mercifully distracted by the *way* they did it. "Look at them. They don't seem malicious or afraid—just curious. It's like they're naturalists examining specimens taken in the wild."

"They don't seem to care much about hurting their 'specimens,'" Kimura reminded her.

"Well, not all scientists do. This may sound silly, Captain, but I'm reminded of, say, British or French explorers from the eighteen hundreds. The kind of people who were fascinated to learn about the strange new animals and peoples they could find around the world—but who were more interested in shooting them or taking them prisoner to put on display back home than in showing any consideration for their well-being."

"Intriguing," Phlox said. "So you think that their motives are actually scientific?"

"That they're taking all those ships and crews as . . . trophies?" Kimura added.

"Now that I think about it, it would explain the

weird pattern of the ship encounters. First they just observe a ship, size up their initial impressions . . . then they take a deeper scan . . . then they send a team aboard to study the crew and their responses . . . and finally they take possession of the whole ship. A careful, deliberate process, assessing their findings in each stage before they move on to the next."

"Then why fire on the ship in their second encounter?" Thanien asked. "To test its defenses?"

"Maybe. Or maybe just to see how its crew reacts. Do they retreat? Do they fight back?"

"If what you suggest is true," T'Pol said, "then it's possible at least some of the captured crews could still be alive, in the aliens' equivalent of research institutions."

"Or zoos," Kimura added.

Thanien bent his antennae skeptically. "If what she says is true, then it's just as likely that they're on display in Mute museums—stuffed and mounted."

U.S.S. Pioneer

Sound traveled easily in the nacelle catwalk. That made things problematic for anyone who sought any privacy. But it also meant that when the fight broke out, Valeria Williams was quick to find out about it.

As she raced down the metal gangway toward the far end of the compartment, joined by a pair of other guards she passed along the way, she found herself unsurprised that a fight had begun. Cramming fifty people into this tight space, in fear for their lives, was bound to create tension, especially with Commander Mayweather hurt and unable to calm the crew. She wasn't even surprised when she realized the fight involved Dax's engineering team: She'd heard plenty of grumbles from people who blamed the "alien intruders" for the danger the ship was in.

But Williams *was* surprised when she and her backup guards pulled apart the combatants and she saw Rey Sangupta amid the engineers, one eye bruised and his lip bleeding. "Rey!" she cried. "What's going on here?"

He held up his hands defensively. "Hey, I didn't start it, I swear."

"The hell he didn't!" Somewhat predictably, it was Crewman Tatopolous, the blowhard from maintenance. "You should've heard him, Lieutenant. Mister Mayweather and Mister Sheehan are fighting for their lives, we're all probably gonna die here, and he's laughing with these inhuman bastards about how it's a good thing because they solved a math problem!"

"No, no," the science officer insisted. "No, that is not what I—that's not what I said, Val. I just, we just—we solved it!"

She stared. "You found a way out of here?"

"No, no, we're still working on that. But we cracked the shield problem. We were trying to figure out how a warp reactor could produce a wormhole, and we realized—well, *I* realized—that you could treat a warp field as a special case of a wormhole where one mouth was nested *inside* the other!" He wrapped a hand around his fist to illustrate it. "And once we started looking at it as balancing the shield equations with wormhole equations instead of warp equations, the math became so much simpler to solve! We were able to come up with a much more robust subspace geometry—one that should work regardless of warp coil calibration, and work for any ship!" He shrugged. "Unfortunately, we also proved the wormhole metric has no directional component, so there's no possible way to determine where it comes out, and nineteen times out of twenty it'd collapse and crush the ship if it even formed at all, so we haven't revolutionized space travel just yet. But we *have* cracked the shield problem."

"Listen to him!" Tatopolous cried. "Just as cold-blooded as they are. He forgot it's these aliens' fault we're in this mess in the first place!"

The group with him uttered cries of encouragement: "Yeah!" "Using us as guinea pigs!" "Think they're so much smarter, but look at them now!"

Williams tensed, a hand on her phase pistol. But someone else stepped out in Tatopolous's path before Williams could. It was the historian, the little blond guy whose name she couldn't remember. "I know how you feel, Alex," he said, his voice so soft that the others had to quiet down to hear him. "I felt the same way. Who do these interlopers think they are, coming here to lecture us on how to run our own systems? Our ships worked fine until their tech was installed, so why should we trust them to know how to fix things?"

This isn't helping, Stan—Sam—whatever, Williams thought, starting to move forward.

But Stan or Sam's voice suddenly got harder, more compelling. "But that was when we were safe and comfortable. It's easy to get protective of what you have when you aren't in any real trouble. Those animal instincts kick in and flail around looking for someone to be afraid of. Outsiders make the easiest targets.

"But when the danger becomes real, when the chips are down, that's when we have to look at the people beside us and realize they're in the same boat we are. That we have to hang together if we don't want to hang separately. It wasn't that long ago that our neighbors came to our rescue at Cheron. When they proved we could count on them when it really mattered.

"And now it's time for them to count on us." The historian stepped aside, gesturing to Dax and his team. "Look at them. They're civilians. Thinkers. They're more afraid than we are. We're the ones who are used to taking risks. To facing the possibility of death in service to a greater purpose. We took on this risk to help the Federation, and they bravely came aboard to take it with us. And now our only hope of making that risk worthwhile is if they can find a way to get us out of here—or at least to ensure that the breakthrough they've made can be transmitted back to the Federation, for the good of all our worlds, all our families.

"We're the ones who face danger every day. So let's show them what we're made of . . . and help them through this."

Tatopolous and the others were suitably abashed. They began to disperse, the historian gently herding them away. Relieved and grateful, Williams turned back to Sangupta and the engineers. "Anyone else hurt?"

The engineers seemed fine. The Vulcans and Andorians had shielded Dax with their greater strength and seemed unharmed. The Tellarite seemed to have enjoyed the scuffle immensely. "Okay," the armory officer said. "Still, maybe you should try to keep to yourselves for a little while. Give tensions time to cool. You come with me," she said, gesturing to Sangupta. "Let the doc take a look at you."

Sangupta gestured to his face. "This? I'll be fine. You shoulda seen the other guy."

"I did, remember? Didn't look to me like you laid a finger on Tatopolous."

"Yeah, but I still look better than him."

"Damn it, Rey!" She pulled him down off the catwalk, making him duck beneath the railing along with her, and over to a small space between a pile of supply cases and a structural member. "You're not making this any easier, you know."

"What?"

"You can see how tense everyone is. It doesn't help when you're treating this situation like a joke. Or like a distraction while you focus on, on abstract science instead of practical solutions."

"Hey, you never know what knowledge might be useful until it is. Come on, this accident solved our whole integration problem!"

"Only if we get out of here alive. That's what your priority should be."

"And I'm always thinking about that. If I come up

with something, I guarantee you'll know about it. But the more active I keep my mind, the better it works. And sometimes stepping back from one problem and tackling another will help you solve the first one."

She rolled her eyes at his infuriating, endearingly cocky grin. How did someone so smart end up acting like such a vain, shallow jock?

True to form, he leaned closer to her, resting an arm against the wall behind her. "You know, for a moment I thought you pulled me back here to talk about us."

She pushed him back. "There is no 'us' anymore. Maybe there never should've been. We're too different."

"And *vive la différence*, I always say. You heard what Sam said: Working together can be worth the risk."

His innuendo was blatant, but she was in the mood to take him literally. "I have to wonder," she said, looking back at the site of the confrontation. "Appealing to Starfleet pride was enough to defuse this fight, but what about all the others? What about the civilians who aren't as used to taking risks? If even Starfleet personnel turn on each other under pressure, how can the Federation work?" She sighed. "Maybe you're right. Maybe the only way is if we keep it as loose as possible . . . let every world stand by itself."

"Hey." The science officer grew unwontedly serious. "That's not what I believe. Loose government, yes, but not segregation. We should all be free to mix as much as we want, as individuals."

"But maybe we're not ready for that to work. Not this closely."

He reached up and tweaked her chin. "But we just figured out how to get our technologies to work together. We just had to find the right way to approach the problem."

Williams had no response. Rey gave her one last cocky grin and went on his way to the medical tent, leaving her to her thoughts.

Shaking it off, she reversed direction, wanting to make one more check on the mood of the crew and make sure things hadn't flared up again. She found that most of them had turned in for the evening, while a few were playing cards together. But she spotted Sam the historian leaning against a structural member by himself, just watching them all. She made her way over to him. "Hey," she said. "Thanks for the help back there."

"My pleasure, Lieutenant." He looked down. "I meant what I said—I agreed with them at first. Treated those engineers like intruders, pariahs. But then I saw what Alex and the others were doing, saw how ugly it became . . . I was ashamed." He shook his head. "I was saying those things to myself as much as to them."

"Still, they were the right things to say."

"Thank you."

To break the ensuing silence, she said, "Umm, I liked what you said about hanging together or hanging separately. That was Ben Franklin, wasn't it?"

"Apocryphally," he said with a shrug. "But one of the signers of the Declaration of Independence, most likely."

"I don't think we'd have a Federation, or a United Earth, if the American Founders hadn't shown the way."

"Well, they were only halfway there," Sam replied. "It was centuries before all Americans were given equal representation."

"But they started the ball rolling."

"Yes, they did." He studied her, and she began to notice that he was more pleasant-looking than she'd noticed before. Not her type by a long shot, too quiet and intellectual, but it wasn't as if fraternization was an option anyway. "Sounds to me like your American roots go back a ways."

"The family's lived in Iowa for generations."

"With a name like Valeria, I would've expected something more . . . Roman."

She laughed. "Good catch. Valeria Messalina Williams, at your service," she introduced herself with mock pretension.

"Wife of Emperor Claudius."

"My family, we're big Roman-history buffs. It's kind of a tradition to give Roman names to our children: Marcus, Julius, Octavia . . ."

"Tiberius?"

"Believe it or not." They shared a laugh. "No Caligula yet, though."

"Nice to hear your family has an appreciation for history."

"Yeah." She rubbed her neck. "You know, I have to confess . . . I'm not sure what a historian does on a starship."

"Well, how can you really learn about an alien world if you don't understand its history? Any world we visit that has written records or other documentation of its past, my job is to study it."

Williams nodded. "Of course. That makes sense." She thought it over. "And I guess . . . if we come across a culture that's similar to, say, ancient Rome or Mauryan India or something, you could offer perspective on how it works."

"Up to a point, sure." He gave a smile that was confident in a far less cocky way than Sangupta's. "Not to mention that we're making history ourselves out here. 'With every light-year,' as Admiral Archer likes to say. Somebody has to write it down."

She laughed, enjoying his smile. Then she blushed. "I'm sorry, Sam . . . I can't remember your full name."

He smiled more warmly and clasped her hand. "Kirk," he said. "Samuel Abraham Kirk."

12

April 5, 2163
Rigel V

SHRAN'S EMERGENCY CALL got Archer out of bed in the middle of the local night. Luckily, the steward at the command center had strong coffee ready for him; it looked like he was going to need it. Looking around, he saw that Commissioner Noar was already here.

"We're surrounded," Commodore th'Menchal reported on the big screen. *"The Mutes must have been able to track us, and they came in force. They've taken out our engines, and they destroyed one of the Rigelian ships as a warning."* Archer lowered his head. *"Then they sent this message."*

Of course, it was edited together from the fleet's own transmissions, most of it in T'Pol's voice. *"You cannot escape. Surrender—all—crew—without further violence. You cannot escape. . . ."*

"Where's the rest of the task force?" Archer asked Shran.

"The nearest reinforcements are here," Shran said, showing him on the tactical map. "At best speed, they're eleven hours away."

"We need to fight our way out," insisted Garos from another comm window. *"With* Rivgor's *firepower, we stand a chance of holding them off until reinforcements arrive."*

"It may not be necessary," T'Pol said. "They could simply be instructing us to surrender their own captured crew back to them."

"We know their methods, Captain," Garos countered. "They have attempted to capture or destroy every ship that meets them."

"Garos is right," Noar said. "We should attack them as soon as the reinforcements arrive."

"If we do that, we'll be committing to an all-out war," Archer said.

"Which is obviously more than justified at this point!"

"Gentlemen!" T'Pol said. "If I may. Lieutenant Commander Sato has made what she believes to be significant headway toward understanding the aliens."

"Has she got a translation?" Archer asked.

"More a hypothesis pertaining to their mindset. She believes the aliens' objectives may be scientific rather than military."

"Scientific?" Shran scoffed. "Tell that to the crew of Thejal."

"Certain . . . anomalies remain about that event, Admiral. I grant that our hypothesis is inconclusive, but I think it imperative to resolve the question of their true motives before we commit to an irreversible course of action." T'Pol took a moment to compose herself, eyes darting around, and Archer's suspicion about what she planned to say was confirmed a moment later. "I would like to attempt a mind meld with one of the aliens."

"What?" Noar cried, echoed by th'Menchal. "Outrageous! We can't waste time on Vulcan mysticism and half-baked theories when the Mutes are holding Starfleet crews at gunpoint. They may have reinforcements of their own coming!"

"And what if she's right?" Archer demanded, confronting him. "Do you really want to be responsible for starting a war if it could've been avoided?"

"*Admiral,*" Garos said, his voice disbelieving. "*The Mutes are clearly testing the Federation's resolve. Showing weakness now could be fatal.*"

"He's right!" Noar said. "We have to meet their aggression in kind! Show them we won't be the ones to back down!"

"That's very Tellarite of you," Shran told him. "But there's more to good strategy than putting up a tough front. It's information that wins battles, but nothing so far has let us get into these creatures' heads. If T'Pol believes she can do it, the attempt could gain us valuable intelligence about their technology, their command structures, their strategies. Maybe even the location of their homeworld." He pointed to the tactical display. "If we start a fight now and those ships are lost, we may lose out on the best source of intelligence we're going to get. We should at least let the captain find out what she can before we go into battle."

Noar maintained his confrontational pose but seemed unsure of himself, his resolve wavering. Archer noted his gaze darting to the comm window where Garos's reptilian features were displayed, almost as if looking to him for guidance. Garos gave no indication that he noticed. "All right," the commissioner conceded, looking as though it took some effort to back down. "You're still in command of the fleet—for now. But I've warned you what might happen if I think you're losing your nerve."

Shran bristled at being so openly challenged in front of his subordinates. But Noar stormed out before anything more could be said. Shran gathered himself and turned back to the screens. "Proceed with the mind meld, Captain T'Pol. But don't take any unnecessary risks. And have your crew stand ready in case the Mutes run out of patience and start shooting."

"*Understood. T'Pol out.*"

Shran turned to Archer. "Do you think she can pull it off? How much experience does she have with these melds?"

"Not as much as I'm comfortable with," Archer admitted. "But I taught her everything I know. Long story," he added at Shran's quizzical look. "At the moment, I'm more concerned about Commissioner Noar. Is it me, or is he getting more belligerent than usual?"

"I've certainly never seen him stand up to me like that before," Shran agreed. "And he was a little too eager to rush into battle unprepared. What do you think's going on with him?"

"That's a good question." Archer had a suspicion, but he preferred not to voice it without evidence.

But then, he always enjoyed the chance to do a little exploring.

U.S.S. Pioneer

Rey Sangupta waylaid Grev as soon as he stepped into the nacelle monitor shack. "Hey, Grev, I need you to listen to something."

"Can it wait?" the stout Tellarite asked. "Captain

Reed has me trying to cobble together a working field coil for the subspace transceiver. Which isn't easy when each of us can only work on the transceiver for forty minutes at a time."

"I know, I know, but this could be important!"

Grev sighed. "All right, what?"

"I managed to boost the sensor grid, get some more detailed readings from outside."

"And?"

"Listen," Sangupta said with enthusiasm, "to what I picked up from the super-Jovian on the EM bands."

He worked the scanner he held, and it played a series of eerie, swooping tones over a background of clicking static. Grev listened for a few moments and shrugged. "It's just normal magnetic field fluctuations from the planet. The space boomers call them siren calls."

"No, that's what I thought at first, but listen! They're different, more complex. And the sources are too localized—localized and moving, and not just following the winds."

"Okay, so how is that useful to us?"

"Grev, I think there's something alive down there! And the computer says the signals are pretty complex. A lot of information. That's why I wanted you to listen. I think they could be intelligent."

"What's that, Lieutenant?" Captain Reed approached them from the other end of the small room. "You think there might be people down there?"

"I don't know, sir. Something alive."

Grev listened a bit more closely to the signals,

running an analytical program as he did so. "Any sign of advanced technology?" Reed asked while he worked.

"Nothing like that, sir. These seem more like biologically generated signals."

"You know what they remind me of?" Grev said after a moment. "The songs of that extinct Earth species, the humpback whales. Intelligent, maybe, but the intelligence of social animals."

Reed frowned. "Then it doesn't help us get out of here, does it?"

"Well, no, sir," Sangupta said. "I just thought it—"

"Lieutenant, your only thoughts should be directed toward helping *Pioneer* escape this radiation field before we plummet into that atmosphere. If you can't contribute anything useful to that effort, at least stop wasting the time of those who can. Is that clear?"

"Yes, sir," the science officer replied, bowing his head. "Understood, sir."

The captain stalked away. Grev sidled up next to Sangupta and patted him on the arm. "Sorry," he whispered. "But really, what were you thinking? Didn't Val already talk to you about this? Abstract curiosity is all well and good, but it's useless if we don't survive."

"I know, I know," Sangupta replied. "But life is about living, not just surviving. Nobody gets out of it alive in the end, so we just have to make the most of the time we get.

"If these are my last days . . . well, if there's something new and amazing to be discovered down there,

I'd never forgive myself if I died without finding out about it. All in all, I can think of worse ways to go."

Grev shook his head. "Rey, you're an incurable romantic."

"I hope so, Grev. I hope so."

Therese Liao was waiting when Tobin Dax returned to the catwalk and removed his EV suit helmet. She bided her time while Captain Reed asked for his status report on the impulse engine repairs; Dax said something about how the gravimetric distortions of the wormhole had knocked the fusion initiators out of alignment, or some such jargon, the upshot of which was that the repairs were taking longer than hoped, especially when the work could be done only during brief shifts in the cumbersome spacesuits.

But Liao had more immediate concerns. Once Dax had concluded his report and was occupied removing the rest of his EV suit, she stepped forward and confronted him. "Doctor Dax. You were out in the radiation for nearly ten minutes longer than you were supposed to be."

"Was I? Sorry. I got so caught up . . ."

"Don't apologize to me. You're the one whose health is in danger. I need to examine you for radiation damage."

"Doctor, that's really not—"

"I know your people have some kind of taboo about alien doctors, but under the circumstances, you're just going to have to set it aside, unless you want to risk radiation sickness or cancer."

Dax's hands went protectively over his midsection for some reason, but he still shook his head. Reed stepped forward. "Doctor Dax, I need all my engineers at their peak if we're to get out of this. I'm sorry if it disrespects some sort of Trill custom or taboo, but under the circumstances I can't worry about such niceties. I'm giving you a direct order to let the doctor examine you."

The Trill deflated. "All right." He let Liao lead him back toward the aft compartment serving as the makeshift sickbay, though he looked like he was being led to the gallows. "Can you promise me that any . . . results will stay confidential?"

"That's a given," she told him. "Doctor-patient confidentiality is a core principle of human medicine."

"Good." He didn't seem any less nervous, though. Was this really a Trill taboo or just a personal phobia about doctors?

Once in the medical compartment, he remained sullen and silent as she ran her scanner over him, and he visibly flinched when she leaned in closer to examine the anomalous structure she detected in his midsection. "What's this?" It was some sort of vermiform organ wrapped around the digestive tract, with its narrow end extending to connect to the spine. "This extra organ in your abdomen. I've never seen anything like it before."

"Hmm?" She showed him the readout. "Oh. Oh, that. I'm, I'm not really, ah, well versed in biology. I think it's part of my endocrine system."

"Then why is it in some kind of marsupial pouch?

And is that . . . some sort of neural connection to the spinal column?"

"I, I really don't think . . . isn't the radiation scan more important?"

"Hold on . . . I'm detecting neurological activity!" She looked up at him. "Where do you keep your brain, Doctor?"

"That's a rather personal question, isn't it?"

More convinced than ever that Dax was hiding something, she intensified her examination. Oddly, he just sat there and let it happen, even as she grew more horrified at what she found. "That . . . that thing doesn't just have its own brain circuitry pattern, it has entirely separate DNA. It's an independent life-form. And it's intelligent!" She took a step back from him, her mind filling with possibilities. Some kind of alien parasite that had taken over this man's body? More alarming still was Dax's behavior. "You knew about this. This isn't something that's . . . infected you without your knowledge. Are you . . . is it controlling you?" She realized with dismay that, to this day, no one knew what Romulans looked like. Were they actually these slug things, taking over the bodies of hapless victims, using them to infiltrate their enemies even now? Was Dax responsible for the wormhole accident all along? And if so, did that mean she'd just made the stupidest and last mistake of her life, revealing to this enemy creature that she'd discovered it?

But after a moment, one undeniable fact penetrated her fear: namely, that Dax looked even more frightened than she felt. She took a few deep breaths, gathering herself. "Doctor Dax . . . what are you?"

He winced. "All right. Just . . . please hear me out before you judge."

Liao stared for a moment. "I . . . I'm listening."

"I'm . . ." He gestured to himself, his whole body, in a sweeping gesture. "This is Tobin." His hands went to his midriff, over the thing inside. "This . . . is Dax."

Her eyes darted from his midsection to his face uncertainly. "Which one am I speaking to?"

"Both of us. Of, of me. It's . . . we used to be separate. Now we're one. One mind."

"It's a parasite."

"A symbiont. An equal partnership."

"Really. And what does the, um, Tobin part get out of it?" The benefits to the vermiform creature were obvious. It had no manipulative ability, no defenses, little evident sensory capability.

"The host. The host gets . . . a lot. Higher intelligence. The wisdom of lifetimes. A new perspective, new skills. And . . . we get to live on."

"Meaning?"

"When a host dies . . . the symbiont preserves our memories, our . . . essence. Part of us lives as long as the symbiont does." He gave a breathy laugh. "I'm actually kind of relieved you found out, Doctor. If anything . . . does happen to me—well, if the ship survives, that is, and the symbiont lives—I need someone I can rely on to ensure the symbiont is returned to Trill as quickly as possible. Under the circumstances, it probably won't be possible, but if there's any way to get it back in time to be implanted in another host before it dies . . . before the last of me dies . . . then it's urgent that, that the attempt is made. Can, can I count on you for that, Doctor?"

"My duty is to protect my patient. If it comes down to a choice between you and the symbiont—"

He shook his head. "I *am* the symbiont, as much as I'm the host. And neither half of me can live without the other. Well, the symbiont can, but only if it gets another host in time."

"That doesn't seem a very fair trade-off."

"Is your way any better? Dying totally and permanently?" He looked around, shaking his head as if at his general situation. "I've been so terrified this whole time. I'm, I'm only Dax's second host, you see. It's a very young symbiont—only a hundred forty-five years old, less than ninety spent joined. It would be . . . well, it would be dreadfully embarrassing if I let my symbiont get killed so young."

"So the symbiont matters more than the host?"

"We can both live on in the symbiont. Neither of us can live if we lose it." He shrugged. "It's how we evolved, Doctor. I know it must seem hideous to you. That's why we keep it secret—to protect the symbionts from aliens who'd see them as parasites, threats. But it's natural for us. It's just who we are."

Liao struggled with the concept. She'd been trying to broaden her horizons, to accept the aliens who were part of the Federation now. But it was one thing to learn to like a guy who looked like a pig and thought rudeness was polite, or a woman with elf ears and a logic fetish. This was a far bigger leap. The idea of what Dax described—having one's identity blended with another creature's, subsumed as a part of it—it nauseated her. It was the most intimate violation she could contemplate—even worse than a Vulcan mind meld, since it never ended.

But there was one thing she couldn't deny: Tobin Dax was simply far too neurotic and timid to be a spy or a mind-rapist. If anything, he was one of the gentlest souls she'd ever met. And if the symbiont was half of what made him who he was . . . what did that tell her?

She turned off the scanner. "I'm detecting no radiation damage, either to you or . . . your other you. I'm clearing you to return to duty."

"So . . . so you won't tell anyone?"

"As I said, my oath forbids it. As long as I'm convinced you don't pose any harm to anyone else, I'm honor-bound to keep your secret."

He smiled, sagging as the tension in his body relaxed. "Thank you, Doctor."

"I do think you should confide in the captain, at least. I'll back you up if you do."

"I don't know. Unless . . . unless he really needed to know it, I'd rather not."

"Better if you control the situation than have it come out by accident."

Dax pondered. "I'll think about it." He headed for the exit, then paused. "Thank you again, Doctor Liao."

"Hey, it's self-interest. We need all the brains we

can get to think our way out of this mess, and you've got a spare in your pocket. So who am I to complain?"

The Trill—both of him—smiled and left. Liao smiled back.

Then the polite façade faded and she breathed hard for a while. Then she made herself study the scans of the symbiont, trying to train herself to stop feeling revulsion at the thought of it.

U.S.S. Endeavour

Following a precedent discovered by *Vinakthen's* medical staff—who were somewhat less reluctant to experiment with their Mute prisoners than he was—Doctor Phlox had adjusted the atmosphere in the decon chamber to proportions that would sedate the aliens, making it safe for T'Pol to enter and attempt the meld. "I must say," the Denobulan physician told his captain as they stood outside the chamber with Thanien, Sato, and Kimura, "I have my concerns over the matter of consent."

"You know that is not a matter I take lightly, Phlox," T'Pol replied. "I do not intend to force my way into the subject's mind . . . not if it can be avoided. Hopefully conveying the intent and ability to communicate will be sufficient."

"It never has before," Thanien pointed out. "Why would you expect it to now?"

"If Hoshi is correct, these beings are driven by a rather aggressive curiosity. The mind meld may be a sufficiently novel form of communication to engage their interest."

"And maybe a closer one to their own," Sato added. "They can understand our verbal communication well enough to send messages with it, but they may not think of it as real language. They communicate with magnetic fields and infrared—they can literally sense what's going on inside each other's bodies at any moment. That's a little like telepathy." She shrugged. "Okay, it's not a great theory, but it's what we've got."

Thanien found it a tenuous basis for such a risk. "Captain, I still question the wisdom of risking a senior officer—especially one with classified knowledge of fleet deployment and capabilities."

"I doubt anything so detailed will be transmitted through the meld, Commander. We are dealing with a highly alien neurology and perceptual framework. What comes across will most likely be basic, universal concepts or rough analogies—our own brains' best approximations for what we sense from one another."

"If so, will it even be possible for you to learn anything meaningful from them? Such as the location of their homeworld?"

T'Pol pondered. "We occupy the same physical space, so I might be able to recognize astronomical landmarks even filtered through their perceptions. However, my primary goal is not to interrogate but to establish a framework for dialogue."

"Captain—"

"As long as our only basis for communication is physical force, the possibility of peace, or even a negotiated surrender such as the one we imposed on the Romulans, does not exist. That leaves only the options of unending conflict or total annihilation—neither of which is acceptable to me. Therefore, an alternative form of communication must be found. Do you disagree?"

Thanien studied her. "I concede that point. But I cannot endorse my captain risking herself."

"Unfortunately, there are as yet no Vulcans serving aboard Andorian ships, and no others on *Endeavour*. Nor am I aware of any telepathic adepts among the Malurians or Rigelians. I am, as the humans would say, the only game in town."

The captain left Thanien with that odd metaphor and his own thoughts. He watched as she donned her breathing mask and entered the chamber after a final go-ahead from Phlox. Kimura, wearing his own mask, accompanied her inside, ready to defend her if the Mutes proved more awake than they appeared. T'Pol approached the motionless aliens with caution despite their sedation. She looked between them, then chose one for reasons Thanien couldn't guess. She closed her eyes, moving her hands over the alien's bulbous head as though searching for something. "What is she doing?" Thanien asked.

"I suppose she must be trying to find the right nerve clusters to access the alien's brain," Phlox said with enthusiasm. "I tried to narrow it down for her, but apparently it's as much an art as a science."

Finally her hands came to rest upon the creature's transparent hide . . . and there was only silence. "Isn't there some sort of mantra?" Thanien asked.

"The aliens don't speak," Sato replied. "I guess

she's trying to get into their way of thinking. Make the connection easier."

"Then how will we know—"

T'Pol stiffened, and the medical scanner in Phlox's hand began to beep. "That's how," he said. "A spike in both their neural activity."

The captain's body trembled, her head twitching. "Is she in pain?" Sato asked.

"I don't dare to guess what she's experiencing," Phlox said, "but I doubt connecting with a mind so alien is going to be a walk in the proverbial park for her. I'm concerned too, Hoshi, but my instructions are not to intervene unless there's a clear danger to one or the other subject." The beeping began to slow. "There . . . she seems to be stabilizing."

For a long moment, there was no movement within the chamber. "Now what?" Thanien asked.

"Now . . . we wait," the doctor replied. "As long as it takes."

Minutes later, Thanien found himself pacing the corridor like an expectant father. He forced himself to stop, resting against a bulkhead out of the immediate line of sight of the tableau within the chamber. Phlox wandered over to him a few moments later, leaving Sato to keep watch at the chamber door's porthole. "It's natural to be worried, Commander. Nothing to be ashamed of." He glanced backward. "I'm worried too."

"I'm not . . . simply concerned," Thanien answered. "I'm . . . confused."

"Hm. What about, if I may?"

"What the captain is doing . . . I think it's a foolish chance to take in the name of some ill-founded hope for peace." Phlox waited patiently. "But it's also . . . one of the most courageous acts I've ever seen. An act of deep conviction and . . . and integrity."

"And that surprises you?"

His antennae sagged. "I've spent most of my life in conflict with the Vulcan High Command, and had my share of run-ins with their Ministry of Security as well. I know what they were capable of. And T'Pol was in service to them both. I've been forced to wonder . . . What crimes against my people might she have been complicit in?"

"I'm sure those organizations did their share of harm to your people, as your equivalents did to theirs," Phlox said. "But I have never known T'Pol to be anything but a woman of profound conscience. A conscience that compelled her to leave the Ministry of Security almost as soon as she'd joined, and eventually to resign from the High Command when it refused to help Earth against the Xindi. A conscience that ultimately helped bring down the corrupt regime that was responsible for provoking conflict with your people. I daresay the peace between Vulcans and Andorians would never have happened without T'Pol."

Thanien considered his words. "I have no reason to question you, Phlox. But . . . it's a difficult thing to accept, with so much history. Kanshent . . . she urged me not to forget the ones we mourned, and the acts responsible for their loss. How can I . . . how can I honor her memory, how can I mourn her, if I let go of those she was determined to honor? If I don't demand some kind of recompense for those old wrongs?"

Phlox was silent for some moments. "My people have faced similar questions," he said, the words not coming with his usual ease. "The Denobulans were at war with the Antarans for generations. Countless millions were killed, atrocities were committed on both sides . . . the hatred was so intractable that our two races refused to speak to one another for three centuries after the fighting ended." He looked down at his hands. "I think perhaps we both felt as much loathing for our own ancestors' actions as for the others', and avoiding our old enemies let us avoid facing those painful truths about ourselves."

"What changed?" Thanien asked.

"We . . . began to speak to one another again. Rather, a pair of us were forced to by circumstance. Reluctantly at first, not without anger . . . but we talked, and after a while we started to listen. And that paved the way for more of us to be willing to talk, and to listen. And both our peoples began to understand that what we hated each other for was far in the past, no longer relevant to the present.

"There were some who demanded reparations for old war crimes, even though none of the victims of those crimes were still alive. But our governments both decided that a demand for war reparations would just re-ignite old tensions—possibly destroy a peace that was still tenuous. Far from healing the wounds, it would simply reopen them, worsen them."

"Our dead deserve to be honored, Phlox."

"But do we really honor them by using them as an excuse to add to their numbers?" Phlox shook his head. "Sometimes, Thanien, you simply have to stop letting the past define your life and live for the future instead. After all, nothing we do can change the past—barring time travel, which in my experience causes more problems than it solves." Thanien stared, but the doctor didn't elaborate on what experience that might have been. "The only thing our choices can affect or change is the future. So it seems to me that the future is where our attention can be most usefully directed."

The Denobulan directed his gaze back toward the decon chamber. "And that's why T'Pol is in there. Because her focus is not on the lives already lost, but the lives she can still save."

"Doctor!" Sato called before Thanien could fully process his words. "She's coming out of it!"

They rushed to the hatch. T'Pol staggered, seemingly unsure of her perceptions. Kimura caught her and guided her gently to the exit. Once they were out, Phlox helped her into a seated position on the deck and removed her breathing mask. "Captain?" he asked, holding his scanner beside her head. "Are you all right? T'Pol!"

After a few more moments, her gaze came into focus. "Doctor. Commander," she said, looking up at him.

"How are you feeling?" Thanien asked.

She reached a hand up to him—and he reflexively took it, supporting her as she pulled herself to her feet. "I am . . . disoriented. But improving."

"Did you make contact?" Sato asked. "Did you learn anything?"

"I gained . . . considerable information," the captain replied, sounding as if she were slightly inebriated. "However, I am not yet sure what it means. I need to meditate on it. After which you and I will need to discuss what I learned, Commander."

"Aye, Captain."

Thanien's first impulse was to question T'Pol, to remind her that they were surrounded by an alien fleet and didn't have time for quiet contemplation. But he found himself holding back.

He realized, at last, that he had no reason not to trust her.

13

Rigel V

"I MUST SAY, ADMIRAL," Orav Penap said as he showed Archer into his place of business, "I'm gratified that you've chosen to take me up on my standing invitation at last. I assure you, my ladies are wonderful at relieving stress. Just the thing to keep you at your peak during these tense times."

"I'm sure," Archer said, trying to maintain his friendly tone. Inside, a number of females and a few males of various species lounged or strolled around in scanty attire, showcasing their wares for the customers. Archer himself had made sure to come in civilian clothes to draw less attention.

Penap gestured to a bronze-skinned, golden-haired female with pronounced supraorbital ridges and hands with a surprising number of fingers. "May I recommend one of our Nuvian masseuses? They are justly legendary throughout the sector."

"Actually I was hoping for something a little more exotic. A little more . . . green?"

The plump Xarantine's eyes widened. "Ah, of course. Our Orion ladies are right this way," he said, leading Archer toward the back of the establishment. "Their talents are in great demand, and out of the price range of the ordinary customer. We don't parade them around for just anybody."

"I'd think it'd draw in a lot of business if you showed them off more."

"Their reputation speaks for itself." Penap stopped him at the end of the corridor, gesturing to a row of lockers. "I'm afraid that all recording and communication devices must be stored here before we enter. The privacy of our clients is of great importance to us."

"I'm . . . sure it is," Archer said, depositing his communicator and scanner.

They moved into a lushly appointed chamber in which over half a dozen Orion women went about their business—a couple practicing dance moves, others trying on clothes, three of them bathing fully nude in the central pool. They all noticed Archer's entrance and merely continued doing what they were doing, albeit a little more seductively. As uneasy as Archer was with the scene before him for more than one reason, he couldn't help being affected by the sight.

And Penap recognized as much. "Ah, yes, they are extraordinary creatures, aren't they?"

"They are something else." Archer sidled closer, focusing on his rehearsed plan as a distraction from the beauty before him. "Just between us . . . they've gotta have *some* pheromones, right? Not as much as the elites, but something."

"Oh, no—well, no more than any other humanoid."

"But there must be some secret to their . . ." He gestured at them. "*That.*"

"Only their innate talents and years of practice. They are all fully dedicated to their craft."

"I just bet they are. But I was just thinking . . . I've been under the influence of Orion pheromones. It went badly, but . . . it had its rewards. I was kind of hoping, in lesser doses, maybe . . ."

The women began to wander closer. Penap was fidgeting more. "I'm sorry, I simply can't help you there, Admiral. But I guarantee you, these ladies will leave you fully satisfied. Just pick your favorite one— or two, if you think you can handle them."

He looked them over—forcing himself to concentrate on their faces—but he didn't recognize the slender, pale-skinned one he was looking for. "Actually . . . I was hoping you could set me up with the same one that Commissioner Noar's been coming to see. He sings her praises very highly. And he seems like . . . a changed man because of her. What was her name again?"

"Ahh." Penap's eyes darted between the approaching women and Archer. "Well, I'm afraid our client lists are strictly confidential. Even if the commissioner has told you her name, I can't confirm it."

"I see."

"But I assure you, any of these ladies will give you just as rewarding an experience. I'll even give you a discount to ease any disappointment."

Archer began moving for the door. "You know what? I really had my heart set on the commissioner's friend. Maybe I'll try again some other time."

He retrieved his gear and made his way out of the

establishment as quickly as he could. *Damn.* So much for getting to question that pale-skinned Orion and find out whether she was influencing Commissioner Noar, and why. *So what's my next move?* he thought. *What would Malcolm do? What would . . .*

"Well, well, well," came a familiar and implausibly timely voice. "What's a nice boy like you doin' in a place like this?"

Trip was in the shadows of the adjacent alley, leaning against a wall in a casual, good-old-boy manner that clashed with the spartan black suit he wore. Archer looked around, made sure no one was watching, and joined his old friend, resisting the urge to call his name. "What are you doing here?"

They clasped hands briefly. "Same thing you are, looks like. T'Pol had her own doubts about what's going on with the task force. She doesn't trust that Garos, and I happen to know she has good reason for that."

"Right." Archer nodded, remembering the strange telepathic bond Trip and T'Pol shared. "Somehow I doubt she would've asked you to investigate. Not without telling me."

"She asked me not to, but my . . . colleagues decided it was worth looking into. Mister Penap in there is a lead I've been following. I take it you're concerned about his Orion women and all the time they've been spending with Commissioner Noar and Minister Knowlton."

Archer stared. He was aware that Earth's defense minister had extended her stay on Deneva, but he hadn't realized the reason why. "Pretty much. I'm not convinced these women are as pheromone-free as Penap claims."

Trip looked at the ground for a moment. "Jonathan, you should let me handle this. An investigation like this . . . it's more my kind of job than yours."

The admiral gave him a wary look. "And why's that?"

His old friend sighed. "Look, if you're worried about my methods, don't be. All I plan to do is get Penap away from the Orions and any influence they might have over him. Get him someplace secure where he can talk freely."

Archer considered. "That's not gonna be easy. Penap will be on his guard now, after the way I nosed around."

"I was tryin' not to mention that."

They traded a sour look. "The point is, getting him alone might be easier if you have some help."

Trip considered. "Like maybe a decoy? You draw their attention while I——"

"I guess I could do that."

"All right."

"But——only if I'm there for the interrogation."

Trip smirked. "What's the matter? Don't you trust me?"

Archer just stared, and the smirk faded rapidly.

U.S.S. Endeavour

"Much of what I perceived in the meld remains difficult to interpret," T'Pol confessed. She stood at the

head of the conference room table, flanked by Thanien
and Sato. Commodore th'Menchal sat by Thanien,
and the seat beside Sato was occupied by Dular Garos.
The two had beamed aboard out of concern that the
Mutes might fire on their shuttles; under the circumstances, it seemed the lesser risk. On the wall screen
were Admiral Shran and Commissioner Noar. "Perhaps this is due to my limited experience as a melder,
or perhaps due to our fundamental differences in neurology.

"However, Commander Sato has been helping me
sort through my perceptions, and we are confident of
one conclusion: The aliens are not motivated by conquest."

That prompted reactions of disbelief and protest
from the visitors and the commissioner. *"Let her finish,"*
Shran told them, though he looked skeptical himself.

"Thank you, Admiral. I do not claim that the
aliens' intentions toward us are harmless. In their view,
we are an inferior and dangerous form of life. They
see us as we would see wild animals."

"But we're clearly not that," th'Menchal objected.
"We have language, technology, civilizations."

"We distinguish persons from animals on those
bases, among others. They evidently do not."

Sato leaned forward. "Their senses let them literally see inside each other, sense each other's reactions
and emotions. We call them Mutes, but in reality
they're in constant communication, linked on a deep
level. To them, that communication is fundamental
to their sense of personhood. It's intimately linked to

their feelings, their thoughts. We don't have that kind of connection, so to them, it's like we have no real awareness or emotion."

"But they bear us no particular malice," T'Pol said. "Rather, their interest is scientific. They have an intense curiosity about the universe, but because they do not consider us capable of true emotion or pain, they feel no compassion toward us either. Hence the ruthlessness of their experimental procedure."

"That's why they didn't retaliate before when their ship was destroyed," the communications officer added. "If some of our people were killed by dangerous animals on some planet, we'd mourn their loss, yes, but we wouldn't declare war on the animals. They aren't people, so what's the point? We'd just try to make sure they didn't hurt anyone else—study them so we could understand their behavior and figure out the best way to protect our people from further attacks."

"This is a very clever set of speculations," Garos intoned. "But perhaps you've forgotten that we are currently surrounded by a fleet of Mute ships demanding our surrender."

"I wasn't finished," Sato told him. "If those animals took some of our people alive, it would change everything. We'd go to any lengths to get them back safely."

"It is not our surrender they demand," T'Pol said. "It is the surrender of their comrades. They may lack concern for us, but their compassion for their fellows is profound. They will do anything to protect one another."

"So what are you suggesting?" Noar asked. *"That you simply turn over their captives and hope they let you go? What about the innocent crews they would 'experiment' on in the future?"*

"Now that we understand why they're attacking us," Sato told him, "we have an opportunity to try to change things. We know they feel compassion and concern for their own kind, and that's part of how they define themselves as people. What we need to do is convince them we have the same capacity for emotion and empathy, even if our ways of expressing it are alien to them. If we can convince them that we're people too, we might be able to get them to stop the attacks. Like the way humans stopped hunting and experimenting on Earth animals once we learned they were more self-aware and capable of suffering than we'd believed."

Th'Menchal frowned at her. "How do you propose we convince them of that when they won't even talk to us?"

"I believe the alien I melded with now understands that we are more than animals," T'Pol replied. "If we release their captives, that individual could serve as a go-between."

Noar scoffed. *"You'd just trust in its good intentions?"*

"No," Sato said. "I've been working with Commander Romaine on a device that would let me mimic their magnetic and infrared communication, transmit emotional cues they could understand."

"You?" the commodore asked.

She fidgeted. "I would . . . go with the released prisoners. Turn myself over as a voluntary captive, try to establish a dialogue. To prove to them, in their terms, that we're true people."

The visitors and watchers reacted with surprise. *"Commander Sato,"* Shran said, *"your courage is impressive, but is it wise to risk yourself like that? Alone?"*

"I'm aware of the risk, Admiral. Believe me," she added, her voice quavering a little. "But there's a body-language component as well . . . it's something I'd have to do in person. And the gesture itself, my willingness to risk my safety to communicate, could be a powerful statement to them in its own right. It would show them that we're capable of more than self-preservation. At least it might make them want to find out how and why I was communicating in their terms. Imagine if you were studying an animal and it suddenly started talking to you in something like your own language."

"I imagine," Garos said, "that many in such a situation would see the animal as a danger and destroy it. I think this is a foolish risk. Commander Sato is too valuable to jeopardize in this way."

"I agree," said Noar.

"What is our alternative?" Thanien asked, breaking his silence. "How many ships, how many lives would we lose if we tried to fight our way out?"

"You do have reinforcements en route."

"And so do they," T'Pol said. "A Tesnian listening post detected a large number of their ships heading in our direction. Their estimated arrival time is shortly after that of our own reinforcements."

"Even if we win," Thanien said, "we will have to

kill many of them to do so. And we now know, thanks to Captain T'Pol, that they hold each other's lives as paramount. If we kill so many, they will no longer be content to treat us as scientifically interesting wild beasts, to be captured and studied but otherwise avoided. They will see us as a threat that must be contained or destroyed."

T'Pol gave the Andorian a look of thanks, which he acknowledged with a nod. "If we fight now, it *will* be the beginning of a war. Our only hope of avoiding that war is to take a chance on communication. It's our job as Starfleet officers—as defenders of the Federation and its allies—to risk our own safety to protect the lives of others. Sometimes, yes, that means fighting. But in this case, we put those lives in more danger by fighting back. I am convinced that Commander Sato's plan is our best chance for protecting those lives . . . otherwise I would never permit her to risk herself."

"There is another way of assessing the risks," Garos said. "I think you give too little credit to *Rivgor* and the other Malurian vessel en route. We've destroyed one of their ships already, working with the lamentably departed crew of *Thejal*. Using what we've learned, I believe we can defeat their armada." He held up his hand. "As for the risk of retaliation that would create, we can avoid that outcome if we quickly identify the location of their homeworld—something that should be possible now that you, Captain, have made a breakthrough in communication with the captives. By blockading their home system, we can force them to halt their aggressions—and then we can follow Commander Sato's plan to open communication with them at our leisure. I think that offers a surer chance of success all around."

"He makes a very good point," Commissioner Noar said. *"Negotiation is all well and good, but it must come from a position of strength."*

"Negotiation with these beings would be far harder if we were responsible for inflicting that much death and suffering on them," T'Pol said. "They may be callous toward those they consider nonpersons, but violence against persons is horrific to them in the extreme. They would not forgive it, and peace would not be possible."

"Forgive me," Garos said, "but you're basing that on telepathic perceptions that you yourself admit are unreliable."

"Given what is at stake, it would be far too dangerous to dismiss the possibility that I am right." She turned to Shran on the monitor. "If we pursue this plan, Admiral, the worst thing that happens is that Commander Sato becomes their captive and matters otherwise return to status quo. But at best, the gains will be considerable. Garos's plan poses far greater risks and far more questionable rewards."

Shran pondered her words for a few moments.

"You can't seriously be considering this," Noar demanded after a while.

"I am," the admiral replied. *"What's more, I'm agreeing with it."*

"You can't!"

"I certainly can, Commissioner. If Captain T'Pol and her people are convinced this is our best chance to avoid a war, I'm willing to let them take it. I've seen them succeed against more impossible odds than these. And I don't want to throw away any more lives if I don't have to." He thrust his face closer to Noar's. "Do you?"

The commissioner didn't back down. "Protecting Federation lives is my greatest concern. And protection requires strength, not surrender!"

"Luckily, you don't have the authority to overrule me."

"Not unless I persuade a majority of ministers to remove you from command of this task force."

"I'd like to see you try!"

"Your wish is granted!" Noar stormed out of the command center.

Shran gathered himself and turned back to the sensor. "Well, that was bracing. But as long as I am still in command, Captain T'Pol, I'm authorizing you to proceed with your plan. Commodore th'Menchal, Mister Garos, I expect you to cooperate with her in turning over your Mute prisoners." He leaned forward. "But don't lower your guard, any of you. If they decide to start shooting once their own people are out of danger, be ready to shoot back. Understood?"

"Absolutely, Admiral," th'Menchal assured him.

"Understood," T'Pol replied.

"Good. Shran out."

Garos rose as soon as the screen was blank. "I still feel this is a mistake," he said. "I fear they will open fire on us, and we'll have lost our best hope of finding their homeworld."

"But you will release your prisoners along with ours?" th'Menchal asked.

"I have agreed to abide by Starfleet's decisions," he affirmed with a slight bow. Then he turned to catch T'Pol's gaze. "I only pray those decisions are not fatally misguided."

Rigel V

Archer and Trip waylaid Penap on his way home that evening, bringing him to an unoccupied hangar Trip had secured at the spaceport. "I resent being treated in this way!" the Xarantine pimp cried once the hood was removed from his bulbous yellow head. "I will register a complaint with Starfleet Command over this!"

Trip forced him into a seat, looming over him. "Does this look like a Starfleet uniform to you?" Penap grew quiet, registering the implications of Trip's stark, unmarked black outfit—or, more likely, the cold, controlled manner of the man wearing it. "You can save your protests, Penap. I've looked into your finances. They hold up to most forms of inspection, but I found the links to the Orion Syndicate and the Raldul alignment. So you might as well tell me what they're paying you for."

"The Syndicate? The . . . why, I had no idea, honestly! I'm shocked. What will this do to my reputation?"

Trip loomed over him. "Your little community-theater act is wasted on me. The longer you keep me waiting before I get answers, the longer you'll be locked away and the darker and deeper the hole's gonna be."

The Xarantine's small eyes stared up at him defiantly. "You have no authority here."

"Your women are compromising Federation officials. That's all the authority I need."

Archer was uneasy at the reminder of Trip's employers' willingness to bend whatever rules they pleased, with Earth's—and now the Federation's—safety as their excuse. He took a step forward. "You should talk to us, Penap. We can make it worth your while. We're a powerful nation. Maybe you've heard about the trade deal we're making with the Saurians. We're about to become one of the richest governments in local space. We can treat you well if you play along."

Penap perked up at the offer of wealth, but after some consideration, he shook his head. "I think you underestimate the Syndicate's resources. Besides," he continued with a lascivious grin, "you've seen my girls. The Orions can offer rewards that surpass any monetary wealth."

Trip tutted. "Fishin' off the company pier? Not a good idea when you keep sharks."

"The secret," the Xarantine replied with meaning, "is to keep them happy."

Trip took a step closer. He didn't grab Penap's collar, didn't get in his face, didn't raise his voice—but the atmosphere in the room suddenly got considerably icier. "The same applies right here, right now. You don't want to make me unhappy."

"I'm not afraid of the Federation. We came to you because of your benevolence, remember?"

"No. You came to us because you know we have the strength to get the job done. Because when someone makes an enemy of us, it doesn't turn out well for them."

"Th-there's nothing you can threaten me with that's worse than what the Syndicate will do to me."

"Don't be so sure. Do you really think we beat the Romulans by being nice? By being afraid to do whatever—*whatever*—it took to win? If you had any idea . . ."

Penap was trembling badly now, his head shaking in despair. "I, I can imagine. I've seen the handiwork of . . . people like you before. Ultimately you're all the same." Trip controlled himself, but Archer could see he was taken aback. "And the people on my side will be no less ruthless if they find I betrayed them. I'm damned either way."

He fell silent, sagging in the chair. Trip reached for him, but Archer grabbed his arm, holding his startled gaze. *Let me,* his eyes said. After a moment, Trip stepped back, letting Archer crouch before Penap. "The Federation can do one thing the Syndicate can't: protect you."

Penap's eyes shot up to meet his. But after a moment, he shook his head. "There's nowhere they couldn't find me."

"Remember who you're talking to. We're explorers. Starfleet has been to places nobody else in known space has ever seen. We know worlds where the Orions and Malurians could never reach you."

The Xarantine's puny eyes darted around as he

thought it over. "And . . . would you provide some of those riches you offered earlier? To . . . help me make a fresh start."

"If your information is good enough, we'll see what we can arrange."

"And I can take some of my girls with me?"

"Don't press your luck," Trip said.

Penap sighed. "All right. Archer, you were right before—all Orion women have pheromones to some degree. The rank-and-file slaves hardly have any—just enough to make them, *heh*, especially interesting. But seeded among them are more . . . potent . . . ladies who, ah, have a knack for getting their clients to do what they want, or tell them what they want to know."

"Just like we suspected," Trip muttered. "It's one big honeypot operation."

"So the woman the commissioner's been seeing?" Archer prompted.

"Her name is Devna. She's one of their . . . subtler individuals, but that unassuming innocence is part of what makes her so effective. Gets her marks off their guard. She attracts clients who crave a submissive partner, someone who can make them feel powerful and dominant. Men like that often enjoy boasting of the secrets they're privy to."

Trip frowned. "But this Devna's after more than just Noar's secrets. She's influencing him. Pushing him to be more dominant, is that it? More aggressive?"

"I'm afraid I don't know her specific objectives, sir. I'm just the facilitator. They don't trust me with the details."

"Imagine that," Archer said. "And you with such a trustworthy face."

"Yes, well . . ."

Archer rose and pulled Trip aside. "I'm not convinced he's told us everything he knows," Trip protested, still in the same cool tones that were so different from the man Archer had known.

"But he told us more than you were getting with your methods," Archer said. Trip declined to answer. "At least we know the basics now. And we have a name. This Devna's the one we should be talking to."

"Agreed," Trip said after a moment. "But you should let me handle that alone." Archer stared, and Trip held up his hands defensively, for a moment looking like his old self again. "Don't worry, I'll leave the thumbscrews at home. I just mean . . . you heard what he said about the pheromones. You're not immune to them. I am."

Archer remembered. "Because of that . . . bond you have with T'Pol."

"Right. Somehow it lets me share her Vulcan resistance to the effects." He shrugged. "Or maybe it just makes me a one-woman kind o' guy. Either way, I'm the only one who can tackle Devna safely—so to speak."

Archer looked him over. "All right. But you'll brief me on what you find out."

"Absolutely." He stepped back, looking uneasy. "I guess you can take Penap from here. Thanks for the help."

"Sure thing."

Trip faded into the shadows and was gone. Archer gazed after him for a moment, reflecting. The man was right about his immunity to Orion pheromones, but Archer sensed there was more to it. There was a barrier between them now. It was as if Trip was no longer comfortable working closely with anyone who didn't wear the black suit.

What are you becoming, Trip? Archer thought. He hoped that Orion pheromones weren't the only thing Trip's bond with T'Pol enabled him to resist.

14

MALCOLM REED RUSHED to the medical tent as soon as he heard that Travis Mayweather was awake. He found his first officer lying on his cot, talking weakly with the doctor, sharing some remark that made her laugh, though he was too weak to do more than smile in return. "Travis," Reed said. "Good to see you."

"Sir!" Mayweather tried to sit up.

"At ease," Reed told him. "You need your rest. Doctor . . . if we could have a moment?"

Liao traded a meaningful look with him. "Of course, Captain."

As she left, Reed knelt by Mayweather's cot. "How are you feeling?"

"Like I . . ." He trailed off, frowning, and finally said, "Like I'm too sleepy to think of a clever description."

"I understand," Reed said with a weak smile.

"So . . . I get the idea things are pretty bad. Radiation field, decaying orbit . . ."

The captain sighed heavily. "To be honest, Travis . . . you might've been better off if you hadn't woken up. We're hours from entering the planet's atmosphere. We don't have time to finish repairs. . . . There doesn't seem to be a way out."

"Malcolm . . . I'm sure you did everything you could."

Just like Travis, to think of comforting others first. Reed stood and paced the confines of the small tent. "Oh, I did everything I was supposed to, all right. Everything by the book. But it wasn't enough. This crew . . . they're good people, they've worked hard, but maybe . . . maybe if you'd been here to rally their morale, maybe we could've . . ." He shook his head. "I don't know if we could've pulled off some miracle repair work, but at least . . . at least I wouldn't feel I've let them down. Failed to inspire them as their leader." He sighed. "I suppose it doesn't matter anymore."

Mayweather stared. "Are you kidding? Sir . . . if this is the end, then this is when the crew needs you the most."

"I know. I know. Maybe . . . if you felt up to saying something to them—"

"No." Mayweather clasped Reed's hand. "They don't need me. They need their captain. They need to know that you're proud of them. That what they did mattered—even if just to you."

"It does. I am. But . . . I don't know if I can find the words."

"The words don't matter. What matters is that you care enough to try."

After a moment, the captain placed his other hand over Mayweather's, giving it one last squeeze. "Thank you, my friend. It's been an honor serving with you."

The first officer smiled back. "No place I'd rather be."

Reed nodded and left the tent. He made his way to the next compartment, where most of the crew was housed. As he passed them, he saw their fear, their growing despair. He saw the need in their eyes as they looked at him—and saw them looking away, afraid they would get nothing in return.

When he reached the front of the compartment, he called, "Attention! All personnel, gather around, please." They began to move forward. "That's right, all of you, up here now."

He made sure that those from adjoining compartments were brought in as well, and soon the entire complement was gathered around him, save for those in the medical tent who couldn't leave—and they had a communicator open to hear his words. Reed looked them over, taking care to meet their eyes. "I know I haven't . . . been the most gregarious of commanding officers. I want you to know that that is in no way a reflection of my regard for you as members of my crew. It's simply . . . it's the way I was raised. Maintaining a certain reserve, a certain discipline . . ."

He trailed off, and after a moment, he started again. "No. That's not the real reason. It has always been hard for me to open up; the Reed men are a reserved bunch by nature. But . . . I became very close to my crewmates aboard *Enterprise*, because they made an ongoing effort to reach out to me—Mister Mayweather as much as anyone. I like to think I mellowed somewhat over the years.

"But then . . ." He forced himself not to turn away from their eyes, never mind the intimacy of what he felt compelled to reveal. "A few months ago, I discovered . . . that due to transporter damage, I can never have children of my own." The crew murmured, as much in sympathy for his situation as in surprise that he'd confide it in them. "This was . . . hard for me to accept. Family—the Reed family tradition, the importance of propagating the line—has always been important to me. Losing that possibility has been . . . difficult to cope with. I fear I may have retreated too much within myself. I brought . . . Mister Mayweather aboard to facilitate my relationship with all of you, but I fear I've used him as a shield instead.

"I think that, in my preoccupation with my family situation . . . I've lost sight of how much Starfleet has become my family. And not just my colleagues and friends aboard *Enterprise* and *Endeavour*. All of you too. I may not have shown it, but I have been very proud of you all."

He paused in contemplation. "My father has never been a demonstrative man. Eventually I came to understand that it didn't mean he cared any less. Still . . . I remember times when it would've mattered to me a great deal if he had shown it more. And I'm sorry I didn't remember those times when I was dealing with you.

"I want you to know that . . . despite our dire straits, I doubt any crew in Starfleet could've done more to extricate themselves from this situation. You have done exemplary work, even if no one will ever know it. But I know it, and I want you to know it, and take pride in it. As I take pride in all of you. You are as important to me as my own family . . . and it has been my singular honor to be your captain."

After a moment of reflective silence, Valeria Williams stood before the group. "Atten-*shun!*" she cried.

And all of *Pioneer*'s crew stood to attention and saluted Captain Reed.

He blinked away a tear as he saluted them back. "Thank you. I'm . . . not sure what orders I can give you for the time we have remaining. Except . . . to continue to do your duty as Starfleet personnel, so that *Pioneer* can go down with honor."

A chorus of "aye"s sounded from the group. "Very well. Resume your duties."

"Um . . . sir?" It was Rey Sangupta.

"Yes, Lieutenant?"

"Permission to propose a crazy, desperate Hail-Mary pass?"

Reed smirked. "I'd say this is the perfect time for one. Go ahead."

"Well . . ." Sangupta pulled out a data slate. "I've been studying—in my spare time, mind you—studying the EM emissions from the planet. The ones I think are signals from some kind of intelligent lifeform?"

"Your Jovian whales, yes."

"Well . . . I'm more convinced than ever that they're there. And . . . they have to be pretty huge to broadcast so powerfully. I'm thinking, if we get Grev on it, and dedicate all our computer resources to decoding their communications . . . maybe we can identify their distress calls. Or at least get their attention somehow." He fumbled for words, then shrugged. "I don't know if it'll do any good. But at least it's something we can *do* in the time we have left." He breathed a weak chuckle. "I signed on to Starfleet to explore. To learn new things and see wonders. If these are my last hours in Starfleet . . . that's how I want to go out."

Reed considered his words, then smiled. "Thank you, Mister Sangupta, for reminding us of our true mission. Very well—go to it. Use Mister Grev and whatever resources and personnel you need."

"Aye, aye, sir." Sangupta held his gaze a moment longer. "And . . . thank you."

U.S.S. Endeavour

"You don't have to do this," Kimura said as he helped Sato into her EV suit.

"Yes, I do," she told him. "You know that."

He sighed. "Yeah, I know. I just hoped if I said it aloud, it might change something."

Sato stroked his cheek. "You've seen me go into danger before."

"Not alone," he said, clasping her slender shoulders. She'd always seemed so small and delicate to him. He knew how strong and brilliant she was inside, but he couldn't look at her, touch her, without wanting to protect her.

She held his gaze. "I'm not alone." With a bit of a shrug, she gestured to the two beings who stood with them in the prep room, under heavy guard and ensheathed in their force-field carapaces. "I have my escorts."

"You really think they understand the plan?" he asked her. "Or that they'll really help you with it? How do you know they aren't just going to toss you in a zoo somewhere?"

"If they do, at least there's a good chance I'll be with the other abducted crews. That'll be a start." She looked over the two silent aliens. "But they aren't fighting us. I think T'Pol convinced her melding buddy over there, and he convinced the other one."

The commander looked where she gestured. "How do you know which is which?"

"Not sure I do. And 'he' isn't really the right word either." Her sublimely dainty lips quirked in that way he loved so much. "I just don't want to call them 'it.' Depersonalization is how we got into this mess."

Kimura took heart. If anything could make this insane plan work, it was Hoshi's empathy, her incredible gift for connecting with alien minds. She thought of it as a knack for languages, but he'd long felt it had to be more than that. Knowing the definitions of words wasn't enough to produce the kind of fluency she could pick up in hours. That took a deeper understanding of how the language's speakers thought about the world they inhabited and the concepts they used to describe it.

He took her finely sculpted chin in his hand and gave her a long, gentle kiss. "You take care of yourself," he told her. "Take care of everyone."

"Right," Sato said as she slipped her helmet on. "No pressure."

Orion homeworld (Pi-3 Orionis III)

"Damn that Vulcan!" Navaar hurled a heavy vase across the lushly appointed command suite. Such histrionics were usually beneath her, but at a time like this, it felt necessary. "If I'd known how much trouble she'd turn out to be, I'd have had her killed back on *Enterprise.*"

"Garos won't go along with their plan, will he?" D'Nesh asked. Behind her, one of their burly male slaves moved automatically to clean up the shards of the shattered vase, so deeply in the sisters' thrall that words were unnecessary to command him. The Malurian was another matter, though. D'Nesh was uncomfortable dealing with a male over whom they had no power.

"He'll have to pretend to," Navaar answered. "But he's a devious little serpent. Deceit and misdirection are his specialty. He'll find a way to make sure the battle escalates."

"Mm," Maras moaned from the couch, where another massive slave was giving her a shoulder rub. "I like explosions. They're pretty."

"Yes, they are, dear," Navaar called, trading a long-suffering smirk with her more intelligent sister. "And we should have lots of nice explosions for you soon." She twisted her hair nervously. "As long as that damn Vulcan doesn't get in the way again."

"What about the ministers?" D'Nesh asked. "Do we control enough votes to overrule Shran if he goes pacifist on us?"

"We have Noar and Knowlton. The Mars defense minister is basically a ceremonial post; he'll go along with whatever Knowlton says. We only need one more vote, and the Andorian will be sure to favor a fight."

"I'd be more comfortable if we had more direct influence over them," D'Nesh said. "Who knew Federation officials would be so hard to corrupt?"

"They're young, ambitious," Navaar said. "Hungry to prove themselves. It breeds idealism. Wait until they get more self-assured, more complacent. They'll be easier prey then."

D'Nesh gave her curly hair a skeptical shake. "Maybe. It's *now* I'm worried about. Penap disappearing so soon after Archer was digging around. What if they get to Devna?"

"Devna has done her work well," Navaar said. "I was going to recall her anyway. We're already in the endgame; in a few hours there'll be nothing more they can do."

The first slave approached, holding the largest shards up to her in his bloody, badly sliced hands. She cradled them tenderly. "Ohh, did you do that for me?" She smiled at her sisters. "Isn't that just the sweetest thing?"

Maras grinned excitedly. "Make him do it again!"

Navaar was happy to oblige. She could use the cheering up.

Rigel V

Devna emerged from the shower to find her chambers occupied by a slender, sandy-haired human male in a black suit. She continued drying herself casually, not making any particular attempt at concealment, and began to will herself to release her pheromones. "Hello," she said. "I wasn't expecting company."

The man held out a robe for her. "I think you'll be wanting this."

Devna smiled. "A gentleman," she said, strolling toward him. "How quaint." She accepted the robe and pulled it on, but she only loosely fastened it. "And unusual, for someone in that uniform."

He studied her. "You're familiar with my employers?"

"I know the competition."

The man in black nodded. "No games. That's refreshing."

The truth was, she had no time or inclination to play games. She was getting ready to leave, her mission completed; right now her only priority was to ensure her safe extraction. So she moved in closer, letting the motion pull open the robe a bit more. "I'm trained to give a man what he wants," she breathed. "I sense you're less fond of playing games than others in your agency."

He stepped back, surprisingly unaffected by her proximity. "Ah-ah, then you can stop playing that one. I'm immune to Orion pheromones."

Devna raised her sculpted brows. "A handy trait.

No wonder they sent you." She turned and glided away, slowly making her way toward the bedside table. "Are you here to kill me?"

"No, so you won't need this." He held up the knife she normally kept in the table. She was starting to be impressed.

"Then what?"

"I want information. Why the Orion Syndicate wants to push the Federation into a war."

"You think I'm privy to that kind of information?"

"I think you're the key to their whole operation. So yeah, you know what to say to Commissioner Noar to get him to do what you want."

"If I'm as important as you say, what makes you think I'd tell you what you want to know? If you plan to torture me, it won't work." She smiled. "I'm very popular as a submissive. I've been conditioned to enjoy pain."

He fidgeted visibly—quite a surprise from a member of his organization. The idea of torture made him uneasy. *Fascinating.* "No one should have to live like that," he told her. "I could threaten you if I wanted. You can't seduce me or outfight me—you're not getting out of here unless I let you. And my people have drugs that could make you talk—and you wouldn't like the side effects." He looked away, failing to conceal a shaky breath. Then he met her eyes squarely. "But I'd rather not do things that way. You're a victim here, a slave of the real bad guys. You don't have a choice. But I can offer you one."

She stared at him, intrigued by his approach. "You think so?"

"Devna, I can be your friend, not your enemy. I can offer you freedom. We can take you somewhere safe, somewhere even the Syndicate can't reach. You won't have to do what they tell you anymore."

Freedom. The wistful thought echoed in her mind. But she shook it off. "You think you'll impress me by setting the lies and tricks aside, by telling me the truth."

"I thought it was worth a try."

"But you're still lying, to me and to yourself. Freedom is a lie. It doesn't exist. We all live within one set of walls or another. You're no less trapped than I am. Trapped by that uniform, by the things you've had to do to earn it, and serve it." She draped herself across the bed. "How can you offer me freedom when you're as much a slave as I am?"

He took a step closer to her. "You're wrong. I chose this life to protect the people I love."

"But you had to walk away from them to do it. I know how your agency works. Officially you don't exist. You can't love, can't be loved. You're nobody, nothing." She smiled, gazing up at him enticingly. "The only people you can really be honest with are people like yourself—like me. It's refreshing, isn't it?"

He examined her a few moments more, then sat on the bed beside her—not to make love, but in a sociable, brotherly fashion. "I know there's no turning back from this life. I figured that out at the end of the Romulan War."

Curious, she moved into a matching position at his side. "What happened then?"

"Something I've never told anyone," he said, meeting her eyes. She saw much struggle within his. "But maybe you're right," he went on after a time. "Maybe you're the one person I can tell."

"I'm a very good listener."

"I just bet you are." Still, after a moment, he began to speak. "Another agent—someone working on the same side, but for a different power—was undercover on an enemy ship. She'd been ordered by the ship's captain to kill me. But instead she put me in an escape pod and gave me a beacon so her allies could beam me off." He took a deep breath, shaking his head. "But after everything I'd been through, all the lies, the betrayals, the constant fear of dyin' . . . I couldn't believe it was finally over. So when I turned on the beacon and it started beepin' . . . for a moment I hallucinated it was a bomb countin' down. When I felt the transporter take me, I thought I was bein' blown up.

"I mean, how stupid is that?" he asked her. "If she'd decided to kill me, she woulda just shot me like she'd already been ordered to! No point wastin' a whole escape pod just to mess with my mind. How crazy paranoid did I have to be not to realize that? And it was weeks before I was convinced the people who saved me weren't more enemy spies. . . ."

Devna waited patiently for him to continue. "That was when I realized—this was my life now. I couldn't be the man I was, not anymore. What this life does to us—I wouldn't inflict that knowledge on the people I care about."

She stroked his shoulder. "You do understand. We're both enslaved."

He met her eyes intently. "But I'm not," he said. "There's one person . . . who knows me more intimately than I ever thought was possible. Who knows my secrets, sees me as I really am . . . and accepts me. Loves me, against all odds. And as long as I have that—have her—then I am free.

"That's why I'm doing this. Because what you're doing is endangering the one source of true freedom in my life. Because I'll do anything I can to save her—and help her save others." He held her gaze. "And I'd like to do that in a way she'd be proud of. Because that will keep me free."

Devna contemplated this odd, beautiful man for a long moment. "You're the strangest spy I've ever met, I think."

"I'll take that as a compliment."

"You intrigue me enough that I'll offer you a trade: Let me go, and I'll tell you some things you'll find useful."

"Like what?"

"You'll let me go?"

"You tell me. Will I?"

She looked into his eyes a moment longer, then spoke. She told him of the joint Syndicate/Malurian operation using Orion women, masked Malurians, or outright bribery to cajole Federation and unaligned officials into pushing events in a more aggressive direction.

"But why?" the man in black asked. "What do they get out of it? If Starfleet gets more aggressive, how does that make things any better for them?"

"As long as you're fighting the big targets, you'll be distracted from the smaller ones," Devna said. "Like the Syndicate operatives planning a major raid in the Deneb system in thirteen days. That Denobulan convoy delivering medical supplies to treat the epidemic? Turns out the drugs they're bringing not only save Denebian lives, they have a powerful addictive effect on Nalori, Boslic, and various other species. Those drugs would be worth a fortune to the Syndicate—and now they'll be largely unprotected."

He took it in. "That can't be the whole reason."

"It's enough for your purposes, isn't it? I never offered you the whole truth."

"So why give me this much? Why should I even trust any of it?"

Devna spoke softly. "Because if you'd been forced to get it out of me another way—a way your true love wouldn't approve—then you would've become more trapped. And for no gain, since I would've killed myself before revealing anything to you. That seemed . . . pointless to me. This way, at least," she continued, with deeper feeling than she let on, "maybe you can hold on a little longer to what freedom you have.

"Then at least one of us would have *some* freedom."

He held her gaze for a long moment. "Devna . . . you don't . . ."

She shook off her moment of melancholy, restored her professional armor, and snuggled up against him. "Besides . . ." She gave him a long, deep kiss, then rose to begin packing her few possessions. "I like the idea of you owing me a favor."

15

Rigel V

SHRAN'S ANTENNAE TWITCHED as he watched the feed
from the task force. The Mute prisoners on each of
the ships had been loaded into shuttles, every step
of the procedure captured on camera and broadcast
to the Mute ships in the infrared band so they would
know not to fire on the shuttles that now flew toward
them—all on remote pilot save for the one from *Endeavour*, which Lieutenant Commander Hoshi Sato piloted herself. Indeed, soon enough the ominous black
ships opened their hangar ports and drew the shuttles
into their bays.

"This is a mistake," Commissioner Noar grum-
bled from behind him. "Now we've lost our leverage and given them a hostage. If they open fire,
Admiral—"

"I know, Commissioner, I know." Noar had certainly been loud enough in announcing that he had
the ministers' support to relieve Shran if he defied
them again. "I'll do what has to be done."

"We're aboard now," came Sato's voice, transmitted to *Endeavour* by her EV suit radio. *"They're opening
the doors. They're coming in—coming for me!"* There was a
tense silence.

"Admiral," Noar rumbled.

"Wait!"

"*I'm okay,*" Sato's voice finally announced. "*Our 'friends' interceded with the others—talked to them. They've escorted me to . . . . I think it's like our own decon chamber. Turnabout is fair play, I guess.*" A pause. "*Now they've closed me in. I can't tell what's going on outside. I'll try to keep you posted.*"

Commodore th'Menchal's visage was on one of the screens. "*Why aren't they cutting off her signal?*"

"*Probably they wish to study our communication,*" T'Pol replied. "*Remember, they see us as creatures of scientific interest, not a military adversary.*"

"*So you believe,*" Garos replied from *Rivgor*'s bridge.

"*Commodore!*" called th'Menchal's communications officer. "*New transmission coming in.*"

"*Let's hear it.*"

Despite what the comm officer had said, the "new" transmission had a disturbingly familiar ring. "*You cannot escape. Surrender—all—crew—without further violence. You cannot escape. . . .*" It was the same message as before, stitched together from T'Pol's and the late Captain Shelav's voices.

"*I knew it!*" Garos cried. "*T'Pol, you were wrong. It is a demand to surrender our ships!*"

"*He's right,*" Noar said. "*These monsters won't be satisfied until they take every last one of our people! Admiral, our reinforcements are minutes away. The time has come to fight!*"

"*Commissioner,*" T'Pol said from *Endeavour*, "*need I remind you that Commander Sato——*"

"*I'm well aware of her situation, Captain! Let me

remind you that it was *your* decision to send her into danger in the first place! The cost of that miscalculation is on your head." He turned to Shran. "Admiral, a clear threat has been leveled against Starfleet ships and their crews. I order you to open fire!"

"You might want to reconsider that, Commissioner!"

It was Archer, storming into the room and coming to rest in front of Noar and Shran. The Tellarite commissioner faced him sternly. "Admiral, you have no authority in this matter."

"But I have evidence, Commissioner. Evidence that your judgment has been compromised by an Orion spy."

Noar bristled. "Whaat?! That is an outrageous accusation, Admiral!"

"You might want to lower your voice," Archer told him. "The spy is a certain . . . friend you've been visiting at night."

That shut Noar up effectively. Archer drew him aside, nodding to Shran to follow. "It turns out Devna's not as free of pheromones as you were led to believe, Commissioner. She's been influencing you, pushing you to support a more aggressive stance toward the Mutes."

"Absurd! No one makes me do anything I don't choose to do, pheromones or no. Devna is a free citizen of Rigel. Her choices are her own, just as mine are."

"Then why did she disappear as soon as we found out about her?" Noar stared. "That's right. She's gone.

And so is her . . . employer, Penap. He's accepted a deal for protection against his bosses in the Orion Syndicate."

Noar looked bewildered. "But . . . this is ridiculous. Why would the Syndicate want Starfleet to go to war with the Mutes?"

"As a distraction," Shran realized. "To keep our attention elsewhere so they were free to go about their criminal enterprises."

"That's right," Archer said, "particularly a major attack they're planning to make on the medical shipment going to Deneb Kaitos."

"Where we drew our ships from for the task force!"

"There's more," Archer said to Shran. "I need to talk to T'Pol and the commodore on a private channel. Make sure Garos is out of the loop."

U.S.S. Endeavour

Thanien listened with dismay as Archer spoke of the intelligence he'd somehow acquired linking Garos's Raldul alignment with the Orion Syndicate in this matter. *"Garos has been playing us all along. He helped organize the unaligned worlds to come to us in the first place, and he's been doing what he could to stir up this conflict."*

"That would explain much," T'Pol said. "Lieutenant Cutler found numerous anomalies when we examined the scene of *Thejal*'s destruction. The evidence was not entirely consistent with Garos's account of events. It now seems likely that Garos was responsible for the destruction of both ships."

Kanshent! Thanien's head spun with renewed grief and rage—and guilt at having allowed himself to be so easily misled by his cousin's true murderer. He barely heard what T'Pol said next, but he realized it even as she said it: The Malurian had made it look like the Mutes had destroyed *Thejal* in order to fire up the task force to violence against them. And Thanien had fallen for it completely.

"*Even if all this is the case,*" th'Menchal asked, "*how do we explain their continued demands for our surrender?*"

"Perhaps it is not our surrender they demand. Our initial conclusion may still have been correct."

"*But we saw the Malurians load their prisoners onto the shuttle and launch it!*"

"Hold on," Cutler said, working her console. "I thought I noticed an odd power surge between *Rivgor* and their shuttle just after it left their ship. I thought it was just a fluctuation in the remote control signal. . . ." After another moment reviewing the sensor logs, she said, "Uh-huh. At that short range, it could've been weak enough to miss if we weren't looking for it."

"*Looking for what?*" Archer asked.

"A transporter beam," T'Pol realized, and Cutler nodded. "Garos beamed the prisoners back aboard his ship as soon as the shuttle launched."

"*And now he's holding on to them so the Mutes will keep making their demands, and we'd be forced to open fire! Commodore, you need to find those prisoners and get them turned over, quickly!*"

"*Understood.*"

T'Pol moved to the comm station, manned by

Sato's backup. "Hail the alien vessels, using the protocols Commander Sato devised." At the ensign's nod, she spoke: "Attention. We are aware that one of our vessels has failed to release its prisoners. The cause of the error has been identified and we are working to secure the return of your fellows. Please stand by."

Thanien came up to her, half listening while Commodore th'Menchal hailed the Malurian ship and ordered its crew to submit to inspection. "Do you think they'll listen?"

"Clearly they have some capability to interpret our language. We can only hope it is sufficient to buy us time."

"Commander Sato," Thanien called, "are you monitoring?"

"I'm here, sir. But I'm stuck in here, alone. They won't talk to me. And they took away my infrared gear when I tried to use it. Maybe they thought it posed a threat. I don't know if I can do anything to help convince them now."

"Signal coming in," the ensign said. But it was just the same surrender demand as before.

"Sir!" Kimura called. "*Rivgor* is moving. They're charging weapons!"

Thanien turned to the screen. The massive Malurian warship was pulling away from the closing *Vinakthen*, bringing its bow to bear on the nearest Mute vessel. Garos didn't waste any time—the ship unleashed a massive weapons barrage against the alien ship. "Captain, Hoshi's on that ship!" Kimura said, barely maintaining his discipline.

"I'm aware of that," T'Pol said. "Intercept *Rivgor*. Target their weapons and propulsion."

But the ship shuddered from a powerful impact against its shields. "The Mutes are firing on all ships!" Kimura cried. "*Rivgor* is still firing—now *Vinakthen* is firing on the Mutes!"

"Commodore, what are you doing?" T'Pol asked.

"We have to defend ourselves!"

"Yes, but against whom? You are doing exactly what Garos wants. He is the enemy here."

"T'Pol's right, Commodore!" Archer's voice declared. *"If both sides' reinforcements arrive in the middle of a firefight, they'll react the same way you are, and then Garos will have his war! You need to show the Mutes that Garos is acting alone. Take out* Rivgor*'s weapons, board them, and find those prisoners!"*

The commodore stumbled as a barrage of blows rocked his ship. *"We'd be leaving ourselves exposed!"*

"That is always the risk," T'Pol told him, "when making peace."

"Do it!" Shran ordered. *"Since when were you afraid of a little turbulence?"*

Th'Menchal grunted in amusement. *"Very well. I just hope you all know what you're doing."*

Rivgor

The distant pounding of fire from two enemies reverberated through the deck. Garos didn't let it throw him off his stride. "Sir," called his weapons officer, Monar, "one of our forward batteries is down."

"So? We have nine more."

Another shudder. "Hull breach in section twenty-three."

"I'm still not worried." One of the lesser-advertised defense tricks of this class of vessel was that most of its volume was typically empty, except when carrying large quantities of cargo or slaves. So the odds of an enemy hitting anything vital were low even if they penetrated the vessel's shields and armor. The ship could even use vacuum itself as a defense: *Rivgor's* un-occupied sections were currently depressurized. Take away the air that propagated heat and shock, and explosions became far tamer. *Rivgor* faced little risk of being blown apart from the inside.

But suddenly the deck jerked beneath his feet—and then again. "The Starfleet ships—their targeting is growing more precise," Monar warned. "They've had too much opportunity to study our design."

"Just like that damn Andorian commodore to plan how to attack us even while we were allies. And they call us treacherous. Evasive maneuvers!"

But as soon as they veered, another ship hove into their path—*Endeavour*, of course. That damned Vulcan female's ship. With Archer no doubt calling the shots from Rigel. *That's three times they've gotten in my way*, he thought. *It's enough to make a man feel persecuted. I'm starting to take this personally.*

He reminded himself, though, that such emotional investment was the kind of trap he tried to lead others into, not fall into himself. After all, he fought for his planet, his people, not his personal interest . . . even if most of his people didn't yet see it that way. "Continue evasive. Keep targeting the Mute ship with Sato aboard." As long as the freakish linguist continued to live, the chance of averting war was still significant.

But *Endeavour* kept itself between *Rivgor* and its target, taking the fire meant for its pet freak. Garos was almost starting to think he'd have the personal satisfaction of seeing T'Pol killed after all.

But then Monar cried, "Sir! The rest of the task force is dropping out of warp! They're closing on us!"

Garos muttered a curse under his breath but quickly regained his aplomb. "Are the Mutes still firing on them?"

"Yes, as well as us."

He sighed. "Then we may have succeeded in starting our war after all. Let's get out of here—but first let's leave a little distraction to cover our withdrawal."

U.S.S. Endeavour

"Captain!" called Kimura. "*Rivgor* has just beamed its alien prisoners into space!"

"*All ships, hold fire!*" th'Menchal called.

T'Pol reacted swiftly. "Ortega, move to intercept the aliens. Kimura, bring them into shuttlebay two." She doubted Garos had let them don their force-field carapaces before dumping them. She could only hope their species' ability to withstand the comparatively low pressure of *Endeavour*'s corridor extended to survival in vacuum as well, at least for the duration of the rescue.

Ortega piloted the ship deftly, bringing it swiftly into range of the aliens and then slowing to nearly zero relative velocity, and T'Pol watched the feed from the external shuttlebay monitor as the outer doors opened to let the three weakly flailing entities drift inside. Kimura had wisely left the inner doors closed, not having time to depressurize the bay. Once the outer doors had sealed, he released the inner doors a crack, allowing the air from within the bay to rush into the gap, giving the aliens at least a small amount of the oxygen they needed. "Get a medical team to bay two immediately," T'Pol ordered. "Status on the aliens?"

"They're holding fire," Kimura answered. "*Rivgor* is gone, though."

"That is a problem for another day," T'Pol told him.

"Do you suppose they understood what we did?" asked Thanien.

"I doubt they understand fully. The messages we have sent them today have been rather mixed." She considered her options, then led Thanien aside to speak privately. "As soon as Phlox clears his patients to travel, we'll turn them over."

"Very well," the first officer replied. "I'll have the other shuttlepod prepped for remote guidance."

"That won't be necessary. I'll be piloting it."

Thanien was stunned. "Captain—they already have Commander Sato. You'd turn yourself over as well?"

"Under the circumstances, I think we need to make

a gesture of atonement if we wish to salvage the peace process."

Thanien tried to understand. "And . . . you think turning over a leader will carry more weight with them?"

"I do not know if they have a sufficient sense of hierarchy for that. But there is another consideration: If Commander Sato's communication gear is no longer in play, my telepathy may be the only way to establish a dialogue." The captain reflected that she should never have let Sato convince her it was logical to remain behind the first time. Archer would have insisted on taking the risk himself.

She turned to Thanien. "Surak was willing to surrender himself to his enemies in order to bring them the word of logic and peace. How can I allow myself to do less?"

Thanien studied her for a long moment, then bowed his head. "Captain. I don't think I had ever quite appreciated . . . how brave Surak truly was."

U.S.S. Pioneer

Once the ship began to impinge on the super-Jovian's atmosphere, the radiation began to subside, absorbed by the growing mass of hydrogen and helium above it. Thus, in the final minutes of *Pioneer*'s descent, the crew left the nacelle catwalk to return to their posts . . . and do whatever they could in the time remaining.

So it was that Malcolm Reed was able to sit in his

own command chair to issue what might be his final orders. "Grev, status?"

"We're transmitting at full power, Captain!" the young Tellarite yelled, something Reed had never known him to do. "But I can't be sure if what we're sending is a distress call or a recipe for grain pudding!"

"Cheer up, Grev!" Rey Sangupta called from the science station, a cocky, carefree grin on his face. "For all we know, these guys love grain pudding!"

The deck was beginning to tremble beneath Reed's feet. "Turbulence is building," Tallarico said, not managing to stay as cheerful as the science officer. "Doing what I can to compensate, but I don't have much to work with."

"Try to tilt our nose up!" Rey called. "Maybe we can skim off the atmosphere!"

"What do you think I've been trying to do, sir? It's only a stopgap at best!"

"Right now, Ensign," Reed told her, "that's our battle cry."

Tallarico dared a glance back at him—and was smiling a bit. "Yes, sir!" She turned back and clung to the control yoke with renewed determination.

"Sir!" Williams called from his right. "Something's approaching! Something damn big!"

"On screen!"

At first, all he could make out were the clouds racing by. But then he realized some of the darker lenticular swells were not moving like clouds. They were cutting through the mist around them, moving with

a will. They drew closer . . . and they were enormous.
Reed could hardly process what he was looking at, and
it wasn't due to the shaky picture alone.

"Wow!" Sangupta cried. "Was this worth the trip
or what? Look at the size of those guys!"

"Look at the size of their mouths!" Williams
shouted back, and Reed realized those dark shapes
on their fronts were in fact openings, with some sort
of wispy structures within resembling baleen filters.
"Great job, Rey!" the armory officer cried as one of
the creatures drew in closer. "Now we'll just get eaten
instead of crushed in the atmosphere!"

"Maybe—but what a way to go!"

"Sir!" Tallarico called after a moment. "It's moving *under* us!" Reed stared at the screen. It had been
hard to tell given the sheer scale of the things, but she
was right: The creature was moving underneath *Pioneer*,
matching velocities. How did something so huge move
so fast?

"What's it doing?" Williams asked. "Is it—"

"It is!" Sangupta cried, laughing out loud. "It's
catching us!"

The ship jolted as it made contact with the upper
hide of the creature. The soft body bowed around it,
Pioneer sinking into a crater of its own making, until
the sensor vantage was obscured by porous blue-gray
flesh. But soon the jostling mostly subsided. "Sir,"
Tallarico said, "we've stopped descending. It's . . . it's
holding us at this altitude."

"*They* are," Sangupta appended. "A couple of other
creatures are holding it up on the sides. We must be

pretty heavy for living blimps like these." He shook his head, grinning in wonder. "But they're doing it, Captain! They're buoying us up like a whale with her calf!"

Reed rose and stepped over to the science station. "Good job, Mister Sangupta. All of you, an extraordinary job." He turned back to the science officer. "Now . . . can you and Mister Grev figure out their word for 'thank you'?"

16

April 7, 2163
U.S.S. Pioneer

THE CREW WORKED QUICKLY to restore thruster control
in order to ease the burden on the noble, vast creatures
who had rescued them. This was as much a matter of
self-preservation as kindness, since if the creatures'
strength gave out, that would be it for *Pioneer*. Apparently the hugh but lightweight creatures—which Rey
Sangupta was calling "cloud whales"—had a form of
jet propulsion that the science team was eagerly studying, surprised to see it developed to such efficiency in
an organic life-form.

Within hours, and after the two cloud whales buoying up the central one had each been spelled by fresh
ones, *Pioneer* was able to lift into the sky under its own
power again, though it stayed deep enough in the atmosphere to be shielded from the radiation belts. While
the rest of the crew shifted to repairing the subspace
radio and warp drive, Sangupta and Grev continued
their efforts to establish rudimentary communication
with the cloud whales, insofar as the creatures' limited
intelligence would allow. But the vast beings were self-
aware and social regardless, and they clearly possessed
an innate compassion that made them better beings in
Reed's book than many geniuses he'd met.

Speaking of geniuses, Tobin Dax and his team proved to be a godsend. Once they were able to get out of the catwalk and really devote themselves to the repairs with the rest of the crew under their direction, they were able to devise some exceedingly clever tricks for bypassing burned-out subspace field coils and jury-rigging substitutes. "We should be able to send a distress call in about sixteen hours, sir," Dax told Reed when the captain arrived in engineering for a progress report.

He followed the diminutive Trill to the chief engineer's desk in the forward corner of the room. "How long until we can get warp drive?"

Dax blinked. "Well, another day and a half, I'd say, if we had to. But once we can call for help—"

"Doctor, if it's all the same to you . . . I'd like to see *Pioneer* leave this system under her own power. It'll likely take days for a rescue ship to reach us, and if we can meet them partway, then we can get Mister Sheehan to a planetary medical facility that much sooner."

The Trill nodded. "In that case . . . I could reassign a couple of people from the transceiver to the engines and we can be under way within thirty hours."

"I'm glad to hear you say that, Doctor Dax," Reed said. "You see, I've been thinking. While Mister Sheehan's prognosis is good with proper care, Doctor Liao says he'll need months to recuperate, and there's no telling when or if he'd be fit for duty again. So I'm going to need a new chief engineer."

With a thoughtful nod, Dax said, "Hm, I see. I suppose I could make some recommendations. . . ."

"Doctor—I'm offering you the job."

That evoked a wide-eyed stare. "Me? No, sir, I can't . . . I mean, I'm a civilian."

"So is Doctor Phlox, and he's served with distinction as chief medical officer on *Enterprise* and now *Endeavour*. Even T'Pol served as *Enterprise*'s first officer as a civilian during the Xindi mission. Starfleet regulations can be flexible about such things, particularly where interspecies exchange is concerned."

"Still . . . I'm not exactly . . . comfortable with dangerous situations."

"You've comported yourself well during this one. Think it over. At least consider staying on a temporary basis, until we see whether Mister Sheehan will be returning."

Dax stood and paced, not wasting any time thinking it over as the captain had asked. "Hm. Hmm . . . I suppose I would like to keep an eye on the upgraded systems. It would be interesting to see my equations in action for a change. And . . . your crew has been very welcoming, for the most part. I feel . . . somewhat comfortable here."

"So you'll stay?"

He folded his hands over his midriff, thinking. "I do have certain . . . needs that would have to be addressed. But I've already discussed that with Doctor Liao."

"I see. Anything I'd need to be in the loop on?"

The Trill studied him, holding his eyes for longer than he ever had before. "I'm thinking about it. Maybe. For now, though . . . yes, I guess I can stay, at least for a little while."

"Excellent." Reed shook his hand. "Glad to have you aboard, Doctor Dax."

"Thank you," Dax said, blushing. But then he gave a nervous smile and headed back toward the warp reactor. "Now if you'll excuse me . . . . I think I've thought of a way I can get warp drive up and running within a day. . . ."

April 7 to 13, 2163
"Mute" homeworld

T'Pol and Sato were kept in confinement for the duration of the ship's journey back to the aliens' homeworld, though the individual that T'Pol had grown able to recognize as her melding partner periodically brought in others of the ship's crew to observe and examine them. They allowed Sato limited access to her communication tools, and several of them sought to meld with T'Pol—in order to confirm the first one's insistence that she was a truly sentient being capable of emotion and empathy, the irony of which was not lost on her. Perhaps, she reflected, it was fortunate in this instance that her emotions were closer to the surface than those of most Vulcans.

After approximately two days' travel, the two EV-suited women were escorted from their confinement chamber and out of the ship. T'Pol got a brief, tantalizing glimpse of the beings' native environment—as Phlox had surmised, a dark planet whose distant sun was visible only as a small, faint bright patch in the overcast. The vegetation surrounding the spaceport was solid black, in order to absorb as much light energy as possible; though T'Pol thought it probable that their photosynthesis relied mainly on infrared radiation.

The authorities to whom the women were handed over—or perhaps the researchers, for their loose but tidy off-white garments resembled the lab coats that many species' scientists employed—treated them more harshly than had the vessel's crew, though some of the latter appeared to raise a protest. Sato's equipment was removed again, and the women were forcibly restrained and dragged at high speed into a clean, orderly facility resembling a research institution. T'Pol caught glimpses of cells in which other humanoids of various shapes were confined, though it was hard to get a clear look in such darkness. Still, it was enough to reassure her that many of the other captured starship crews were still alive.

Once placed in a cell of their own with a suitable atmospheric composition and pressure, T'Pol and Sato were forcibly stripped nude, subjected to thorough and uncomfortable physical examination at the aliens' gloved hands, then left alone, locked inside the austere cell with only minimal floor padding, a water tap, and crude facilities for attending bodily functions. Sato struggled to remain calm and suppress her humiliation, relying on the meditation techniques T'Pol had taught her over the years; but there were a few moments when the captain simply needed to allow Hoshi to weep on her shoulder. The aliens—or, rather, the natives, in this context—watched them curiously through an airtight wall that was cloudily translucent to the women's eyes but presumably transparent to infrared and magnetic signals.

For over a day, T'Pol and Sato had only one another for company, but eventually her melding partner and its shipmates began escorting other natives in to meld with her. These natives were not dressed in the gray and brown jumpsuits of the ship crews but in more varied attire, presumably civilian garb, in drab colors and patterns that often clashed to T'Pol's eyes but were presumably quite aesthetic in infrared. The argument that Vulcans, at least, had full personhood was beginning to earn a broader hearing, though it was difficult to persuade them the same was true of nontelepathic species such as humans; apparently the ship's crew had not been fully convinced by Sato's technological mimicry. T'Pol did her best to share her experiences with other races through the meld, but it was difficult to convey the kind of emotional link that would reach them. She shared her thoughts of the non-Vulcans she had bonded with on a personal level over the years: Sato for one, as well as Phlox and Jonathan Archer. She kept her experiences with Trip Tucker in reserve, concerned that they would be too complicated and ambivalent to convey the simple message needed here—and simply wishing to keep them private.

Still, many of the natives remained skeptical. "Their resistance is understandable," T'Pol admitted to Sato as she lay wearied after a long melding session. Hoshi sat next to her with her arms wrapped around her knees, still feeling the need to protect her modesty. T'Pol found this illogical, for there was nothing that these aliens could find sexually desirable about either of them, but she understood her friend's sense of vulnerability and did not criticize her for it. "They consider themselves a highly ethical people toward their own kind. The prospect that they have been abusive, even murderous, toward other beings of equal sentience disturbs them deeply. For many, it is easier to reject the notion."

"Sure," Sato said. "Whatever we feel, we don't show it the same way they do, so they can pretend it isn't the same thing."

T'Pol looked at her. "What if we could?"

"What do you mean?"

"We cannot hope to mimic their magnetic communication. But there are Vulcan biofeedback techniques I could teach you that would allow you to regulate your internal heat distribution to a limited extent. The more muscle activity or blood flow you can concentrate in a certain region, the warmer it would appear to them."

"I get it. If we could mimic their 'expressions,' so to speak, then maybe they'd have a harder time denying that we have feelings like theirs." She thought about it for a moment, then scoffed. "It seems silly, though. That they'd be fooled by something so superficial."

"We are dealing with politicians, not just scientists. They deny our emotional awareness because of a difference in superficial display. If we remove the basis for their denial . . ."

Sato chuckled. "You're right. But it's still just a start. If we're going to convince them to free all their prisoners, we're going to need to prove that those species are real people too. You couldn't teach that heat-regulation trick to all of them."

"It would be difficult."

The communications officer's brow furrowed. "Maybe what we need is an analogy. A way to show them what they have to look for to read humanoid emotions. The mimicry would just be the first step, to show them how our own emotional expression parallels theirs."

"You mean, while we mimic a given heat signature, we concentrate on displaying the equivalent humanoid emotional expression."

"Something like that. But they wouldn't register tone of voice, and our expressions wouldn't convey the same sense of interconnection they associate with their emotions." Sato straightened, snapping her fingers. "Pheromones! We all exchange them without even realizing it."

"And specific patterns of pheromonal and hormonal secretion are associated with specific emotional states, which would allow them to detect the differences between those states. Very good."

Sato sighed. "But we'll still have to convince them to take us to the other prisoners."

It took another two days for T'Pol to teach Sato the biofeedback techniques, and then meld with the natives in order to inform them to scan for their hormonal and pheromonal signatures. The civilian

officials seemed suitably stunned by the mimicry;
T'Pol imagined it was similar to the reaction of
humans upon their initial success at teaching sign
language to their cousin apes. Essentially, beings
they had always considered lesser animals were now
"speaking" to them in a fair approximation of their
own terms. For many of them, she realized, this
drove home the truth of human and Vulcan sentience more persuasively than even her own telepathy had done, for it was more recognizable to them,
more comprehensible to those whose imagination
and experience of the exotic was less than that of the
scientists.

Eventually, the women won permission to see the
other prisoners. Rather than being given their EV
suits, however, they were given force-field carapaces
like those used by the natives. The vest-like protective gear provided limited but, given both women's
small size relative to the natives, just barely adequate
anatomical coverage. More important, the carapaces
shielded them from the planet's toxic atmosphere as
they were escorted from one cell to another. The first
group of prisoners they met were Ithenites—roughly
a dozen small humanoids with shiny, copper-hued
skin and hair. Said hair was quite unkempt, the males
sporting several weeks' beard growth, and all of them
were gaunt and mostly nude. This must have been the
crew of the Ithenite freighter that had disappeared
three weeks earlier. A taller-than-average male, about
four-fifths T'Pol's height and wearing a crude loin-
cloth apparently made from bedding material, strode

forward. "You're Vulcan! And human! Are you here to rescue us? Is the Federation finally here to make these monsters pay?"

T'Pol knelt to match his eye level. "I am Captain T'Pol of the Federation vessel *Endeavour*. This is my communications officer, Lieutenant Commander Hoshi Sato. May I ask your name?"

"I'm Kadlin. Garet Kadlin, captain of the freighter *Noyrit*. These things, they took our ship, brought us here. They've violated us, tortured and starved us. They've murdered three of my people with their obscene experiments, crippled four others. Please tell me you're here to burn this planet to the ground."

She traded a look with Sato. "The situation is . . . more delicate than that." She went on to explain.

When she was done, Kadlin stared in outrage. "Are you serious? You turned yourselves over to these torturers and you think you can talk them into letting us all go?"

"I know how it must sound," Sato told him. "But we've made considerable progress. We wouldn't be here talking to you if they weren't genuinely willing to listen. They didn't mean to be cruel to you; they just didn't understand what you were. If we can prove to them that we're as much people as they are, that we feel like they feel, we can bring an end to this."

"I will instruct you in the necessary biofeedback techniques," T'Pol told him. "Then it will simply be a matter of demonstrating your emotional bonds with one another. Showing them your capacity for empathy, for sorrow."

"I can't believe this," Kadlin spat. "A Vulcan, telling us that love will set us free? After what these monsters have done to my crew, my friends, I only have hate left in me! And it's all they deserve!"

"Your anger is valuable too," she told him. "You are right to be outraged at the wrongs they have unknowingly inflicted. You need to demonstrate that outrage, make them understand your pain in terms they can perceive."

"I'll do that, all right, by caving their misshapen skulls in!"

"Enough violence has been done already, and it has accomplished nothing except the escalation of this conflict. These beings have a high regard for their own ethical standards and are horrified by the prospect that they have violated them unknowingly. So show them your anger—our way. Make them understand how much it has wounded you to see your loved ones suffer and die. That will shame them deeply. It will hurt them. And it will convince them to bring an end to their abductions and experiments so that no more of your people have to suffer. Is that not a satisfactory revenge?"

After giving the hirsute Ithenite a few moments to think, Sato shrugged and added, "Besides . . . Starfleet probably doesn't know where we are, or they'd have been here by now. This is pretty much the only option we have."

Kadlin gave a rasping sigh. "Very well. Show us how it's done."

April 13, 2163
U.S.S. Essex

Captain Bryce Shumar turned as Soval emerged onto the bridge. "Commissioner. Are our guests settled in?"

"Insofar as Saurians ever 'settle,' I would say yes," the gray-haired Vulcan replied. "They seem as eager to return to their homes as I am to put an end to this assignment."

Shumar chuckled. "Well, we'll have them back home within a week."

"Excellent."

"Cheer up, Commissioner—if you'll pardon the expression. I think the talks worked out quite well, once the Basileus realized the limits of his leverage and decided to play along after all."

"I wish I shared your confidence in the outcome, Captain Shumar. I have my doubts that the Basileus is truly satisfied with the trade deal."

"He may be, once he sees how it benefits his people along with the rest of Sauria. I admit he's a dangerous, ambitious person, but I do believe this joint agreement will have a stabilizing effect. After all, neither side benefits if they attack the other and forfeit their trading privileges."

Soval lifted a brow. "That presupposes that they feel they are the ones dependent on trade with us. If anything, the reverse seems to be the case."

"He has a point, Captain," Caroline Paris said from where she stood by the helm console. "The Saurians don't lack for confidence in themselves."

"And that's what makes them such worthwhile allies," Shumar answered, "sorts like the Basileus notwithstanding. They're smart, resourceful, incredibly adaptable—and I daresay they've already thrived from alien contact, not been damaged by it. They're too self-assured to let their customs or beliefs get shoved aside by alien ways."

Soval stepped forward, contemplating his words. "I have heard similar sentiments expressed by my fellow Vulcans about another species. Yours, to be precise."

"They had a point," Paris said. "We don't seem to be speaking Vulcan or quoting Surak."

"And look how far you have come so quickly. How much you have changed the galaxy."

"For the better, I hope," Shumar replied.

"I am . . . more confident of that now than I once would have been," was Soval's hesitant reply. "You have proven your maturity, for the most part."

"For the most part?" Paris protested.

"Don't prove his point," Shumar teased.

"But it has not always been so," the commissioner continued. "I have seen the pattern before in my study of your history. Your Western European region, a thousand years ago, was a primitive backwater compared to contemporaneous human societies in Asia and the Middle East. Its peoples were often seen by their contemporaries elsewhere as violent, uncivilized savages. In time, however, the Europeans gained access to the knowledge and inventions of the more advanced cultures to the East—medical and scientific knowledge, movable type, the magnetic compass, gunpowder. Far from being damaged or overwhelmed by this alien knowledge, the peoples of Europe embraced it, making themselves a stronger, more enlightened society."

"True."

"But they did not stop there. Their ambition to compete with their more advanced and prosperous neighbors eventually drove them to surpass those neighbors technologically—and ultimately to subjugate them, either economically, militarily, or culturally. Within a few centuries, they had effectively conquered your entire world."

"That's putting it a little harshly, don't you think?" asked Paris.

"I speak from the Vulcan perspective as observers of your world. After first contact, we often told you that we were holding back your progress into space for your own protection against the dangers that lay out here. But that was only part of the reason."

Soval met their gazes keenly. "Sometimes a policy of avoiding contact with less advanced civilizations is not about protecting *them* from *us*. Consider how strong, how intelligent, how long-lived the Saurians are. Yes, that has let them adapt well to contact with other worlds.

"But what might happen, I wonder, if they adapt *too* well?"

April 17, 2163
U.S.S. Endeavour, orbiting Gamma Vertis IV

Thanien had been deeply relieved when a signal from T'Pol finally reached the task force. For all his efforts to maintain faith in her, he had spent several sleepless nights afraid that he would never see the captain or Sato again, and that the conflict with the Mutes would only continue to escalate.

But then the call had come, requesting that *Endeavour* and *Vinakthen* travel to an uncharted K-star system in order to retrieve the surviving captives from many abducted ships. The system had only a catalog number in Federation databases, but the Rigelians counted it as the third-brightest star in a minor constellation they called Verti, so it was entered in *Endeavour*'s charts as Gamma Vertis. The message specifically requested that no other ships come, for the situation was still volatile and too large a military presence would be dangerously provocative.

"The release of the prisoners is only the first step," T'Pol told her first officer as she rose from the sickbay exam table, making room for Sato—who had been holding Kimura's hand throughout T'Pol's examination—to take her place under Phlox's scanner. "The Vertians, as we may now call them, have begun to accept the idea of our personhood and have provisionally agreed to suspend their . . . sample-collection missions—but only if we can assure them there will be no retaliation against their world. They have observed the violence humanoids often inflict on one another, and indeed this was one of the main reasons they became convinced we could not be truly sentient life—for no sane Vertian would harm another."

"That's right," Sato put in. "They know we're intelligent animals now, but we're still pretty wild by their standards, and that makes them afraid."

"From what I have heard," Thanien said, "the worlds whose citizens were taken by the Mu—the Vertians have legitimate cause for outrage. It will not be enough simply to leave them be and hope they do the same. The victimized worlds are entitled to some form of reparation." Phlox threw him a look, but Thanien stood his ground. Forgiving old sins was one thing, but these sins were more immediate.

"As I said, the process has only begun," T'Pol told him. "There is much still to resolve, and many hurdles of communication and psychology to transcend. But the essential thing now is to negotiate an agreement that will prevent further violence."

"Which is something the Federation can still help with," Sato added. "But at least we can leave it to the diplomats instead of the military now." She smiled. "You can't really get anything done without communication, can you?"

"Are we sure," Thanien asked, "that we can really trust the Vertians, though? If they still see us as wild beasts, how do we know they aren't simply handling us in their own interest, rather than negotiating in good faith with equals?"

T'Pol pondered. "I grant there is reason for mistrust on both sides. But one thing that is clear about the Vertians is that they are experimentalists by nature. They probably have as many doubts about the prospect of peace as we do. But they are curious enough to be willing to try it and observe the results."

"Hm." Thanien considered it. "Then I suppose that is one area where we do have common ground."

Once Phlox cleared T'Pol to leave sickbay, she and Thanien headed for the bridge. "Captain," he asked in the lift, "may we speak in private?"

"In my ready room," she said, "once I have checked in on the bridge."

A few minutes later, after the captain had acknowledged the welcomes of Cutler, Romaine, and Ortega and gotten up to speed on the ship's status, they were alone in her ready room. "I wanted to apologize, Captain," Thanien said. "My behavior in the wake of Captain Shelav's death was unacceptable. I let my old prejudices about Vulcans color my thinking." He shook his head. "No—rather, I used that anger as a diversion from my pain. Either way, I allowed my emotions to compromise my judgment. It is important that I not let that happen again. Perhaps . . . I could benefit by heeding your more logical example."

T'Pol raised her brows and nodded. "I agree."

Thanien blinked, then cleared his throat. "I believe this is the part where you concede you could learn a thing or two from my emotional example as well. That our respective reason and passion can complement each other?"

The captain contemplated him for a moment, seeming reluctant to confide something, before finally speaking. "In fact, Commander, I am much more aware of my emotions than I tend to let on. I . . . have always struggled with emotional control more than other Vulcans—at least, more than most Vulcans would admit. But more than that . . . years ago on the Xindi mission, I suffered . . . chronic exposure to trellium-D, a substance which permanently impaired my emotional suppression mechanisms. I have learned to manage those emotions, with much assistance from my studies of Surak's teachings. But while I am able to maintain my surface equanimity, my emotions are always a part of my decision-making process."

Thanien thought it over, looking at her in a new light. "I see."

She met his eyes. "Commander . . . Thanien . . . neither of us is defined by a single trait, such as logic or emotion. We are not racial stereotypes but fully re-alized individuals with many facets. What I need from you as my first officer is to be engaged with every facet of your own being—emotion, reason, discipline, intu-ition, all of it—just as I endeavor to be with mine. I need us both to understand each other as individuals with all those traits. That, as I learned from my years as Jonathan Archer's first officer, is what will make us effective complements for one another. Do you under-stand?"

Thanien smiled. "Yes. Yes, Captain T'Pol, I under-stand now."

T'Pol almost—*almost*—smiled back. "Good. Then shall we return to the bridge?"

"It would be my pleasure."

Epilogue

April 19, 2163
Federation Executive Building

"THE DENOBULAN CONVOY reached Deneb V without incident, Mister President," Admiral Gardner informed Thomas Vanderbilt. "Our ships caught a few Nausicaan raiders testing the waters nearby but scared them off with no shots fired."

"I assume they weren't the force the Orions were going to send," the president replied dryly.

"Probably just some overambitious types who didn't have the sense to back off when the Orions did."

"Still, too bad we couldn't have kept them in the dark that we'd found out. Caught them in the act."

"Fake a war with the Vertians just to catch some drug smugglers?" Gardner asked.

"It does sound disproportionate when you put it like that." He sighed. "I'm just worried about what the Orions will be doing next. Would've helped me sleep better if they had fewer ships and weapons to do it with."

"Whatever they're planning, Starfleet is ready. The borders are well defended." The admiral paused. "If I may ask, sir, is the commission any closer to appointing a new defense commissioner?"

"We're reviewing candidates."

Gardner noted his sour expression. "Mister President?"

"It just doesn't seem fair that Noar had to resign. He was manipulated—drugged, essentially."

"Because he had the poor judgment to get himself in a compromising situation . . . sir."

"I suppose. It just feels more like politics—avoiding a scandal, even if it ruins an otherwise exemplary career."

"Some things are universal, I guess."

"Maybe. At least I won't have to worry about politics much longer."

Gardner stared. "Sir?"

"You might as well be the first to know, Samuel. I won't be putting my name up for re-election next year."

"But . . . why, sir? You've been doing a fine job under trying circumstances."

"Have I? Look what almost happened under my watch."

"You made a reasonable decision to guard against an apparent threat. You protected the Federation, just like you protected Earth during the war."

"But that's just it. We're not fighting the last war anymore. Maybe that didn't sink in until now." He rose and looked out the window at the vista of Paris beyond. "It wasn't the warriors who saved us with the Vertians, Sammy. It was the thinkers and the talkers. Same with *Pioneer*—being scientists and communicators was what saved them, and saved their breakthroughs for Starfleet."

He turned back to the chief of staff. "So I've realized—Jonathan Archer is right. Again. In this complicated, mysterious galaxy, with so much out there we can't assume we understand or know how to cope with . . . knowledge will be our best defense. We need to move beyond our wartime mentality and become explorers again. And we need a president who can define a peacetime role for the Federation."

Gardner tried to take it in. "Sir . . . we'll always need a strong defense. The Orions and Malurians won't be going away, and we don't know how long the Klingons will stay preoccupied."

"Of course we will. But that can't be all we are. If this last month has proven anything, it's that if you go looking for a fight, you tend to find it."

The admiral held his gaze, realizing his mind was made up. "I understand, sir."

Vanderbilt clasped his shoulder. "I'm not sure you do. But I trust you to do your duty."

"Thank you, Mister President."

He dismissed Gardner. Once he was alone, he gazed at his desk and tried to imagine who might take his place. Councillor T'Maran or Thoris? Earth's Prime Minister Samuels, or Centauri's Ambassador Sloane? Commissioner Soval might be a good choice, if he weren't so valuable where he was.

Although Vanderbilt found he couldn't shake the image of Jonathan Archer sitting in that chair someday.

April 25, 2163
U.S.S. Pioneer, San Francisco Navy Yards
   Orbital Facility

Malcolm Reed showed Admiral Archer and Captain T'Pol into *Pioneer's* mess hall, where a few of the crew were taking time off between repair shifts. He was pleased to see that Tobin Dax was dining and carrying on a lively conversation with several crew members, including Grev, Val Williams, and the historian Samuel Kirk. He noted how Kirk was looking at Williams and hoped he wouldn't have to have another talk with her about shipboard romances—although at second glance, she didn't seem to return his interest. They broke off conversation when they saw the admiral and visiting captain, but Archer said, "At ease, everyone," and took a moment to greet them all, pausing to invite Williams to dine with him and her father sometime.

Soon the three of them were in the captain's mess. "I finally get to return the favor, sir," Reed said, offering a seat.

"Thank you, Malcolm."

"Yes, thank you," T'Pol said. "I appreciate the opportunity to visit *Pioneer* at last. It lives up to your descriptions."

"I'm glad to have you, Captain. And thank you."

Archer looked around. "Well, your crew has fixed the ship up very nicely after what you went through."

"Thank you, sir."

"And the discoveries you brought back—not just the solution to the integration problem, but those cloud whales." He shook his head as Reed poured his iced tea. "Amazing."

"We owe them all our lives. It's refreshing to encounter beings of such kindness."

T'Pol offered an appreciative nod. "Our time negotiating with the Vertians was illuminating as well.

They are beings of great compassion. It is regrettable—and something of an object lesson—that they were trapped by such a narrow definition of who was worthy of their compassion. But their own history is virtually devoid of war and persecution. It makes for a fascinating study."

Archer shook his head. "I envy you, Captains. Still out there, discovering all these amazing things. Living the adventure."

"Yes, sir," Reed said. "And thanks to Doctor Dax and Mister Sangupta, we can now do it more reliably and safely."

"Indeed," added T'Pol. "Starfleet can finally embody the principle of Infinite Diversity in Infinite Combination—different worlds' technologies meshing harmoniously to create a greater whole."

"And not just the technologies," Reed said, "but the people as well. A symbiosis, you could say," he added, reflecting on the fascinating secret Doctor Dax had confided to him not long before.

"An interesting analogy," T'Pol said.

"I know you had concerns about connecting with your crew, Malcolm," Archer said. "Looks to me like you had nothing to worry about."

"Well . . . I had my moments of doubt. But we're past that now."

"Nothing like a little life-or-death crisis to bring a crew together."

"Indeed, sir."

"I'm so proud of you both," Archer said. "You and your crews. You've proven how valuable exploration and peaceful contact are to the Federation. It's like you're keeping the spirit of *Enterprise* alive in both your ships."

"That's a lovely thought, sir," Reed said. "Nevertheless, I'm sure there are still those who disagree."

"Oh, yes. I don't think Admiral Shran will ever be a pacifist," Archer chuckled.

"There's value in that too, sir. There are still dangers out there, both known and unknown. We have to be ready."

"I'll grant that. But we have to be ready for peace too." He nursed his tea for a moment. "These are critical years. What we do now, the decisions we make, will determine the course of the Federation for centuries to come. We have to make the right choices." He smiled. "And that's why I feel so lucky that we have people like you and your crews out there making the big decisions."

"Don't sell yourself short, sir," Reed said.

"Malcolm is correct, Admiral," T'Pol added. "Your decisions can make a far wider difference than ours."

Archer nodded. "I believe I can do a lot of good where I am now. The Federation is still feeling its way . . . still vulnerable. It needs all the help and support we can give it."

Reed lifted his glass. "Amen."

The three of them clinked glasses. "I will always miss being an explorer," Archer said. Then he smiled. "But I joined Starfleet to seek out new life and new civilizations, like Doctor Cochrane said. Well, the Federation is a new civilization forming right before our eyes—and I'm getting to explore it from the inside. And that, my friends, is one hell of an adventure."

April 26, 2163
Smithsonian Orbital Annex, *Enterprise* NX-01 exhibit

Archer found Trip in engineering this time, not the bridge. That was fine with him; he was happy to let Porthos run around in the more spacious chamber, although admittedly his old friend was getting somewhat elderly for a beagle and wasn't as sprightly as he had once been. Seeing that, here in the familiar engine room with the historic Warp Five engine encased in clear polymer, reminded him of how much time had passed since he had begun his journeys aboard this ship, and how much had changed in that time. While many of the changes were for the better, they had come with a cost.

A bigger cost in some cases than others, he thought as he looked at the man that only he and a few others still called Trip. "I guess you've heard," he said. "The medical supplies got where they were supposed to go, and thousands of people who would've died from Denebian fever are now recovering."

"I may have overheard a news item about that somewhere," Trip replied.

"A lot of people owe you their thanks, Trip. Myself included. I may not be crazy about the people you work with . . . but it's good to know I can still count on you when I need to."

"That's what I'm here for," the other man said,

giving a reserved smile. Still, the sense of careful distance between the two men didn't go away. Porthos trotted over, looked at Trip for a few moments, then opted to sidle up to Archer instead. The admiral knelt and scratched his head, but he respected his wish— and Trip's—to maintain the distance.

Still, the concerned look in his old friend's eyes drew his attention. "What are you thinking?" he asked.

"Oh. It's just . . ." He considered his words carefully, something which had become far more of a habit for him than it had once been. "I'm not convinced our problems with the Orions are over. Devna gave up the Deneb operation way too easily."

"In exchange for her freedom."

"Yeah, but there's no way the Syndicate would let her live if she gave up something really important to them. That suggests that Deneb wasn't their endgame—just a bonus they could easily live without. I think—*we* think—that their real goal was to create a rift with the Vulcans. Make the Federation so warlike that they'd secede. And the Federation might not have survived that kind of a rift. Jonathan, if the Orions were aiming that high, they won't stop after this."

"Trip," Archer said, a touch of sternness creeping into his voice. "Starfleet Intelligence can handle the Orions."

"And so can we. Is there really that big a difference?"

"Yeah, I think there is. Because SI has to justify its actions to a government elected to represent the people. Now that I've worked with you, now that I've gotten a hint of the sort of things your 'Section 31' is willing to do . . ." He shook his head. "I'm just not comfortable with an agency that doesn't let the public have a say in what's being done in their name." He met Trip's eyes. "And I don't think you're comfortable with it either."

Trip was silent for a time. "There are things about this gig I'm not crazy about. But we don't go any farther than we have to."

"Not yet. But who gets to decide how far is too far? Without some, some mechanism to keep a check on your agency's decisions, who knows what it could become in the future? And what happens once the extreme threats are passed? What are you gonna do to justify staying in business then? What if Section 31 becomes more about protecting its own secrecy than protecting the Federation?"

"That's why I gotta stay with 'em," Trip said. "I know it's not gonna be easy to keep the Section on the straight and narrow. But I'm doin' everything I can to keep 'em that way."

"The best way to do that would be to bring them into the light. Fold them into the new Starfleet along with all the other services."

"And what happens when the only way to get a job done is in the dark?"

"What happens when you wield that hammer so long you see every problem as a nail?"

The two old friends mutually broke off, recognizing that things were growing too tense between them. After a moment, Archer picked up Porthos. "I'm going to ask you this once," he said, the solemnity of his tone catching his friend's attention. "Leave the Orions to Starfleet. What we're building . . . the nobility, the decency of it . . . it's still fragile. We've seen how easily it could go astray. And the means inform the ends, Trip. Protecting the Federation is something that needs to be done in the light."

The man who had been Charles Tucker considered his words. "I hope you're right," he said, though his voice bore little optimism. "I'd sorely love to be out of a job."

May 21, 2163
Rivgor, orbiting Psi Serpentis B

Garos watched as Navaar and her sisters finalized the agreement with their shipboard guest. "You're sure you can supply us at the necessary levels without the Federation finding out?" D'Nesh asked.

The Basileus of M'Tezir straightened, pride showing on his ridiculous goggle-eyed face. "Those trusting Federationers will be easy to fool. Have no fear; my nation's mineral wealth is inexhaustible. And the Federation does not expect to get all of it; there are reserves they have no interest in tapping due to the danger to my subjects or to the natural habitats of animals." The Saurian monarch scoffed. "As if those are any less mine to command or discard as I please."

Navaar smiled broadly. "Well then, it sounds as if everyone will get what they deserve. What could be more equitable?"

The Basileus leaned forward menacingly. The Three Sisters' huge Orion guards stepped forward, prompting the Saurian's own bodyguards to follow suit, but Navaar halted them with a slight gesture. Garos remained where he was, uninterested in risking his own well-being on behalf of non-Malurians. "Providing you live up to your end of the bargain," the Saurian snarled.

"Don't worry," D'Nesh said, looking irritated that the monarch was as immune to her mammalian phero-mones as Garos was. "Our advisors will teach you how to build the weapons and ships you asked for. The rest of N'Ragolar won't be able to stand against your armies." Beside her, Maras simply filed her nails, un-concerned with anything else.

"As it should be," the Basileus murmured, half to himself. "As it was destined to be."

"It doesn't bother you?" Garos asked. At the Sau-rian's inquisitive glare, he elaborated. "Having to rely on the tools of such weak, fragile beings as us in order to master your world? What does that say about your own strength?"

The Basileus faced down the Malurian with con-tempt. "What do you know of strength—you whose people hide behind masks and trickery? You may be less hideous than these mammals, but you cower and connive just as they do. So you cannot see. Yes, your races are weak, but that drives you to build stronger tools to compensate. Tools that you have used to mas-ter the very stars and build great empires." He straight-ened. "Just imagine what those tools could achieve in the hands of beings of true power and ambition."

"And you fancy yourself the one who will find out?"

"Who better?"

Navaar maintained her poise and charm, smiling in feigned admiration at the petty tyrant. "Then this may be an even more auspicious agreement than we had thought. We are honored to serve you, Basileus."

The Saurian considered, then gave a sharp, dismissive gesture. "Forget that antiquated title. With the new destiny I intend to carve out for myself, the tradition of subsuming my own identity within the ancient lineage of kings no longer seems appropriate. It is time that I reclaim my true name.

"Call me Maltuvis."

Navaar rose and bowed. D'Nesh followed suit, giving the distracted Maras a tug on her flimsy waistband to goad her into doing the same. "It is our honor, noble Maltuvis," said Navaar. "Rest assured we shall fulfill our obligation to you with thoroughness and pride."

"You had better. Those who disappoint Maltuvis do not live to regret it." With that, the erstwhile Basileus left, taking his bodyguards with him.

The sisters traded a look and broke up laughing, but Garos was less amused. "I see what you're doing, Navaar. With the Mutes no longer a threat, you need to groom your next interstellar menace to provoke Starfleet. But is that wise? They know we've attempted to goad them in that direction. They won't be so easily manipulated next time."

"Oh, but that's why I chose the Saurians," Navaar said, twirling her hair in the way she imagined to be seductive, oblivious as always to the fact that it had no impact on him. "It's the Federation that brought them knowledge of the stars—that's teaching them, encouraging them, showing them the power their resources give them. They're the ones whose insistence on fairness led them to include Maltuvis as an equal partner and put him in a position to act on his ambitions. So whatever consequences Maltuvis's hunger for conquest may lead to, the Federation will be compelled to intervene—or else to stand by and watch for fear of losing all those lovely resources he will control. Either way, they will blame themselves."

Navaar's smile widened. "And so will all his victims."

STAR TREK: ENTERPRISE

RISE OF THE FEDERATION

will continue

Spring 2014

ACKNOWLEDGMENTS

Thanks to my editor at Pocket Books for inviting me to tell the story of this virtually uncharted period of *Star Trek* history and finally complete my Trek grand slam by writing for all five canonical series. *Rise of the Federation* follows from the continuity of the previous post-series *Enterprise* novels *The Good That Men Do* and *Kobayashi Maru*, by Andy Mangels and Michael A. Martin; and the duology *The Romulan War*, by Martin. Characters and ideas drawn from canon are too numerous to list exhaustively, but a few key ones for clarity: Admiral Forrest's aide Williams (Jim Fitzpatrick) was introduced in *Enterprise*: "Broken Bow," by Rick Berman & Brannon Braga, and was named in honor of William Shatner. Garos (Wade Anthony Williams) is from "Civilization," by Phyllis Strong & Michael Sussman. Navaar (Cyia Batten), D'Nesh (Crystal Allen), and Maras (Menina Fortunato) are from "Bound," by Manny Coto. The "Mutes" are the nameless aliens from "Silent Enemy," by André Bormanis; I have herein identified them with the mute civilization on Gamma Vertis IV referenced in *The Original Series*: "The Empath," by Joyce Muskat. Maltuvis was a historical dictator mentioned in *TOS*: "What Are Little Girls Made Of?" by Robert Bloch. Devna (voice of

Nichelle Nichols) is from *The Animated Series*: "The Time Trap," by Joyce Perry. Bryce Shumar and Steven Mullen were referenced in *The Next Generation*: "Power Play" (Teleplay by Rene Balcer and Herbert J. Wright & Brannon Braga. Story by Paul Ruben and Maurice Hurley).

Takashi Kimura was established in production art for *ENT*: "In a Mirror, Darkly, Part II," by Mike Sussman, as the future husband of Hoshi Sato, and introduced as a MACO major in *The Romulan War*. Thomas Vanderbilt was named as the first Federation president in a piece of unused production art for *Star Trek Generations* and established in *The Romulan War* as Earth's defense minister. Caroline Paris was alluded to in *Voyager: Mosaic*, by Jeri Taylor, as an ancestor of Tom Paris. While Tobin Dax was referenced in various episodes of *Deep Space Nine*, his physical description is drawn from Jeffrey Lang's "Dead Man's Hand" in the anthology *The Lives of Dax*, although the specifics of that story have been superseded by *Enterprise* screen and prose continuity. My description of the Malurians, whose true faces were only partially glimpsed onscreen, is influenced by the artwork of Bettina Kurkoski in "Communications Breakdown," a story in Tokyopop's *Star Trek: The Manga—Kakan ni Shinkou*.

The "*Columbia* class" is essentially the conjectural NX-class refit designed by Doug Drexler and depicted in the *Ships of the Line 2011 Calendar*, although I have positioned the shuttlebays slightly differently. Drexler's "Drex Files" blog at drexfiles.wordpress.com provided valuable reference for alien ships and species from the

ENT era. *Star Trek: Star Charts*, by Geoffrey Mandel, established the primary stars for systems including Sauria, Orion, and Deneva and introduced the "Beta Rigel" concept; the StarMap site at www.whitten.org/starmap identifies "Beta Rigel" as Tau-3 Eridani based on its placement in Mandel's book. The physical attributes of Saurians were established by Robert Fletcher in his costume-design notes for *Star Trek: The Motion Picture* and have been developed in prose by myself and David Mack.

Thanks to Dave Mack for offering valuable insights on Tellarite psychology and explaining the qualities of a good brandy to this teetotaling author. Thanks to Kevin Dilmore and Kirsten Beyer for their input on the story outline.

A final note: This book is not in continuity with the book *Federation: The First 150 Years*, by David A. Goodman. I did not have the opportunity to peruse Mister Goodman's work while writing my own, and he chose to depict this era of Federation history differently than the Pocket novel continuity had already done in previous volumes. It's worth remembering that *Star Trek* tie-in novels, comics, and games over the decades have often depicted multiple alternative versions of a given event, which I think is a good thing, because it gives the readers more choices and a more interesting mix of ideas than a single, uniform continuity would provide. It is the lesson of *Star Trek*, after all, that diversity in combination is something to be celebrated.

ABOUT THE AUTHOR

Christopher L. Bennett is a lifelong resident of Cincinnati, Ohio, with bachelor's degrees in physics and history from the University of Cincinnati. He has written such critically acclaimed *Star Trek* novels as *Ex Machina*, *The Buried Age*, the *Titan* novels *Orion's Hounds* and *Over a Torrent Sea*, and the two *Department of Temporal Investigations* novels *Watching the Clock* and *Forgotten History*, as well as shorter works including stories in the anniversary anthologies *Constellations*, *The Sky's the Limit*, *Prophecy and Change*, and *Distant Shores*. Beyond *Star Trek*, he has penned the novels *X-Men: Watchers on the Walls* and *Spider-Man: Drowned in Thunder*. His original work includes the hard science fiction superhero novel *Only Superhuman*, as well as several novelettes in *Analog* and other science fiction magazines. More information and annotations can be found at http://home.fuse.net /ChristopherLBennett/, and the author's blog can be found at http://christopherlbennett.wordpress.com/.